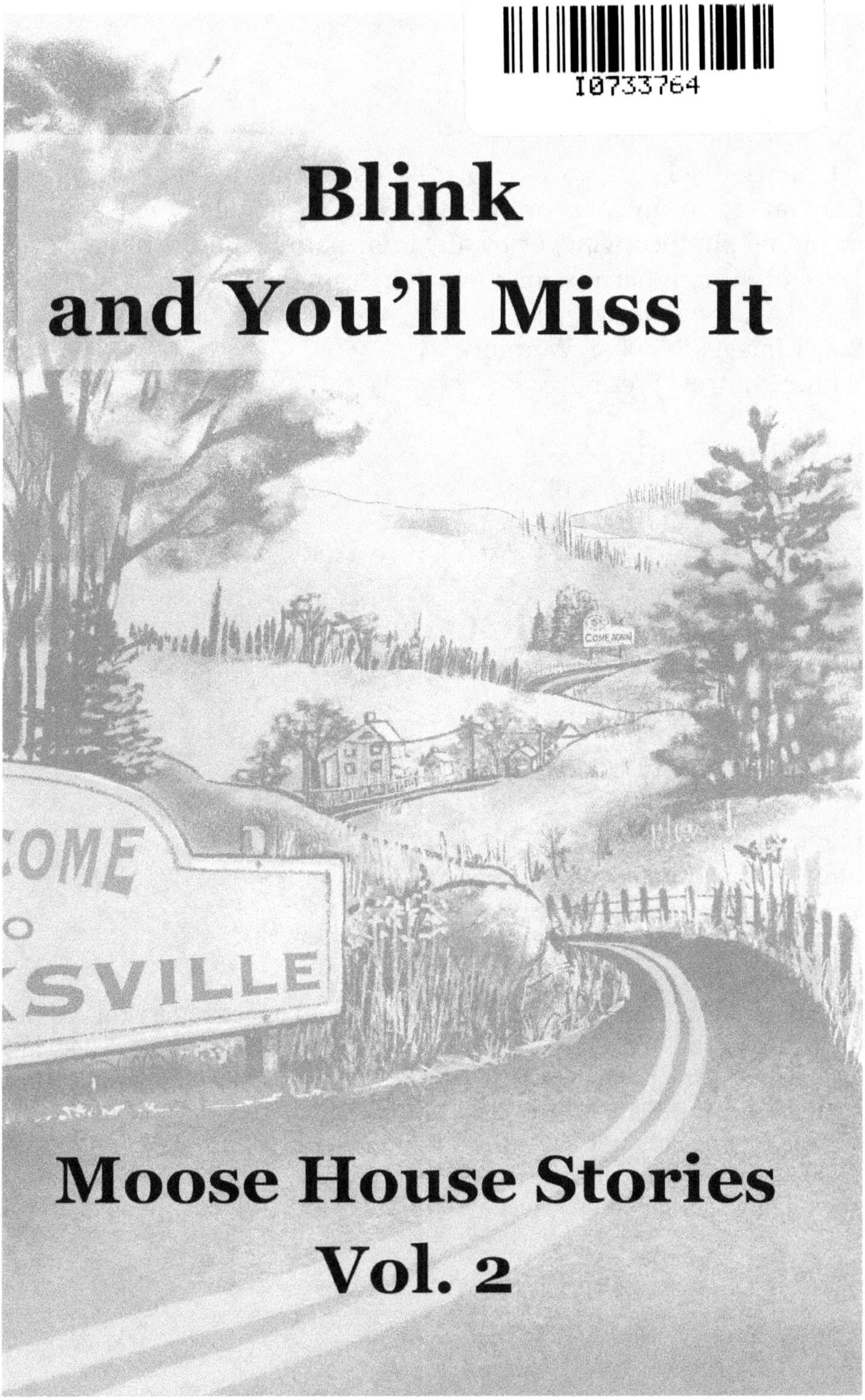

Blink
and You'll Miss It

Moose House Stories
Vol. 2

Cover image: Rebekah Wetmore
Editor: Andrew Wetmore

ISBN: 978-1-990187-35-3
First edition October, 2022

MOOSE HOUSE PUBLICATIONS

2475 Perotte Road
Annapolis County, NS B0S 1A0

moosehousepress.com
info@moosehousepress.com

We live and work in Mi'kma'ki, the ancestral and unceded territory of the Mi'kmaw people. This territory is covered by the "Treaties of Peace and Friendship" which Mi'kmaw and Wolastoqiyik (Maliseet) people first signed with the British Crown in 1725. The treaties did not deal with surrender of lands and resources but in fact recognized Mi'kmaq and Wolastoqiyik (Maliseet) title and established the rules for what was to be an ongoing relationship between nations. We are all Treaty people.

Tell us a story

Moose House set these writers a challenge: tell us a story about something in rural Nova Scotia—a thing, what people do, what people believe—that folks from a more urban area might not understand or appreciate.

You don't have to say, "Tell us a story," twice to a Nova Scotian. Manuscripts flew in from all across the province, from long-time writers and from folks for whom submitting a story was a brand new adventure.

We take you all over the provincial map and sometimes backwards in time. You will look in on maple syrup sapping, magic at a donut shop, and where ghosts walk along the shore. You will see the first steps in a struggle for women's right to get an education, a right we now take for granted. You will learn what the most horrible four-word expression is, and the unbreakable rules for hanging wash on the line.

I once heard folk musician Pete Seeger give a concert at a little community hall in Connecticut. He started to sing a song about the Hudson River, near his home, then he stopped. He said, "You know, you don't always have to sing other people's songs about other places. The place where you are is worth singing about, too." Then he launched into a very silly song about the Housatonic River, which flowed by where we were.

Read and enjoy these tales as much as our authors enjoyed writing them. And consider them an invitation: where you spend your time, where you hang your hat, where your heart was broken and mended—tell us a story about that.

We can't wait to hear or read it.

Andrew Wetmore
Editor

For all who love a good story about a good place

These are works of fiction. The authors have created the characters, conversations, interactions, and events; and any resemblance of any character to any real person is coincidental.

Blink and You'll Miss It

9

The water's edge

10

Blue Rocks

Anne MacLeod Weeks

It was an unexpected whirlwind. A phone call to the house one afternoon, when I was visiting my dad. He said he had heard I was home. Did I want to go out for a beer?

Well, sure. After all, he was definitely buff.

We met at the Knott and sat in the corner booth to the left of the front door. Cozy, but also close enough to escape if necessary. I had no idea what to expect. Of all my brother's friends, he was the one I knew the least.

We caught up, and he told me about his business, his politics, his dreams, his desires. He told me he thought my red hair was beautiful.

I rode my bike home wondering about it all. The cool, moist, coastal air cleared my head, energized me, and by the time I reached Blue Rocks, I needed a scotch to wind down for bed.

His calls that summer were like clockwork. Thursday afternoons. Would I like to go fishing? Would I like to go for a motorcycle ride? Would I like to walk the beach? I always said yes because what else was there to do?

He taught me how to refinish the bottom of a skiff. He taught me to eat smoked eel. He taught me to love listening to old sea shanties. He taught me it was okay to be authentic.

It was late August. I was going to head back to work, leaving my dad to his own devices for the winter. I knew the Thursday routine would have to end and, I suspect, so did he.

Maybe if I took the lead, it would feel less abrupt, less insincere, less cruel. I called on Wednesday morning. Would you like to paddle to the yurt on the island?

I packed a dinner of smoked mackerel, Geser's honey crisp apples, Dijon mustard, the boulangerie's crusty red fife, Soilmates Farm arugula and radishes, sliced almonds, and a bottle of Tidal Bay. I brought a pashmina shawl to keep out the chill and added a small stack of birch kindling.

We paddled the canoe out to the island's landing and lighted the lantern to take us along the path to the yurt. Settled in, we set the campfire.

The darkness enveloped us, and the stars were clear. The hunter, the great bear, the bull, and the three sisters. The quiet.

In bed, under the Hudson Bay blanket, hearing the last crackle of the fire, I sighed. He turned to me, his eyes as dark as the night.

Would you like to?

Yes, I would.

In the clarity of morning, I saw that he had taught me that being buff was actually not enough, but I knew I didn't want to admit it. The dichotomy of someone who worked with his hands for a living, rough calluses that left small scratches on my cheeks when he caressed my face, with a mind that could finish a New York Times crossword in fifteen minutes, was more than I could handle. I couldn't synthesize it all.

Paddling back to the mainland, I could only think about returning to work, to routine, to an identity I found tolerable. I could feel the distance growing between us as the waterway widened and narrowed. The rhythm of the paddle across the water's ripples lulled me into a trance-like state, burying my doubts and pushing me back to the city.

When Thursday came without a call, I knew he knew.

I packed my car, hung my bicycle on its rack, and headed back to a life that was supposed to be, one without polarity or contradiction, and, possibly, one without love.

Read on

Chris Bristol

I make my home on a small island in Nova Scotia, surrounded and protected by the Atlantic ocean. The air is clean, smelling like an unattainable scent advertised on an air freshener, and the water from my drilled well, my favourite beverage, is a cold, clear delight. There exists a sense of being safe here, as if the ocean creates an impenetrable field which blocks out the negative aspects of the mainland lifestyle. The climate is warmer in the winter and cooler in the summer because of the gulf stream.

The possible occupations, in descending order of financial remuneration, are fishing, working in the fish plant, or working in the summer at one of the tourist traps, with luck for long enough to secure unemployment for the winter.

Being isolated as we are, the population here is atypical, nothing like what you would find elsewhere. Yes we have internet and other media connections to the modern world, but the mentality is stuck in the 1950s. There is no police presence here, nor does there really need to be. The community tends to look after its own and there is no crime *per se*.

Most of the residents are under-educated, with many of them close to illiteracy, but they make a lot of money fishing or too little at the menial jobs available, and therefore they either do not see the need or have the means to seek higher education. The wealthier ones live comfortably, drive the latest vehicles and have big screen televisions, and the poor are the same as the poor are everywhere. Many of the people here have never lived anywhere else and only a few have explored the outside world.

My friends from away, living in distant urban areas, shrug their shoulders in disbelief wondering aloud how illiteracy is possible in the oh-so-connected world in which we all live.

There are many causes for illiteracy. On this island I have my personal favourite, but let's let the story unfold and you can decide for yourself where to place the blame.

I must admit that reading has never been a big attraction on the island, but through a program known as the Bookmobile, a renovated school bus carrying a variety of books ranging from history to education to fiction, there exists at least an opportunity. Partying is a much more common activity, and always will be.

When the hippies made smoking marijuana popular in the 60s, it eventually found its way to the island as well, competing handily against the older generations' proclivity for getting drunk.

While you can manufacture alcohol at home with a bit of skill and patience, growing marijuana is simply a matter of throwing some seeds in the ground. No police meant no one looking over your shoulder. The police do fly their helicopters over the island during the fall harvest, but hiding a dozen plants in amongst the scrub vegetation and weathered evergreens that abound here is easy.

Hiding your paranoia is a little harder for some, like the owner of the Fisherman's Catch restaurant, Ray Williams.

It was a sunny, drowsy afternoon in the late summer of 1981. The water in the harbour glistened like sequins on an undulating, tight-blue dress. The ever-present breeze was quiet this day, hardly enough to move the mosquitoes waiting impatiently in the shade, but still able to disseminate the tangy smell of sea salt.

Ray, 48 years old, just stretching to six feet tall, with thinning blonde hair brushed straight back and hanging below his collar, stood next to the cash register scanning the visitors in his restaurant, silver-grey eyes darting back and forth nervously, as if afraid of missing some vital clue.

The noise started as a soft thumping, and, as it grew louder, Ray's curiosity pulled him outside, where he squinted his eyes against the burning sun as he scanned the immediate area for the source of this ominous sound.

Suddenly a helicopter appeared over the edge of the western horizon, like a huge predatory insect. It grew steadily in size as it approached, and the next thing he knew there was dust flying all around as it landed in the far corner of the parking lot.

Instinct kicked in. Ray hurried back inside, panicking but trying not to show it, focusing on his breathing, and went speed walking straight through the seating area, into the kitchen, out the back door. Breaking into a run, he crossed the short stretch of gravel and disappeared into the woods.

Heart pounding, branches whipping his face and arms, he headed directly to his marijuana patch. Frantically he ripped out the ten plants which would have been ready to harvest in less than a month, the smell of fresh vegetation filling his nostrils, and stashed them under the low hanging branches of an evergreen.

Sweaty and drawing ragged breaths, Ray forced himself back towards the restaurant, arriving just in time to see two men walking casually across the parking lot, each with a bottle of cold pop in hand. The helicopter lifted gently and swung through a half circle, its path taking it back to the mainland.

Ray's wife, Gina, two years younger, with thick auburn hair and a ready smile revealing a chipped front tooth, stepped outside and stood beside him. "Please tell me that you didn't rip up those plants."

Ray's face twisted into a grimace saving him the need for words.

"Well, thank goodness I planted my own. Maybe this winter we will have more than leaves to smoke."

"Hey, I just don't want to get busted!"

"What are the chances of that? We live on an island where almost everyone has a VHF radio. The minute the cops show up on the other side and wait for the ferry the whole island knows. And even if they find your plants, how can they connect them to you?"

"They caught Billy two years ago."

"That was on the mainland, and since then no one has tried to move any pot off the island by car. And anyway, ours is for personal use, so no trafficking for us. Just cool it. We are safe here."

After the helicopter's pass over the island, the residents waited anxiously over the next few days to see if any ground forces would show up. There was a big raid on the mainland as the police destroyed a crop containing over two hundred plants, but no squadron of police vehicles showed up to take the ferry, and all breathed a sigh of relief.

This was the time of year when the tourists changed from summer crowds to fall crowds, and over the weekend fresh recruits with loud voices and boundless energy had arrived *en masse*.

Michael Stockton was at the restaurant having coffee and chatting with Ray on this busy Monday morning. He was ten years younger and several inches shorter than Ray, but he was stocky and well muscled from working on a local lobster boat. His father, Tommy, was the island's bootlegger, and since the cork does not fall far from the bottle, Michael was a marijuana grower, and was rumoured to have the biggest operation of any of the residents.

Since people on the island generally grew their own supply, Michael's clientele was primarily on the mainland. Locally he was more famously known as the food bank, helping underpaid seasonal and fish plant workers stretch their less than minimum wages in the inevitable slow times.

Fall was always a nerve-racking time of year for marijuana growers. Over the years the island growers had learned to plant many small patches, which not only helped keep them undetected, but resulted in fewer losses should any of the patches be discovered.

When to harvest was a gamble—better yield versus the risk of mould from early morning dew. It was also the most likely time to get raided and vigilance was high, with islanders taking turns watching the mainland ferry slip to see who was approaching.

"Heard you had some excitement the other day," Michael said.

"Go ahead, rub it in. I panicked, all for nothing as it turned out."

"No, I'm not here to make you feel bad. I planted some extra this year, so come and see me when you run short."

"Thanks, man. I appreciate it."

"Someday they are going to legalize pot and put me out of business," Michael stated.

"That will be a long time coming, if ever," Ray replied.

"With all the money they spend on law enforcement and all the taxes they could collect, I'd bet sooner rather than later." Michael drained his coffee cup and stood up. "I have the 10 until noon shift to watch the ferry. Talk to you later."

From his second-floor bedroom window Michael could see the ferry slip on the mainland clearly, and, with the aid of binoculars, could easily identify any possible problems headed their way. He got comfortably seated and scanned the shore on the other side of the water. All looked quiet this morning, with a smattering of tourists waiting for the next ferry, a few commercial vehicles bringing supplies and services. All normal.

A few minutes before the ferry was scheduled to load for the next trip a tired, but familiar-looking converted school bus drove into view and came slowly down the hill, stopping at the rear of the other vehicles lined up and waiting. Michael smiled. It was the Bookmobile. He had a few books to return, and had special-ordered a couple of others he hoped would be available today.

The ferry loaded the waiting vehicles, hoisted its on-ramp and pulled away, starting the ten-minute trip to the matching ferry slip on the island. It would be another hour before he would have to pay attention again. Time enough to visit the Bookmobile.

Gathering his borrowed books from the table in the living room, he left the house for the five minute walk to the parking lot beside the post office where the Bookmobile usually stopped.

On the way, he talked to a couple of people enjoying this morning's sunshine and by the time he arrived at the post office the Bookmobile was nowhere in sight. Martha, the post mistress, was outside enjoying the sun and having a cigarette.

"Where's the Bookmobile?" Michael asked.

"It drove right by, heading towards the store."

Michael started walking in that direction and caught a glimpse of the bus heading down the street above the main road. It stopped, and Michael cut through the lane connecting the two streets.

As he approached it from the rear, the back door of the bus

opened, and three police officers jumped out and dashed up the sidewalk, heading straight for Billy Jenkins' house.

Michael pulled up short, hopped over the small fence surrounding his girlfriend Natalie's property and banged on her back door. As she opened the door, Michael pushed past her questions and went into the living room where her VHF radio was. He grabbed the microphone.

"Alert, alert. Cops are on the island. They are hiding in the Bookmobile."

With that announcement, the island exploded into life. ATVs shattered the silence and the residents were on the move.

From the front window, Michael watched the Bookmobile as it started forward, heading for what could only be his home. He had started taking in some of his crop yesterday. The first buds of the season were down the basement drying on screens.

He went out through the front door slowly, stopped next to the tree by the front gate and twisted his head around it to look up the street. Sure enough, the Bookmobile was stopped outside his house and police were already banging on the front door. He turned back and saw Billy being led outside in handcuffs. People were pouring outdoors to see what was happening, astonished to see police on the island.

Unable to see a way out, Michael went up the road towards his home. One of the officers was positioning a battering ram to knock down the front door.

"Hey, wait a minute. It's not even locked," he called out.

One of the other officers ran over, grabbed him firmly by the arm and started to drag him towards the house.

Michael easily twisted free. "Take it easy. Where do you think I'm going to go?"

As they entered the house, Michael was trying to come up with a way to distract them from going down the basement, but could not think of any bone to throw them. The fact that they were here in his home meant that they had some sort of inside information.

When one of the officers opened the basement door, the pungent odour of drying marijuana wafted up the stairs. One officer pushed Michael down the stairs with a firm hand clamped on his shoulder. The other two crowded in behind. About an ounce of fresh buds greeted them in the laundry room.

Michael first heard and then felt the handcuffs as they clasped his hands together behind his back.

"I am arresting you for possession of a restricted drug, and cultivation of a controlled substance for the purposes of distribution."

Back outside, Michael joined Billy Jenkins in the back of a paddy wagon which had arrived on the next ferry. Billy looked worried, as this was his second offence.

Michael had no reassurance to offer, glad only that this was his first arrest, and together they sat in contemplative silence. Before they left the island, four others had joined them.

The next day, photographed and fingerprinted, everyone was back home. Newspaper reports claimed that the police had arrested and charged six people, confiscated four pounds of marijuana and located and destroyed seven hidden gardens.

Now that the worst had happened, the harvest on the island got into full swing. Overall they had lost about ten percent of the crop. The extra Michael had planted this year made up for his losses, and so he would still be able to stock the food bank's shelves as usual.

Through his lawyer, Michael had agreed to plead guilty to simple possession, and the other charges were dropped. But he never got a chance to return the books he had borrowed.

On the first Monday of the following month the Bookmobile climbed the concrete ramp to access the island.

As it reached the top, from out of the rocks on the water side of the wharf an explosion of people burst forth. In their hands, protected by fluorescent yellow or pink rubber gloves, they held equally brightly coloured beach buckets filled with a combination of rotten food, dog poo and rancid lobster bait, which they threw like ugly insults, painting the Bookmobile with an unmistakable message.

As quickly as possible, the beleaguered bus performed an awkward u-turn and got safely back aboard the ferry, never to return.

A fine kettle of fish

Trena Christie-MacEachern

Sorry for your troubles.

Duncan loathed that expression. He took it as a derogatory comment like *it's your loss*, or *better you than me*, instead of its obvious intention. So Duncan's response to anyone offering those four words was a grunt or a grimace, or a limp hand indicating disinterest.

Most dismissed his crude behaviour as that of a boy still in shock, grieving the sudden loss of his father.

He didn't even get teary-eyed until they showed up. All fifteen. They were shaved, sunburned, smelling of tobacco and rum, dressed in their Sunday best. They bowed their heads while mouthing those four words, taking his mother's hand and then his sister's, and then his. Only then did Duncan bawl like a baby.

Old Archie, with his ruddy complexion, thumped him hard on his back. "Be strong," he said gruffly, "for your mother's sake."

It wasn't what they said that got him worked up, nor was it because they left their gear and their boats to send off one of their own, or the fact they all gave from what little they had as an offering to his mother. No, it was what Duncan dreaded most of all, something he had put out of his mind years ago. He may have been seven or eight at the time, he couldn't quite recall, but when those men came walking in single file, he knew that day had come.

"C'mon, Duncan. Get your nose out of them books," his father had bellowed from the bottom of the stairs. "They're not going to be doing you any good when you're out on the water."

But the fact was, Duncan had no intention of becoming a fisherman like his father, or like his uncles, or like their father before them. Fishing wasn't in his blood despite the lineage. He felt that deep down to his very core. No, he was going to be a college man.

"No time, Dad. I've got a test on Monday. Ask Dinah. She'll do it."

It wasn't the first time he had suggested his sister. Duncan knew she was better suited to the profession. She could walk along the washboard as gingerly as a gull even in the roughest seas, bait the traps, and band the lobsters as fast as her father, maybe even faster. But no, fishing was not for women, no matter how much Duncan willed it, prayed to make it so.

To appease his father, Duncan did try, but the stench of the fish and the roll of the waves churned his stomach, causing his face to turn as olive as rockweed; fostering what Duncan already knew— and hated. So he had put out of his mind once and for all that he would ever become a fisherman. Period.

He'd daydream up in his room about the towering skyscraper he would have an office in one day. The futuristic condo with its mirrored walls and shag carpets, the cool cars he would be driving like the Ford Mustang or maybe the new Pontiac Firebird in classic black and gold striping. He didn't know what he wanted to become yet, he'd get to that.

But his father's sudden passing after a day of misbehaving, attempting to light a cigarette while manoeuvring MacLellan's Turn, put an end to Duncan's dreams. Ian was not wearing a seat belt and went through the back of the windshield when his truck hit the culvert.

While recovering in hospital with broken ribs, his Uncle Sandy said, breathing erratically, "I don't think he knew what was happening." He pressed a hand to his bandaged chest. "He was still in the middle of one of his stories."

"Just sell the gear, ma," Duncan pleaded, biting down on a fingernail.

Mary was sitting on the couch, her shoulders rounded. She was holding a balled-up tissue in her hand. She dabbed her pink, swollen eyelids, which reminded Duncan of the new-born baby mice they had discovered in the attic. It had been two days since the funeral.

"We can't, Duncan. We won't get anything for it."

"C'mon, ma." Duncan tapped his foot nervously, pressed his hands to his face.

"You have to do it, Duncan. Daddy had debt..." She trailed off, the worry etched deep in her face.

She was looking at the floor now, opening her mouth, then closing it, and then, in barely a whisper, blurted, "Duncan, we'll lose everything."

Duncan closed his eyes and let out a heavy sigh. He needed a prayer. He needed some kind of sign.

Then his mother said, "Simon, the Murphy boy, said he'd help."

Duncan stood up and stomped out the door, slamming it behind him.

Duncan didn't make things exactly easy for himself starting out. He didn't really try to fit in. He came to the shore long-faced and pouting, grumbling under his breath, complaining about the hard work and cold mornings. "Well, this officially sucks," he barked when the season started late because the ice didn't leave the harbour, a sure omen.

Then, for good measure, Duncan hauled his sister down to help paint the buoys and mend the traps while he sat and read. He would put the season in, however, pay off the debt for the petrol and the bait, and maybe, just maybe, put aside a little cash to help over the winter. He had promised his mother that much.

"I can't believe that's Ian's boy," they said as he'd made his way aboard the *Stella Dawn*. He still couldn't tell the difference between port and starboard, mackerel and herring, but he didn't care. He made it a point to tell everyone his plan wasn't to stick around and become one of them: bitter, beaten, stuck. No, sirree. He would be leaving this place as soon as the season was over and he counted the days, marking them off on his calendar in his bedroom.

When he'd be the first to leave in the evening, they'd holler and laugh, "What's momma cooking for supper tonight?"

Duncan paid them no mind. He'd smile, holler back, "Twenty-two more days, fellas," feeling smug, not giving a rat's ass what they thought of that either.

But when the sun was out in all its glory on that final day of fishing, the water a perfect shade of blue and flat-calm with not a cloud in the sky, Duncan felt a shift. Maybe it was his pride and ego becoming aligned, or the fact he had made it through the season. Or, maybe because he had stayed true to his word and this was the last God-damn day on this boat and he could finally go back to his regular life.

He started up the *Stella Dawn*'s engine and, once Simon Murphy was aboard, steered out to the coordinates his Dad had taught him years ago, the ones he now knew by heart, only to find—nothing. Nothing but clear, cool, salty waters for the eye to see.

Every ounce of colour drained from Duncan's face. He tossed his gaff against the back of the boat and screeched at the top of his lungs. "Fuccccckkkkkkkkk!" His voice echoed across the waters.

Simon took a cigarette from his package, brought it to his parched lips and lit it. Duncan grabbed it from him, drew in a deep breath. His brain got woozy and light-headed.

He stared into the deep waters of the North Atlantic, where his buoys had been cut—all one hundred and fifty of his traps left to rot on the ocean's floor.

Simon offered the four words Duncan detests as seagulls cried overhead and the waves lapped against the hull of the *Stella Dawn*.

A Portuguese Cove ghost story

Roberta McGinn

I went back to Portuguese Cove a little while ago. The old house with the old ghost was gone. Subdivisions stood in its place.

The ocean was still there. I used to jump off the cliffs and swim, and walk along the shore, along the cliffs over the rocks. The water was so attractive, so very charming and enticing. Like Alan.

I worked at the theatre then. I would hitch-hike home to the ghost-infested house each night unless I could get a ride with Ron, the crazed man who rented the house, and worked as a bouncer at the tavern. Ron tuned into a Zen Zone every night to get us home alive. When we arrived he would fall over. Dead drunk.

Sometimes, though, when I had to hitch a ride, I walked a lot of the way. The moon was as bright as day, reflecting on the snow, and throwing back brilliant light. From the top of that hill I could see out over a great sweep of barren lands lit by moonlight. The ocean shimmered on the horizon. The ghost light allowed me to walk late at night up over Camperdown Hill, past the old, abandoned military tower, and down into the hollow full of rose bushes, and the old house.

The house was unlit, leaning into many years of abandonment prior to its current motley occupants. Out-of-work theatre people and various hangers-on came and went, initially enticed by the rent-free living, and generally driven out by minimal heat, no electricity, the outdoor privy, and a complete lack of any organization.

And the house was haunted. The worn, wide-planked, bare wooden floors groaned and creaked for no apparent reason. Candles, the only source of light, would snuff out, leaving deep darkness in rooms where ragged remnants of rotted window curtains allowed in shadows of uncertain origins and macabre shapes.

I loved it. I was content there. Until the day Ron brought home Alan.

Ron often brought men home for me, rather like a cat presenting dead mice as presents to its person. I had about zero interest in any of them, and came to actively dislike some.

Alan was different. He was a writer, currently finishing up a play that he hoped to have performed at the theatre where I worked. That was his initial interest in coming home with Ron: my connection to the theatre.

He soon learned that I was merely the costume mistress with little influence, but by then it was too late. I had already lured him upstairs to my freezing little bedroom and roundly seduced him.

The ghost in the house had kept a low profile up to then. No eerie manifestations; just the usual annoying activities of spirits with little else to do.

Alan drew it out. When not up in the bedroom with me, or working on his play, he began activities that astonished the other more transient residents. "Why is there so little firewood? How about we get some really good oil lamps going here? I bet these wood floors would polish up a treat! That looks like good soil out there. Let's get planning for a summer garden."

This was just the beginning of his enthusiastic settling into the house and into my life. And to the more active presence of our resident ghost.

The level of ghostly activities increased, causing further housemates to abandon us and head back to the City. Landlord Ron had acquired a girlfriend elsewhere, and soon enough Alan and I were living in the house by ourselves. I guess that was what our ghost was waiting for, as it was about then that it started pushing the manifestation envelope.

I saw it first. I was alone in the house one afternoon, a fresh spring wind whipping about outside, sweeping into the many cracks and openings, the flapping curtain next to me appeared suddenly to not be a curtain, but, rather, a person. A tall, pale woman enveloped in a wispy garment that may once have been a house dress. Her black hair floated in wild entanglement about her head. Her eyes, large and tear-filled, turned to me. A long, thin arm reached out to me. Her mouth opened and a wailing cry filled the room.

That part could have been me, though, as I fled from the room and out the door, collapsing onto the cold and wet ground.

Alan, who had been working on pruning the wild rose bushes, heard my yelps and rushed over. Once my incoherent babblings had settled down, and my pounding heart resumed a more normal beat, Alan was able to coax me to explain my actions.

"Moving white curtains, whistling winds, your active imagination; I'm guessing there is our 'ghost.'"

This logical explanation by the practical man was unhelpful to me at the moment. Sensing this, he did help me up and gave me a big hug. I knew that I had seen the Spirit, though, and that it was still here.

I began to think of her as Isabelle, and she continued to make her presence known. Not always as dramatically as at first. At times she seemed to be just hanging around. But she was watching. And she was waiting.

Alan neither saw nor felt her, so I hid my fears. His continued enthusiasm around and about the house, and his loving attentions towards me, encouraged me to join him in the various projects he initiated. We built up an impressive woodpile. Oil lamps shed a warm glow. New curtains in the windows. The delicious smells of coffee, soup and homemade bread wafted about. The house was shedding some of its decrepit, mustiness and began to be downright homey.

Isabelle seemed pleased, if a ghost can be pleased. As my encounters continued, she took on a more corporeal, almost gracious appearance, revealing herself to be a tall woman with black hair hanging loosely down her back, modestly garbed in a sensible dress of indeterminate colour that fell to mid-calf, and sturdy, worn black leather boots.

My initial trepidations, indeed terror, were subsiding somewhat with each encounter, and as spring warmed into summer, Isabelle's ghostly presence became almost normalized. Alan, on the other hand, remained entirely unaware of her existence.

In this way the three of us settled into our home. Me, Alan, and Isabelle the ghost. Alan was absorbed in completing his play, puttering about the house fixing things, and tending the garden we had managed to get started. It had been many years since anyone had paid attention to the house, once a respectable, comfortable, and well-loved family home. Isabelle had been sadly neglected, too, the only remaining resident, albeit in non-traditional form, and one-time living householder. Since her earthly demise, she had remained attached to the place, drifting aimlessly about and unable to prevent the gradual decaying of her former home. Alan's loving attentions to the house and grounds caused a lightening of the Spirit's demeanour, a transubstantiation of her incorporeal form, a trending towards beingness.

Isabelle did not let Alan's delightful presence in my life and in the house go unnoticed, nor his blithe, unintentional blindness to herself. Her trailing about the house, while seeming to be without meaning or direction, began, it seemed to me, to become Alan-focused. With the subtlety of a teenager with a crush, she followed him about, casually brushing against him, making what I think she thought were admiring comments, but which instead sounded like the mewling of a sad puppy.

I watched these developments with intrigue and alarm. Having no previous experience with supernatural beings, I did not know where this might lead, and, more worrisome, how it might affect me and Alan. His continued obtuseness to Isabelle's presence led me to question his perception of my own presence. *How could this guy be so unaware?*

The warming weather often drew us out to walk by the ocean. The great, smooth, granite shore invited lovely, long treks along its edge.

Our absence from the house seemed to disturb Isabelle. The sad aura that hovered about her took on a darker shade of grey. Her attentions to Alan became, in my view, downright annoying, as did his astonishing and cheerful oblivion to her presence.

"Isabelle," I said to her one sunny day, "why not join us outside of the house for a time?"

She shrank against the wall, at my suggestion, seeming terrified at the notion of 'going outside'. Perhaps ghosts could actually not exist outside of the home in which they dwelt. Perhaps 'outside' to a ghost was akin to a fourth dimension inaccessible to more corporeal beings.

"Me and Alan will very likely spend much of the coming days in the outdoors, as the sublime Nova Scotian summer progresses. You will be mostly alone in the house. Without Alan," I added unnecessarily and rather spitefully.

Impelled by her growing need to be with Alan, Isabelle began little forays towards the front door of the house. When Alan strode outside, leaving only the screen door closed, Isabelle floated over and gazed anxiously out, scurrying, if a ghost can be said to scurry, back into the room at the least gust of wind, rustle of leaves, or scent of roses.

It was these very elements, coupled by her longing for Alan, that eventually compelled her to venture forth, although only so far as the porch. I watched with some concern as to how this outside environment, unfelt by her since she had passed away, would now envelop her being. Would the wind simply pick this nebulous ectoplasm up and carry it away, never to haunt again?

Apparently not, as Isabelle bravely sallied forth, seemingly enamoured by the enchanting scent of wild roses, and the presence of Alan.

We now became a little trio as we traipsed about the garden; Alan and me working hard and Isabelle languishing by the rose bushes. Now, as she hovered about both inside and outside, I began to find her rather *de trop*. Secure in my opinion that a corporeal female out-trumped what was, after all, nothing more than a bit of ethereal wispiness as far as Alan's perceptions were concerned, I once again offered a wee bit of advice. The poor dear seemed so sad and alone.

"Perhaps," I offered, "you would like to accompany us on our shore walks. The luminous light, mercurial cloud formations and hypnotic oceanic soundscape may act to project your visual presence solidly into our own dimension."

Taking me up on my well-meant suggestion, Isabelle drifted along the next day, as me and Alan headed out to the shore and the lovely ocean. She emanated attar of roses, and this mingled delightfully with the salty air. And, sure enough, this transparent bit of spirit presence began to morph into something resembling a human being. A young woman, in fact, with alabaster skin, eyes uniting green ocean and blue sky, a mouth like the ripe strawberries we were yet to harvest, hair as lustrous as the seaweed floating on the tide, wearing a plain summer dress and sturdy boots.

Alan noticed.

Each day, as summer meandered on, the ghost I knew as Isabelle accompanied us on our walks, in the garden, and eventually, back into the house. Without questioning who she was or where she had come from, Alan increasingly focused his attentions on this wondrous apparition, and less on me.

It was not long before I realized that the wheel had turned and it was I who was now *de trop*. My lovely Alan and the previously anxious, sad ghost, were besotted, and I was the one neglected and unseen. My presence on our ocean walks was unnoticed, my loving attentions to house and man, ignored.

I clung to the only hope I held: their inharmonious bodies. This was Isabelle's tragedy, and I saw the torment she endured. I did not see the workings of her illusory mind. I did not see that Isabelle had a plan.

The three of us stepped out the next day for a stroll by the ocean. The water was shiny smooth and lusciously clear, with sunlit shallows and enticing depths, Inspired by a rose and salt gentle breeze, a promising summer hint of warm sun, and the glassy sea, I enticed Alan to leap with me into the briny deep.

Down, down we fell, the water embracing us with exquisite chill. *This is the only place where I can be alone with him*, was my thought, as we reached up towards the sunny surface, through the smooth, glossy forest of seaweed.

Seaweed that seemed suddenly to be long black hair, enveloping a lovely face with eyes of ocean green and sky blue, and a mouth as inviting as ripe strawberries. Isabelle.

Entwining herself around Alan, she pulled him back into the depths of the sea and into her arms. He smiled at her and then at me as they plunged downward into the blue.

I never saw them again.

Back then

The black sedan

Bob Bent

Tom bites into the crisp flesh of a Gravenstein apple, savouring its tartness. A trickle of juice dribbles down his freshly shaved chin and he wipes it away with the back of his hand, squinting into the mid-morning sun. The Gravensteins are still too green for the market, but they'll be ready by the end of the week if the weather holds.

The sky is wide and blue, with only a few pillows of cloud resting on top of the South Mountain. Along the edge of the orchard tufts of goldenrod and delicate, pale-pink bells of dogbane shine in the late August sun. Robins sing from the tops of apple trees and scratch for worms in the short grass while sparrows flit from tree to tree, chasing each other like children.

Only thoughts of his son put a blight on the shiny surface of his day. The last time he'd heard, young Tom was in England, completing his pilot training. He wrote that soon he would be flying into combat.

Old Tom would be overseas too if it weren't for his bad knee, compliments of German shrapnel at Passchendaele. A renegade cloud blots out the sun, dimming the goldenrod and dogbane, silencing the robins and sparrows.

The low purr of an automobile interrupts his thoughts and Tom limps from the orchard to watch a black sedan roll solemnly down the long dirt driveway toward the farmhouse. A solitary crow laboriously flaps its black wings low over the orchard, heading east, up the Valley. One crow sorrow. But that thought disappears with the crow.

Between flashes of sunlight on the black sedan's windshield

Tom catches a glimpse of an officer's hat and feels a sudden sickness in his stomach. He knows what it means when an officer in a military sedan comes to call.

He stops to toss his half-eaten apple into the long grass, then leans against the machine shed for support as his mind stumbles, thinking of the three women in the house, possibly looking out the window. He rights himself and directs the black sedan to the far side of the barn, out of sight.

The officer is young, with the thin single stripe of a Pilot Officer on the sleeve of his freshly-pressed, Air Force blue uniform. The white collar of a chaplain confirms Tom's worst fears. They don't send chaplains to tell a father his son is wounded. Besides, pilots are never wounded. They either survive, or they do not. In his hand, the young chaplain holds a white envelope.

"Let's go down here," Tom suggests and leads the chaplain past empty apple crates stacked neatly against the faded red barn, then along the dirt and grass road leading through the orchard to the river.

"I'm afraid I have bad news."

The discomfort of the young officer is obvious, and Tom stops him with a slight raising of his hand, his mouth tight. "It's all right. I know what the letter says. Young Tom's dead."

He takes the envelope from the chaplain's hand, opens it and scans the letter. *It is with deep regret…*

He turns and looks through the apple trees toward the back of the farmhouse. Above the orchard he can see the dark window of the attic where Tommy liked to play when he was very young. He covers his mouth and chin with his calloused hand and squeezes hard.

How will he ever tell them? Ann, his wife, young Tom's mother, who has lived in dread ever since their son announced his intention to join the Air Force; Laura, his little sister, now a young lady of sixteen, still worshipping her big brother, her hero; and Pamela, a sweet girl, young Tom's wife, their life together ended before it began. How could he possibly tell them?

He stops and is silent for an endless moment before murmuring,

"I suppose our luck couldn't last forever."

The young chaplain looks at him for an explanation.

"My three brothers and I served in the first war. We all came home alive." He pauses to remember, then adds, "Although my knee never healed and Norman..."

He stops there and thinks of his younger brother; once strong and full of harmless deviltry, now haunted and useless. With enough coaxing he can get Norman to pick apples and help with the pruning and spraying, but other than that Norman does nothing. Margaret gave up on him years ago and moved to Halifax.

Tom's thoughts return to the three women in the house. He needs to have something to tell them, so he can keep talking, all day if possible, for once he stops talking the unbearable grief will crash in on them. He shuts his eyes tight for barely a second, then shoves his left hand into his overall pocket, fussing with the jackknife there.

"It doesn't say much."

The young chaplain stops, too. "I know." He looks around at the apple trees and ripe fruit, uncertain what to do; the aroma of ripening apples too fresh and sweet for the task at hand. "I'm sorry. This is the first time I've had to do this." His fingers entwine in front of his shiny uniform buttons, as if in a collapsed prayer. "He crashed somewhere in North Africa. He's buried in the Military Cemetery in Khartoum. That's all I know. I'm sorry."

Tom nods. *North Africa.*

Then he goes back in time: little Tommy, barely five, walking down this orchard road beside him, leading the oxen by himself; splashing and swimming in the river up ahead with his school friends; playing hockey on the pond across the road, then at the rink in town, centre for the high school team; high school graduation, just two years ago, not the top student but close enough, popular with the girls, and finally picking Pamela; Tom, not so young now, so he thought, old enough to join the Royal Canadian Air Force, home only twice from his training in Dunnville, the last time in December, to marry Pamela; Pamela, in the farm house with Ann and Laura, making the first apple pies of the summer with the dew-drenched Gravenstein drops he'd gathered earlier that morning, not knowing her Tommy was gone; only two weeks together in Halifax after the wedding before young Tom shipped out to England.

He has an overwhelming need to sit down somewhere, to collapse, but there's only the ground—and the chaplain is with him.

Tom had enlisted, too, in 1914, and married Ann before leaving for the trenches of France. But he'd come back, albeit with a shattered knee, and young Tom had been born, and Laura. Young Tom would never come back.

He rubs his forehead hard enough to hurt, but barely notices, instead seeing the framed photograph on the mantle. Tom, standing at the edge of the orchard with an awkward grin and an apple half raised to his mouth—at home, on the farm that now would never be his.

Tom and the young chaplain walk without speaking, each on their own path, a strip of grass and many years between them; Tom lost in thoughts of his son, not knowing how he would comfort the three woman making apple pies in the farm house; the young chaplain, too young and inexperienced to know how to ease a father's pain. And he'd left his Bible in the sedan.

They stop at the river and the young chaplain admires the view; the blue water with its rippled reflection of fluffy white clouds, another orchard across the river, and a pasture with fat brown and white cattle grazing lazily.

"I'm from Toronto," the young chaplain says. "I've never seen this many greens before. It's beautiful."

"I suppose it is," Tom agrees half-heartedly.

It was much more beautiful yesterday, when he didn't know his son was dead. Today his eyes see only tattered Queen Anne's lace edging the path along the river, their ragged leaves dying around the edges.

They return the way they'd come, with nothing left to say; Tom watching the back of the white farm house, limping more noticeably now, the knee suddenly aching; the chaplain watching his polished black shoes.

When they're almost back to the yard, Tom wanders silently into the orchard, leaving the chaplain standing alone in the narrow road. He reappears a few minutes later, his large hands full of green Gravensteins, which he dumps carefully into a small wooden basket.

"Here. Take these. They're not quite ripe yet." It comes out sounding like an apology, so he adds, "I like them best that way."

So did young Tom.

He turns away, gazing back at the orchard, then slowly shakes his head. The young chaplain watches him, saying nothing, until Tom finally turns and looks toward the farmhouse.

"Do you want me to come in with you?" the young chaplain asks.

Tom's gaze doesn't leave the house. "No, I'll do it." A short sigh, then, "Thank you for staying a while. I know it was hard for you."

The chaplain nods. "Thank you for the apples."

Tom watches the black sedan roll up the driveway and turn onto the main road, then takes a deep breath and limps slowly toward the barn. Inside the barn he sits on an upside down apple box and reads through the letter a second time, squinting in the dim light.

Then he sits there for another five minutes, doing nothing, like his brother Norman, tapping the edge of the letter on his sore knee, before he pushes himself up and trudges toward the farmhouse, the letter hanging from his right hand.

In memory of ElRoy Fenwick Bent
1 September 1922 to 19 August 1942

Bubblegum Road

Danielle Pierce

"Here," Pap says. "Park 'er here."

It takes me a minute to see it: a road so old and crumbling that nature's repossession has camouflaged it.

"This is where you grew up?" I ask my grandfather as I park on the shoulder. The ocean in the background fills the cab with white noise as soon as I shut off the truck.

"Yap." Pap nods and begins fussing with the seat belt. His hands shake so badly with tremors that it takes him a few tries to get it unsnapped. I hop out and go around to help him down.

Standing before the wild road, Pap chuckles and it's the sound of stones being sucked into the sea. The rumble of it breaking in the morning air prompts a cacophony of gulls to answer him. Two of them step into the salty breeze and fly over our heads. With their wings spread, heads turned into the wind, they hang in the pinkish morning sky like a painting.

Looking at the state of the road I question whether it's safe to take my elderly grandpa on what is, essentially, a hike. He'd warned me that the road would be in hard shape and that we would have to walk.

"I think I could drive the truck down here easy, Pap, if you want to get back in—" I yell, hoping to be heard over the elements. The wind whips my hair around my head and strands of the wheat-coloured stuff stick to my lip gloss.

"No no, no no." He dismisses the idea with a gnarled hand before heading purposefully down the road.

He grows smaller as he walks away. He's been growing smaller with each visit I pay to the home. When I was a little girl, he was a big man with a broad chest and people called him a workhorse. Now, at ninety years old, his chest is concave, the curve of his spine arcs like a bow and his head sticks out from his neck like the tongue of a bell. I jog to catch up with him.

Pap's gait is slow but consistent. We walk in silence for a while and I try in vain to listen to the quality of his breathing over the incessant rushing of the sea.

Finally, when the truck is long out of sight, he stops.

"That there's where the military housing used to be." Pap stares and points at an empty scene alongside the road. I wish I could see the image he's recreating in his mind. Other than thickets of bayberry bushes and twisty alders bent on reclamation, there's no evidence of houses of any kind—a stark vacuity in place of the landscape he's remembering.

"They were long skinny trailer-type things. A'course, you'd never know they was there from the looks of it now."

Pap pulls a blue handkerchief with a print of cowboy hats and rearing rodeo horses from his pocket and swipes along his top lip, blowing his nose. "That's what the army's like, though. They show up one day with thirty-odd trucks carrying the trailers on back, set 'em all down in a row, and there they were: a fully manned army base in the middle of nowhere—MY middle of nowhere!"

The indignity of it tortures him still, though the army base shut down decades ago. "Looked like a damned motel and probably got as much action!" he says.

"Well, it must've made things more interesting for you and your brothers out here..." I use my arms to frame the stark scene around us.

The sweet pastel streaks in the sky have turned into the steely grey tones of a dreary November day. We're both dressed warm, though Pap refused to wear the snow pants I'd brought with me to the home. The wind cuts through everything I'm wearing and a chill crawls in under my collar, slithering down to my feet.

The ocean follows us along what used to be the main access road for the base, thudding against the shore. The repetitive blunt force lets out a crash that competes with the wind.

"And when they were done with the place, they were gone just as fast." Pap says, an epilogue to his earlier train of thought. "They even picked up the pavement!" He looks down at the cracked road and kicks a couple of loose pieces of asphalt down what might've been a driveway, or where he might've once kicked a ball.

He continues walking and I stay close so I can hear him.

"When we were kids, we used to pick bubblegum off this road and chew it," he says. A quirk in his jaw is all I get for a smile these days. "The guys at the base used to chew gum to hide the reek of alcohol when they were driving back from the disco."

Pap stops another minute to stare, filling the space with his memories. He stands totally still despite the raging wind pushing me around. I wrap my arms tight around myself and wait.

"The road to our house was covered in bubblegum," he chokes out with another clumsy quirk of his jaw. There's a depth of emotion in his eyes that reminds me of deep wells, and I put one of my gloved hands on his shoulder.

"Gotta love that A.B.C. gum," I holler into his ear.

"We didn't have much as kids," he says as he starts walking again. He lets me take his arm for a bit, but keeps his head hanging low against the gales of the past. "We used to forage for berries if we wanted something to eat, you know. And if we were thirsty, we'd stick our head in a ditch and drink whatever water was running through it."

Pap shakes his head as he remembers and I'm surprised there's no jangle. "And we never got sick! The amount of monkey meat I ate as a kid! Criley."

"What kind of berries grow around here?" I ask, curious about what could thrive in this harsh environment.

"Oh there's blueberries and gooseberries, them's the sour ones, and we used to always just put a handful of rose hips in our pockets when we were going out huntin' or trappin' 'cause you could just pop a few of 'em in your mouth and it'd keep you going. There always was shore roses about."

What fractured bits of pavement left of the old road ends and gives way to an uneven trail that looks like it's only seen the grizzly tires of a four-wheeler in the past ten years. I go to turn around, but Pap steps resolutely onto the path.

"This here was our driveway," he says. I hurry to overtake him on the track, which is uneven and overgrown. I look around in search of a walking stick when I see him bracing his hands against his knees to get up a steep part of the path and find a nice piece of driftwood for him. He grunts his thanks and we slowly pick our way along the winding trail.

"It doesn't look like anyone's been down here recently," I shout over my shoulder, but Pap just grunts.

We trudge on in silence until I trip over a barely protruding rock and nearly face-plant into the thorny briers shouldering the path. I catch myself with a quick correction step, my hands outstretched, ready to break my wrist before busting up my face.

"Side-hill gougers almost got you!" Pap barks before letting out another riptide laugh.

"The what?"

"The side-hill gougers," he says again, as if repetition will explain it all. When he sees my confusion, his eyebrows knit together and come down over his eyes, casting a shadow of disappointment into the lines of his face. "Don't tell me your dad never told you 'bout the side-hill gougers?"

"Never heard of it—or is it a them?"

"The side-hill gougers are folks who live in the woods—tricksters, like. They got one leg longer than the other, making 'em real good at running fast across hills and tripping people up," he explains. "Depending on what leg of theirs was longer, they'd be either right-hilled or left-hilled."

"Oh, so you think one of them tripped me just now?"

"Yep; a left-hilled one I'd bet." Pap stops a moment to catch his breath.

"If the gougers are getting me, I'm a little worried about them getting you, Pap. Do you think we should turn around now?" I ask, looking ahead at the uneven ground.

"Ha! Let the gougers try!" Pap huffs, and busts past me in a burst of energy. "Quit your worryin', we're almost there."

"Sure, it's just I have to get you back to the home before four—"

"This is my home!" Pap barks.

There's nothing left of the family homestead but a few rocks, broken and standing up like jagged teeth amongst thickets of alders. I wish I could picture anything cheerful on the plot of land my grandfather surveys.

"Does anyone have a picture of the place?" I ask, but Pap's immovable stoicism as he looks out at the rocks is my answer. He has the only picture.

A shroud of barrenness is the only thing that seems to have persevered in this place. Were there ever warm, sunny days with nothing but a balmy sea breeze on your cheek? The harsh coastal winds and the lashing tongue of the ocean's storm surges were a constant imposition on daily life. The area was ravaged and rebuilt many times before the handful of families who'd tried to settle gave it up and left it to the sea and wind.

I look out at the greenish-grey water along the horizon and the roll of it makes me queasy. I wrap my fingers around the stem of a nearby bush and try to snap it, but the wood bends against the pressure instead of breaking.

As he looks at another relic I cannot see, Pap stands perfectly still in the howling wind. While the wilderness around us rustles and protests the incessant gales, only his jaw moves.

His cheeks are sucked in and his teeth grind at something, his jowls jumping.

Before I can think of anything worth saying, Pap turns on his heel and starts walking back down what used to be his driveway, now barely a footpath.

I walk close enough behind to catch him if the gougers decide to take a swipe at his aged, brittle body, but he is still a surefooted man. When the deserted road rolls out ahead of us, he spits a gob of fleshy orange seeds on the ground, then reaches into his pocket and pops another rose hip in his mouth before reaching for my hand.

I hold on tight and we start the walk back towards the truck. His watery eyes sweep the road from shoulder to shoulder, searching for bubblegum.

Catching her breath

Virginia MacIsaac

What other people tossed away, Tessie took in. She had to.

But Mama was the tough one, a master negotiator who always got what they needed though it wasn't always what they wanted. Tessie tried making things look nice, but that fridge, and that stove, and those taps were already pitiful before she got them.

Inside the little bungalow, built as part of a social housing project, Tessie rocked gently in an old wooden chair, eyes closed. She was imagining sitting in a kitchen with a blue patterned floor that shone like sun on water, buttercup-yellow curtains in the window, freshly painted walls, and a thickly braided mat to keep her feet warm. On the stove sat a tall, shiny tea pot. She had described this to Mama many times.

She heaved a deep sigh and opened her eyes to the old kitchen table, marred and scarred, trim missing around the walls, and floor tiles scrubbed bare of any pattern. She quickly remembered to give thanks for each of them.

Reaching out, she opened the oven door a crack to check on Mama's supper. She was keeping it warm until Mama woke. She frowned at the stove and the cracked oven glass that distorted the reflection of a 42-year-old woman, still a girl in her mother's house.

She glanced over at the clock. Closed her eyes and returned to the warm glow of the daydream.

Her table was polished until saucers could step-dance their way across the top. Cookies were heaped in a big glass jar for the neighbour children who would sit and swing their chubby legs and tell her their stories.

The smell of warm molasses cookies, or maybe it was just Mama's supper, pulled her out of her daydream. She looked around, thinking nothing ever changed.

That wasn't quite true. Her flaming red hair had dulled to nutmeg grey, her ivory skin was smoked into a spotty parchment across the wide cheekbones inherited from her Granpap. Her body had never narrowed at the waist and thrift shop belts couldn't change that.

Tessie finished high school as a good reader, a good cook, and a knitter with a great appreciation of colour. She had been ready for that lofty goal of making the most of herself and getting a good little job. It turned out she had a ready-made one taking care of Mama because the cancer bell tolled for Papa.

Mama and Tessie were left alone. Together. Tessie made some crafts and Mama made some bargains.

Rocking vigorously now, Tessie glanced at the clock again. She had given Mama her bit of supper and put the dishes away. On the next forward rock, Tessie stretched her arm to the side and flicked on the radio and heard...*with a threat of frost in low-lying areas.*

A quiet evening, she thought as she stared out the window to where the cool autumn breeze chafed the hardwood branches and nudged lingering leaves to the ground. In the west the blue sky was faltering as shards of left-over sun scraped the bottoms of heavy clouds. Along the shore a thin grey mist hung low above the olive crests of an ocean roll.

On the next swipe of the rocking chair, Tessie turned the volume up a notch. Her show, *Highland Tonight,* an hour of fiddle tunes and Gaelic singing, would be on soon. She would breathe in the tunes. They would lift and fall and weave their way to her. The music would travel to her feet, rise to her knees, and run out the tips of her fingers as she kept time. Tessie turned the up the volume one more notch and hummed herself a little tune to the rhythm of the rocking chair.

"Tessie!" Mama bellowed.

Tessie entered the bedroom as Mama was trying to heave her huge body off the bed. "Come on, Tessie!" she rasped. "Help me, for

God's sake. I don't want to piss the bed."

Tessie slid her shoulder under the sleeve of Mama's rumpled nightgown, and they made their way down the hallway.

A few moments later they returned, Mama breathing hard. Back in bed, her head lolled to the side as if held to her body only by the mottled skin at her neck. Her eyes pinched shut.

Tessie tried hard not to shudder as she imagined death itself crawling around under the bed covers. She thought it would quickly climb into her mother's tortured body if she turned away. Fear slid into her arms, making them heavy. Her heart thudded in short, quick bursts like the cover of a pot getting to a boil.

Mama moaned and opened eyelids as wrinkled as walnut shells, in a face lined with as many ruts as the old Interval Road. Tessie patted her wiry mass of hair then, picked up a water glass from the stand by the bed. She heard a great tune playing in the kitchen.

"Mam, I'll get you a smoke."

"And tea, Tessie, hot tea. I can hardly breathe."

"Mary Ellen used to take ginger in her tea, Mam? To help her lungs."

"No, she took her ginger with hot water."

"I'll get you some."

"No, just make tea, hot tea."

"Like this morning? Did that help?"

"It did so. Go next door...and ask for a thimble of brandy to put in the tea."

Mama lifted her head a speck as if she would try to do it herself, then sunk back on the pillow.

"There's nobody home there," Tessie said, hoping it was true.

"Call anyway. There might be somebody."

"There's nobody."

"I need something more, Tessie. Call Sandra."

"She's got nothing. It's Sunday."

"Then call J.R."

"He's gone to Dallas."

"Isn't anybody home around here?" Mama was in no mood for Tessie's humour. "Call the priest, then. Call Father Iain. He should help me."

With prayer or pledge? Tessie pondered, remembering the uncle forced by in-laws to swear before the priest that he'd stop drinking the alcohol that drove him crazy and drained his pockets. Which reminded her that Mama's cheques hadn't come for a few months and Tessie didn't know what to do about that.

She watched Mama's whole body racked with coughing that left her sprawled out, gasping for air. Mama's lungs were likely the size of prunes by now.

"Just you settle down. I'll go get the tea and call Father." The power of the priest was not to be questioned.

Before she reached the hall, her mother's voice had recovered enough to reach her.

"Tell him to bring wine."

Tessie trudged to the kitchen and turned the kettle on. She waited for someone to answer the phone in the glebe house. When Fr. Iain answered, the kettle whistled, and a new set of tunes began.

She delivered her message, hung up and walked into the living room for Mama's smokes and hers. On the walls were Pope This and Pope That and dead priests' prayer cards which kept their faith renewed daily.

Back in the kitchen, Tessie put the smokes on the counter, got the tea ready, and listened to the tunes. Before she had finished making the tea, Mama called for her to bring the crucifix to her room.

Tessie set a cup and plate for the priest.

He arrived and prayed with Mama and shared tea and stories. As he was leaving, he told Tessie her mother's pain would be over soon.

Tessie prepared Mama for the night and she wondered about illness. Later that night Mama told her He always answers prayers even though He might be late. Tessie silently agreed—*He could be years late.*

The next morning, Mama Flora was finally at rest.

~

Tessie was ploughing through wet snow and blasts of rain, her heavy legs churning towards the little store to pick up groceries and smokes. She hoped George would continue credit until Mama's cheques appeared. He'd just have to. The wind pulled stands of thin hair from her paisley scarf only to drive it between her teeth as she fought for breath.

At the funeral, Mama's cousins filled the front pew and sang loudly. Mama's younger sister, Eliza, had arrived from Halifax by bus. She and Tessie sat quietly at the end of the second pew. The old pallbearers wore shiny black suits topped by deeply solemn faces.

Tessie sat through Mass with chin level and back straight as a board. At the graveside, she tossed a handful of dirt on Mama's coffin, whispered to her, and watched shovellers start filling in the hole before she moved off.

She offered an arm to her little aunt and shoved her other hand in her coat pocket, where her tissues rested unused.

The good neighbours had dropped off squares and sandwiches at Tessie's during the funeral. As they admired the sweets, Aunt Eliza asked her if she liked to cook. Tessie looked around the little kitchen and didn't answer.

After they sipped on tea and nibbled ham and cheese sandwiches, Tessie felt a bite of date square sticking in her throat. Her mouth was dry, and her eyes were getting moist. She took a big gulp of hot tea.

When she could talk again, Tessie asked why Eliza's husband, Uncle Fred, hadn't come to Mama's funeral.

"Fred was really sorry, but he had work to finish," Eliza explained.

Tessie frowned without realizing it while she stared at Eliza's wool sweater, styled hair, soft leather shoes with matching beige slacks.

"You know your Mama and I sent each other letters and cards. Even up to a month ago."

Tessie nodded, yes.

"Come back to Halifax with me. She would like that."

Tessie shook her head, no.

"Winter is coming, Tessie. And until the paperwork is looked at, you don't know if you can stay here."

Tessie had already wondered about how to get oil and pay bills. Mama usually signed the cheques and handed them to her for the bills. Mama had said they'd turn up, but they hadn't.

Tessie grabbed a tissue and wiped her eyes. She tilted her head to Aunt Eliza, a reluctant yes.

Eliza helped Tessie pack a suitcase and Tessie gave the house key to her neighbour, Sandra, in case the government came looking for it. Next morning the two ladies climbed aboard the bus for Halifax.

Tessie watched traffic flowing along the Trans-Canada Highway outside of Antigonish and her fingers gripped the window ledge. "The last time I went this fast was when Johnny 'Fly' drove Mama and me to town and back."

Eliza smiled. "Your dear Mama was wise and practical. There are buses in the city, Tessie. You can walk if you want, but you don't have to."

"What about my music? Can we get 101.5 on the radio?"

"Sure. Fred will set it up. Or get a CD player. You'll find lots of music."

Tessie wasn't so sure. She wondered how many people in Halifax knew about the great dance fiddler Buddy MacMaster. Or Alex Francis MacKay. Or Sandy MacLean. She guessed they knew Dave MacIsaac since he lived there. She just wanted to get off the bus before she threw up.

Eliza patted Tessie's arm and closed her eyes for a nap.

~

A taxi dropped them off in front of a neat little brick bungalow. A stone walkway, sunflower hedge, and rose bushes winding down brought a flash of anger to make Tessie's guts roil again. She knew her aunt and uncle weren't rich, but this was so much more than her mother ever had a chance for. *Couldn't they have helped a little more, just for Mama's sake?*

Tessie wanted to turn around and would have climbed back on the damn bus if she didn't feel so weakly sick.

Aunt Eliza unlocked the front door and called out to Fred. She pointed to a cushioned bench and Tessie sat on its edge, feeling the heat of resentment again even as grief was chilling her to the bone. Her mind ceased to work, and she felt her body begin to shake.

Fred came in, said hello, and took Eliza's coat. Quietly, Eliza and Fred spoke about the bus ride and the funeral.

Then Fred asked, "Tessie, are you all right? We're hoping you'll stay for a while."

Tessie squeezed her clasped hands and tried to be calm, but her low voice trembled. "I don't really fit here."

Eliza stood up. "Tessie, let's warm up with some tea. It was a long trip."

She guided Tessie slowly across the hall and said, "Fred couldn't come to the funeral with me because he was renovating." She pointed to a red toolbox on the floor.

Tessie thought nothing could make her feel any worse, but when she entered the kitchen, a sharp pain pierced her chest. Her eyes watered and she gasped.

Fred gently patted her on the back. Tears rolled down her cheeks.

"Mama?" she said when she could finally catch her breath.

Fred nodded. Tessie reached for the tissues to blow her nose and wipe her eyes. She looked around at cream-coloured walls, bright yellow gingham curtains, a thick braided mat on shiny blue flooring.

She shook her head in disbelief.

A small, tea table was set for three and a large jar filled with molasses cookies sat on the counter top.

"From your Mama's cheques," Eliza whispered.

Tessie's blue eyes filled up again. She looked down at the floor. She took one deep breath and then another. Her head shook.

Eliza said sternly, "I know it might be hard at first, Tessie, but why not try?" She moved to give Tessie a quick hug.

Tessie shook her head. She cleared her throat. Another deep breath. "Aunt Eliza, it just won't do." But her voice squeaked.

She looked up at Eliza and Fred. For the first time in a while, her damp blue eyes held the strong hint of a twinkle. She pointed to the squat, brown kettle sitting on the stove.

Uncle Fred quickly moved over to her and held up an index finger. He turned, went into the hall and three seconds later was back with a shopping bag. "I got home just two minutes before you ladies arrived."

He dug in the bag and pulled out a stately, stainless-steel tea pot and handed it to Tessie.

"Here we go, Tessie girl, you make the first pot."

Surprised jackers

Eunice Amero

After supper, when everyone was ready to relax for the evening, Old Buck said to his son Benny, who was sitting back in the living room on an old worn out chair and picking his nose, "How about we go hunting tonight?"

"Dad, did you forget about last year when we got caught and they took our licenses away?"

"I'm not worried. No one will be around tonight, it's too cold," Old Buck said.

"Okay, but if we get caught, don't say I didn't warn you. You know how dangerous it is."

"I know what I'm doing. Stop worrying, let's go."

"Buck, you should listen to Benny because he's right," Milly, his wife, told him.

"Stop complaining. No one is going to catch me."

Old Buck was a stubborn man and nothing could stop him from doing anything he laid his mind to do.

"If you get one, come home. You don't need to get two to get in trouble again," Milly cried, as Old Buck was going out the door.

When Old Buck and his son got in the woods they climbed a tree, holding their gun and light. "No one will see us up here, Benny."

"Let's hope not." Benny sounded worried.

They sat for a while without seeing any deer.

"Let's go home dad, I'm cold," Benny said.

"That's what you have to put up with when you go deer hunting. Hold on, we'll see one soon."

The night was calm, quiet and frosty. Old Buck could hear

Benny's teeth chattering. Soon they saw two deer standing in the field, and what a sight to see. The men couldn't get over what they were seeing. They stared and stared and couldn't believe their eyes.

What they really couldn't get over was when the deer started to sing. "We wear sunglasses at night, so we can't see your light. So a jacker won't get us in sight and it could be tonight," on they sang, "So we wear sunglasses at night..."

The men were so shocked they couldn't move once they got to the ground. They stood frozen as they watched the deer proudly walk across the field.

Then they heard them sing again. "Put out your lights. You know it's not right, and you could get caught, believe it or not, unless you're as keen as us, then you will be in trouble with the law."

As the deer went farther in the field, Buck and Benny couldn't run fast enough to get out of the woods. When they got home and tried to make Buck's wife Milly understand she said, "Did you shoot them?"

"Nooo," Buck said.

"Why not? You've always done it before."

"Milly, you don't understand," Old Buck said, shaking his head. "These deer were wearing sunglasses and they sang to us."

"It's true, mama," Benny said.

"You are both crazy. Now how are you going to get one?"

"We'll have to do it the honest way. Hunt in daylight."

From then the men decided to go hunting in the daytime. "At night those deer are too smart, son."

The letter

Linda H. Y. Hegland

Benjamin's mailbox had been leaning precariously into the ditch at the end of his property for more time than he cared to count, at least three seasons. Arlington Road, running atop the North Mountain, was not plowed often in the winter. But, inevitably, every winter, his mailbox got pushed over by the plow when it did happen. In the spring season, bulrushes and tall ditch lilies would grow up around it. Finally, he just left it.

He still walked to the end of his lane every day, regardless. The trip to the mailbox, though it lay in the ditch, was a habit very much like lifting the coffee pot onto the wood stove or brushing his remaining teeth. He just did it.

This past spring a family of swallows had taken up residence in the box, the flap having flown off the recumbent mailbox in a strong gale. Each time he walked out to the road, the swallows would fly at his head and flap their wings in his face. He would bat them away with his hat, like clearing a way through a cloud of gnats.

"Yeah, yeah, keep your pants on. I ain't gonna hurt ya," he would mutter.

An 'undeliverable' notice pinned to his sagging screen door one day took him to the post office in Bridgetown where he learned that the undeliverable mail was a notice of his land taxes, past due. This prompted him to remedy his errant mailbox.

While red-winged blackbirds sang to him from the open, grassy field across the road, he hacked the mailbox out of the ditch detritus and fixed it with a length of binder twine and two rusty nails.

Benjamin wasn't expecting a letter. He only ever got those occasional tax notices, and never a letter. Then this morning, a grey morning moist with unshed rain and silent of birdsong, a small yellowed envelope sat in that recently-righted, rusty letter box.

He drew it out of the box between two fingers with great trepidation. He was 78 years old, and in all that time he had never, not once in his life, received a personal letter of any sort.

His name was handwritten, letters looping and whorling across the front of the envelope, the ink pale blue and flowing like a stream: Benjamin Ezekiel Clement.

There was no doubt the letter was meant for him, he was quite sure that his was not a common name. It was probably beyond uncommon.

The address simply read "last house, blue, at the end of Arlington Road, North Mountain, Annapolis County". The stamp was faded and peeling at its edges, its place of origin obliterated.

He turned the envelope over—no return address. A red wax seal, old, worn, and brittle sealed the flap.

He turned the envelope back over and studied his name again: Benjamin Ezekiel Clement.

"Beck"—BEC—is what he had called himself all his life, not even Ben. He did not feel he was a Ben, certainly not an Ezekiel.

But, there on the envelope his name, in those large looping letters, was undeniable. Found he was, in the blue house, at the end of Arlington Road, Annapolis County.

He wanted to leave the letter in the box. He wanted to pretend that he had never made the walk down the lane from his house. He put it back more than once.

He absently lifted his slouched hat to a tractor rumbling past. Haying season. The driver, a boy not more than 13, nodded back.

He turned back to the mailbox. He pulled a tick from the back of his neck and split it in two with his blunt fingernail. Kicked the post barely holding the mailbox crookedly aloft.

At last, sighing, he took the letter, fastened the mailbox deliberately and slowly, and turned towards the house, his old barn cat weaving herself like a shuttle back and forth between his slow, bow-legged steps.

"Well, my old harridan," he said to her, "let's see what this is about."

He let the cat into the house, a rare occurrence, usually only occasioned by wintry weather or coyotes near at hand. But today he felt like company. He wanted another presence in the room when he opened the letter.

He laid the letter on the oilcloth-covered table, stepping to the sink to fill the coffee pot.

"Some cream?"

The cat assented, a purr growling like an asperous tractor engine deep in her chest.

Once the water boiled and the coffee settled, Benjamin poured a cup and sat at the table with the letter placed in front of him. He could think of no more minor bustlings to keep him from the eventuality of opening the envelope.

The cat leapt to the table and settled beside his elbow, making an elaborate production of grooming her cream-flecked face. Instead of brushing her to the floor, Benjamin absent-mindedly rubbed her tattered, tom-chewed ears and hummed to himself, staring at the letter.

Then, so quickly that the cat flattened her ears and hissed at him, he jumped to his feet and fetched a knife from the drawer beside the sink. He settled again at the table—the cat having forgiven him, lying with her paws tucked neatly beneath her bony chest, watching Benjamin and the process of opening the envelope with great assiduity.

He wiggled the knife beneath the brittle seal and pried it up. It fell to crumbled pieces. He opened the envelope and extracted a single page. A small gold ring fell to the vinyl tablecloth with a muted "ping". The cat reached out her paw and stopped it from rolling off the table.

Benjamin picked up the ring. It was tiny. It sat like a ludicrous halo atop his little finger. Inside the loop he was barely able to make out the word "Sara". The ring was old, so old—the gold of it muted and worn.

Benjamin knew of no Sara. He unfolded the letter, the page so dry that he had to be careful not to handle it roughly, the edges crumbling to flakes despite his care.

The same pale blue ink flowed in the same stream-like way across the page; some words were too faded to read.

> Dear Benjamin (though I have been told you feel that is not your name)
>
> You do not know me, nor I you. It is not in me, usually, to interfere with other peoples' lives, with their fates. We have never met and likely never will. And though it may sound cruel, I do not believe that I would like to meet you. I have seen the results of knowing you.
>
> But I am prompted to write because of two events that cannot be neglected, two events that pique my sense of duty. And though you were never made aware of the story, I feel that it is unconscionable that someone live out a life without knowing what consequences they have left in their turbulent wake. Your ignorance of consequences is through no fault of your own, I confess, but in many ways I am an in-tolerant, single-minded man. An unreasonably moral man.
>
> One event is that a woman, the mother of another wo-man whom I love with an unabashed dismay, has died. She died with heavy burdens that should not have been hers alone to bear. She died in poverty, worn out and broken down, of a sickness that ate at her from the inside out, steal-ing her beauty and the quickness of her mind. When she was staring at the ceiling in her last hours—at the crack that looked like a lightning bolt and the ever-widening wa-ter stain staring back down at her—she told me a story and she gave me a ring. The ring that is contained in this letter, a diminutive ring, an infant's ring—a mere trifling.
>
> The second event concerns the woman I have said I love, the daughter. She stares towards the horizon a lot lately—like she's searching for something. She entertains a longing that she cannot define. Something missing. Something never there. She stares at the woods behind our house, too,

and comments how that one by one the trees will lose their leaves and then the snow will fall, or maybe not. She doesn't seem to care, though always before she has fretted about the small birds and how they will bear the winter—holding her hand to her heart, imagining the rapid drumming of theirs.

Her name is Sara and she is your daughter.

Yours, Simon

Benjamin's eyes widened, he gasped. His daughter? What was this person speaking of?

He put the letter down and moved to the stove to refill his cup. He shook his head slowly back and forth, as though he could shudder the letter and its words from his mind. He stared out the window into the growing dusk, falling gently to the ground in soft drapes of dark, over the hard dirt and basalt rock of the hillocks behind his house. He imagined this woman, this daughter, staring too.

He had farmed the scrubby soil of this place for 60 of his 78 years. The apple trees that had once paid for his living were now ancient, the bottom having fallen out of that industry decades ago. They now offered bitter, inedible fruit and scant protection from the wind.

In all those years he had rarely left the loneliness of the farm. He went to the farm market in Annapolis Royal in the fall to sell his grain and seeds, his vegetables, and small wooden carvings of bears, and foxes, and owls with which he occupied his winters. On his way back he would buy fuel for his truck and a bit for his house, a book to read away the cold, and a new blanket. In the spring of a year he would go to buy seed and supplies from the co-op in Middleton. And every few years he would hunt around the co-op barn to see if there was a mousing kitten, if the winter or a badger had taken his existing cat.

Other than that, he never left. He was alone. Always alone. And sometimes, just sometimes, lonely.

But before he had taken himself off to that blue house at the end of Arlington Road, before he had become the town's eccentric hermit—the subject of stories with which to scare children, he supposed, he had been, instead, the town swain. Crackin' handsome, wild and alluring. He had had plans for greatness, for a life of distinction and affluence. Things a small town in rural Nova Scotia could never hope to provide. In those times, Benjamin had drunk hard and often; he had driven fast; he had slicked down his hair and dallied with many a chaste heart.

His mother stayed silent, just thankful that she didn't have the RCMP at her door, telling her her son and his car were wrapped around a pole. His father encouraged him, egged him on, vicariously thrilled with how Benjamin sowed his wild oats. Ironically, his father failed to note how sowing some actual wild oats in a field of green cover ruined it for hay. How destructive wild oats could be.

But one night when Benjamin was eighteen and at his most discontented and trenchant, when swilling corn liquor until his eyes bugged and driving fast enough on illicit purple gas to decimate entire generations of rabbits held no satisfaction, he committed a hideous indiscretion.

He charmed a young girl, out from the hippie houses built in the woods at the back of North Mountain. He took her to the Friday night dance at the community hall in a place called Paradise. Late that night, the peepers singing the last waltz, he danced her out the door and into the fields. He pulled her to the ground. But he was not appeased with just shattering her heart. He wanted to annihilate her soul.

Watching himself from above, outside of himself and looking down in an alcoholic heedlessness, he saw himself become someone he couldn't comprehend. Someone whom he didn't come anywhere close to recognizing.

And when it was over; when she attempted to hold her torn dress across her bruised breasts. when she held her hand to the blueness about her lips where he had pressed down hard to stop her from screaming, when she looked at him with tears and snot and blood clotted on her face and with her eyes like those of a heifer sensing the first clout of slaughter—he ran.

Benjamin had grown cold, the fire had gone out. He inhaled a shuddering breath. Unhitched his shoulders. Drew a rough hand down his coarse, stubbled face. He stared at the page in front of him as though he were reading his own epitaph. He ran his finger gently under the name "Sara".

With an overwhelming punch of pain felt deep in his gut, which then upper-cut into his heart with such impact he felt it wobbling like a world off its axis, he felt a loss—a loss he hadn't even known was his to feel. A daughter: Sara.

Was this man, Simon, writing to bring him into Sara's world? Was he writing to say that wrongs could be righted? No...

Benjamin re-read Simon's affirmation that people should be aware of the consequences of their actions. How their thrust into the world, right or wrong, left a scar. Like carving love initials into a tree. Deep in the bark there forever even if the love had long since faded and become something else. Benjamin read again the barely veiled accusation, the pity in the tone.

Benjamin looked again at the frail, aged paper; at the yellowed colour; at the antiquated writing and the brittle bits of a seal— nobody used sealing wax anymore. He saw that this letter had been an immensely long time in coming to him, more than decades.

He saw that the gods of fate and irony had cruelly played him, by losing a letter that could have turned the drift of his life. The loss was more poignant, piercing. His opportunity to amend was long gone. The letter was old and worn out. His daughter too—if she even still existed.

Benjamin took the letter with him out the back door, his old cat at his heels. He sat on the creaking, rotting steps and stared out at the umbra as dusk deepened into night.

Here he and his cat had sat many evenings together. They gazed out at the birches at the edges of the fields; the bunchberry and burdock in stubborn humps at the fence lines. They had watched the fog rolling up from the Bay of Fundy. They had watched light-ning storms that lit up the skies as bright as sun on chrome. They had watched foxes skirting the periphery of the land at the margin of their eyesight. They had watched swallows dipping and diving in an avian ballet.

Tonight, fireflies lit up the field in front of them like sparks rising from a fire. A ghost of a moon had risen above the barn.

Benjamin took the brittle letter and its fragile envelope and held them flat in his large, calloused hands. Then, from the edges in, he slowly crushed the paper into shattered bits barely more substantial than dust. He then lifted his hands into the air and blew it all into the night air. The pieces flitted and darted about until they were indistinguishable from the fireflies. The cat raised a paw and batted a couple of vagrant pieces away from the stoop.

He and his cat watched until the freshening near-morning wind that turns the night into dawn. The new-day wind blew the last of the fireflies and scraps of letter out across the mountain until there was nothing left of either.

Benjamin took the tiny, golden infant ring and pushed it with his finger deep, deep into the ground at his feet. He pushed and rubbed at the soil until you could not see that it had even been disturbed. He scratched the cat roughly round the ears, groaned as he creaked to his feet, and turned toward the house to stoke up a fire and put the coffee on.

The dress

Clo Carey

Fifteen years it had taken for Hope to come back. Years of big-city loneliness, homesickness for the tang of an ocean breeze and beach pebbles bruising the soles of her feet. An ache that had stilled as soon as she stepped off the plane.

Now her anxiety mounted again, memories flooding back the closer she got to her grandparents' place.

The local store's parking lot was full, everything else empty. The new coat of paint on the fire hall was the only notable nod to progress.

Turning left, she bounced her car up the overgrown track until first the barn and then the farmhouse, cedar shakes weathered to a timeless grey, came into view. She presumed her mother owned it now since her grandmother's death, but there was no rock here that she would be hiding under.

Hope paused on the veranda, its boards spongy underfoot. She looked back at her rental car parked out front, her only connection to the present, the escape route.

Her gaze swept the landscape. The barn roof had collapsed, grass seeding along the exposed ribs. The old tractor, overgrown with weeds. The house derelict. The place empty since that day.

This, then, was the seat of all her childhood nightmares. A child abandoned by her mother, taken in by grandparents who begrudged the extra burden on their hard-scrabble lives. They referred to the Bible for every decision; every cruel task meted out, every duty called upon, every punishment.

Taking a deep breath, Hope cranked the rusted doorbell, daring the ghosts to rise. She pushed on the warped front door. It creaked open. The smell of must and long disuse assailed her nostrils, the air still and stale.

She tiptoed down the hallway, looking neither right nor left, and entered the kitchen, little changed but for the deterioration of time. A cupboard door hung by one hinge; black mould bloomed on the back wall; a mouse disturbed, scuttled for cover. This farmstead was so far removed on South Mountain that even vandals had not found it.

Touching nothing, Hope moved back towards the stairs and up, each step a test of nerves as treads creaked, then cracked beneath her feet.

A turn at the top and there it was, still suspended in the window of her old room. The dress.

She closed her eyes, recalling the excitement. The high school prom. The invitation from the coolest guy in her class. The purchase of the dress. Each action cloaked in its own secrecy, hidden from grandparents who forbade joy of any kind.

Hope and Beth, skipping school and hitching a ride to town from one of the Oickle boys who would keep the secret in exchange for a kiss. Searching the racks of the thrift shop for that perfect dress, and then searching again.

There it was. A cloud of pink organdy and lace, smuggled back and hidden with care in the darkest depths of her wardrobe.

On the night of the prom, Hope and her grandparents ate their soup and, evening penances done, her grandparents prepared to attend their Saturday night prayer vigil at the temple. Feigning cramps, Hope begged not to have to go. She took to her bed with a list of bible verses to study and waited until she heard the buggy, with old Jupiter between the shafts, clop down the avenue.

Running to the wardrobe she took out the dress and hung it on the curtain rod. She buried her face in its folds revelling in the fabric, soft as a whisper against her skin. Dreams of stolen embraces fired her young body.

"The sin of pride is not permitted in this household."

Hope spun around, shocked to see the bulk of her grandfather filling the doorway.

"You will atone for your lying ways and for the desire to display your body in this shameful garment." He lunged forward, the kitchen carving knife raised in his hand, aimed at her gorgeous dress.

"No!" Hope screamed, sliding the dress along the rail in an effort to prevent the damage that must follow. With nothing to stop his charge, the momentum pitched her grandfather straight through the open casement window.

There was a sickening crunch. Then silence.

Gently pushing the dress to one side, Lucy had glanced down at the spot where her grandfather lay dead.

A terrible accident, they had said at the time, though some wondered at the kitchen knife clutched in his hand. *God's vengeance for missing the prayer vigil*, others muttered.

Hope said nothing to the contrary, biding her time until she could run. The funeral over, she had climbed on a bus and waitressed her way to a prairie landscape.

Now she smiled, unhooked the dress and, folding its flimsy fabric over her arm, headed down to the car.

Aspirations

Linda Turner

Every head turned as Phemmie strolled into the tavern. Some incredulous, some hungry with anticipation, and most irritated that she had walked into their lair to take up space.

McGeorge's was not a woman's place. Lawyers gathered here during the week to talk over court cases. Still, no other venue could have served the purpose. No parish or community hall would make itself available for a meeting such as this.

Nor would Phemmie have withdrawn from the challenge, in spite of the disquiet fluttering in her intestines. No, Hugh McLeod would not win without the fight of his life.

A week ago she'd gone to speak to Master Michael McCulloch, who had taken over Pictou Academy since his father, the former Principal, had succumbed to the lure of Halifax's Dalhousie Institute. While she was there, McLeod had sat in the hallway, listening with every pore, a strained dance of drawing himself closer then pulling back lest young McCulloch see him.

McLeod must have heard it all...her insistence, beseeching consideration for formal entry to the halls of higher learning. If Pictou Academy was as it touted itself, "open to all and without discrimination", surely in the 1830s that should mean open to women. Or so Phemmie believed.

Not surprisingly the new principal had insisted the Grammar School sufficed for women, asserting it prepared them well to teach subjects women were "allowed" to teach.

She knew the real reason. Pictou Academy wanted to spit out its alumni to take up society's most influential positions beyond the Shiretown, and viewed it as wasteful to forfeit even one seat to a female student.

"And if teaching is not my goal?"

"Not the goal? Then pray tell what *is* the goal you speak of, Miss McIntyre?"

"The goal, Mr. McCulloch, is to assist in the field of medicine."

His chortle annoyed her. "Well now, *that* is a topic of which I've not had the pleasure of discussing in *any* context."

He closed a book and took fountain pen in hand in a gesture that strangled any encouragement. "We are extremely busy, Miss McIntyre, and I must respond to Mr. Audubon immediately, and so you see—"

"Of course I understand it would be wrong to keep the prominent ornithologist waiting in the bushes."

Everyone in Pictou knew about John James Audubon's journey to McCulloch's home, his lavish praise of the Scot's private bird collection, and his effusive gratitude at being offered his choice of specimens.

"May he regret the feathers he will need to dust," had been Phemmie's reaction.

"I am to conclude, am I, sir, that the Academy maintains its stand of rejecting female students...indefinitely?"

"And may it be ever thus. Even the granddaughter of a Judge in the Old Country receives no ticket to gain entry through the doors of Pictou Academy."

She gritted her teeth, but knew better than to storm out. She'd been raised with better manners than were on display toward her. "I beg your pardon, sir. Thank you indeed for your valuable time."

She backed away one step at a time.

"Never going to give it a rest, are you, Miss McIntyre?"

She knew that voice, abhorred it. Of course Hugh McLeod would be sitting there, ready to gloat. Ignoring him would only spur him on, and she did not fancy him straggling along as she walked back to Mrs. Cameron's rooming house.

"You've not some advice for me, then?" She faced him square on.

"Aye, I've better than advice. I've a proposition."

"And what, pray tell, might your proposition entail? Be quick, for

I've not got all day."

"As I see it, you're wishing to show the good men of the Academy that your fine lady's mind can hold the stuff as well as the finest of learned gentlemen who don the black gowns."

"That is evident. And you have a suggestion, I suppose?"

"I've but an idea...if it's better left with me, so be it."

"Nay, out with it." She refused to let McLeod see her desperation.

"As I see it, only a duel, as in the olden days, might hold a wee chance to achieve your goal. Not a battle of guns or swords, of course. No, no. Rather a duel of words and thoughts and perceptions, using the knowledge that you're convinced you hold. Our Literary and Scientific Society would be most interested in such a debate."

"Mind ye," he added, "I might be running with the hounds to think you might actually know of men's affairs: politics, business, the economic headaches of the day. You're likely not schooled in such affairs?"

"I know the Anti-Burghers took a proper licking in the fall election, and we've seen the last of them."

McLeod considered this. "And what tidbit can ye provide from the scientific world?"

"I've just had my copy of Lavater's *Physiognomy* returned to me, thus my ability to cite the man's words may have a few cobwebs, but that shall return as it was part of my earlier studies."

McLeod knew little about Lavater, but interrogated her. "What credit grant ye to the grand philosopher, then?"

"Of course, Lavater promotes careful observation and serious contemplation of 'the general form of the countenance, the relation of its countenance parts, and their curved lines, or positions'. "

With that Phemmie stared at McLeod as if he were one of her microscope specimens.

"You resemble a scholar, Madam."

It was a flimsy attempt to flatter. Phemmie knew his goal was to embarrass her publicly, to trick her into a situation in which he could show her up. Yet she couldn't afford to resist, with the paths to her goals dwindling.

"Please be on with your idea, kind sir. I've made you lose enough of your time."

She had decided on the spot to agree to his plan. Now that the appointed Saturday was here she questioned her sanity. It would indeed be a battle of words, with few rules. A "heyday with headlines", he'd called it.

From any newspaper story published in the colony recently, each would provide three words. The opponent needed to unequivocally identify the story, provide commentary, and throw a challenge to the other.

Jotham Blanchard, editor of *The Colonial Patriot*, was the logical choice as judge, given he was already familiar with all relevant content.

True to form, Blanchard had been quick to propose an idea to draw a crowd and turn the session into a charitable event. "Each who shall come will pay the fee of a shilling. All to be given to the newspaper coffers to replenish the debt that had landed our publisher, William A. Milne, in jail several months ago."

In every issue Blanchard demonstrated his loyalty and frustration, poking the conscience of locals who left subscriptions unpaid while the business teetered on bankruptcy and his publisher sat in debtor's prison. The match could provide a forum to rouse the guilty to payment.

Phemmie was thinking that to draw in an audience who would support her with over 50% of the votes was difficult enough, let alone if people had to pay. Yet she would not be seen as unsupportive of Milne or Blanchard.

To back down was unacceptable. So too was to be made a fool of. She comforted herself by concluding that if at least one person heard the message that some women wanted to study science, it would be worth it.

Phemmie hadn't always had access or time to read the news, but late many evenings she'd at least scanned the headlines. What caught her attention was seared into her mind.

Her thoughts veered off to concern about her brother William's failure to return from the West Indies or to send word. She could have used his support, and that of his friends who also worked in the rum trade. They were somewhere between Pictou and the West Indies.

The few women she'd spoken to were shocked she would put herself in the middle of such a ridiculous scheme. They'd remained stone-faced at the notion of being in attendance. Her cousin Isabella had begged her not to embarrass herself or, worse, bring shame on the family by dragging their name into such a foolish enterprise.

When time came to head to McGeorge's, there was still not a murmur about or from William. The men her uncle did business with also bailed out, saying their crops and flocks needed tending. If only it was another day, they lamented; but she knew they were glad to have an excuse.

~

Blanchard looked at the gathered crowd. Somebody had provided a chair for him, knowing that with his battered health he'd tire quickly. Some relentlessly jested about his handicap, overlooking his clear intelligence and accomplishments as the newspaper's editor. He endured the abuse every day.

Finally Blanchard pounded gavel to table, his voice as threatening as old Reverend James MacGregor's when he'd preached the evils of slavery in his native Gaelic.

"This debate begins now. Debaters, come forward."

McLeod, dressed to be admired, stood.

Phemmie had decided the look of a grieving widow was appropriate, knowing it could be the death of hope to enter the Academy during her lifetime.

Blanchard reviewed the rules. "Hear them now for they'll not be repeated."

Each debater was to provide three words each from three news stories. The other was to respond with the context and significance to demonstrate they'd read the story. That each chosen story should raise a question "worthy of vigorous debate" and sure to spark a retort from the opponent was the other requirement.

McLeod bowed to Phemmie. "Ladies first, of course."

"I prefer that Mr. McLeod be the first to submit."

"Very well." McLeod breathed into his body as if to inflate his presence. "I present you, Madame, with the three words: OFFICER...CHOLERAPHOBIA...CONDUCT."

Phemmie knew this. He was toying with her, surely. "Certainly, sir. You speak of Vox Populi, that courageless scoundrel too low to use his own name, to whom the Public Health Officer felt obliged to respond concerning accusations that he had turned a blind eye to cholera's presence on a ship while its captain warmed his palm with pounds. It is unthinkable that any man of good conscience, and particularly one hired for that role, would behave thus. I know not with whom you hold allegiance, Mr. McLeod, but, in my view, both articles were a waste of good ink. Why invent blame for an act that could not have occurred?"

McLeod nodded. "Fair enough, my lady. I have no desire to keep my opinion buried. I therefore ask how otherwise can an observer of deeds of an unjust, dishonest, immoral and illegal nature bring such activities to light, if their words are blatantly ignored? Further, how can anyone in this room say what another has or has not done? Is Vox Populi not justified, nay, obligated, by his own wise counsel to bring such scandal to light without professing his identity when doing so would be offering himself as victim to bloodthirsty stone-throwers?"

Phemmie momentarily wondered if McLeod had been Vox Populi, given his preposterous stance. "My disagreement with your honourable self lies not in an observer speaking truth, but in such a one failing to use his own name."

Phemmie and McLeod glared at one another.

Blanchard, realizing the evening would be long if he didn't intervene, said, "Madame, please advance with your first story."

"Happily. Mr. McLeod, please explain what is the story behind these words: ST. ANDREWS...FEAST...ACADIAN."

McLeod was momentarily puzzled, but quickly recovered. "Indeed! You refer to the newspaper's coverage of local festivities on the feast of our Patron Saint. I hope you do not intend to insult him to whom we are indebted, nor to tarnish the importance of the gathering. I hope your lack of generosity does not extend to purporting it is wrong to honour traditions and history. Yet you mingle the Scots and the Acadians, and perhaps what you mean to say is that the Acadians too celebrate their history. To find it worthy of criticism would prove ye have neither heart nor appreciation for the tragedies and gains from which national pride must grow."

"My understanding," Phemmie said, "is that our preparatory task was to read deeply into the articles, and to query the details. Tradition is a fine thing, particularly when collective pride is generated. I would be loath to criticize the heart of who we are."

"Instead," she continued, "I refer to Raising a Toast to the Acadian *Women*. I ask you why the gentlemen chose not to raise a toast to their own fine and splendid wives, who toil every hour to ensure their families thrive? Or the Acadian men whose dykes we benefit from? Better yet to the Mi'kmaq women and men the papers say behaved admirably at last summer's Regatta, when they beat us in every canoe race? Please explain why Acadian women merit the toast on a night of Scottish pride, and not these others?"

McLeod gazed through her. "Shall we continue?"

Blanchard nodded him on.

The debate continued with what seemed to Phemmie like benign banter. Each time she expected to impress the audience, the flame sputtered out. What use was it to verbally defeat McLeod when the crowd had already decided?

It was useless. She wasn't even a toddler's shoe size closer to convincing the guardians of the Academy that she belonged there. Yet she felt, as powerfully as the sea's surge, that the strangling definition of a Pictou Academy student as male must be untangled. She'd needed to start somewhere.

Suddenly the jarring noise of multiple footsteps could be heard outside the window, and then clattering up the stairs.

The door opened and she saw not ties, not top hats, but a sea of bonnets. In the lead was young Miss McKenzie, the jailhouse keeper's daughter. Rumours were that she had developed a strong affection for the imprisoned publisher.

She nodded at Phemmie and led a string of six women into the corner. Among them was Margaret Pierce, soon to be Mrs. Jotham Blanchard. The widow had treated him so kindly when he'd gone to plead the Pictou Academy case in London that later he'd sent his father to bring her to Pictou to marry him.

As for the other women, the only common thread Phemmie saw was that they were all spinsters, unmarried women clearly undaunted at the thought of stepping from street to hotel after sunset. There was no law to stop them, but there were custom and propriety. Crossing the threshold obliterated that taboo.

It was bold, unthinkable, and of greater risk than they likely knew. But they were there.

Jotham Blanchard, face flushed, knew what the moment required. "The time to vote is upon us. The winner, as agreed to by the good Lady and the kind Gentleman, will be responsible to request of the other a letter of support of a nature that shall please the winner, addressed to the institution of the winner's choice, with indications of the competence and intelligence meriting consideration."

Phemmie was without any outward emotion. Votes were counted quickly but she continued to look in front of her, unable to speak.

Eventually, with a gesture, Blanchard lowered the volume of chatter, and silence moved into the room like fog from the harbour.

"It lies upon me to thank our two esteemed opponents." He nodded first to Phemmie, then to McLeod. "All the more do I, on behalf of our good Publisher, thank those whose donations shall go far to alleviate his suffering."

"On with it," someone cried, "or we'll go home and take our shillings with us."

"As ye wish, it shall be done." He consulted a slip of paper. "I announce that our good fellow Mr. McLeod has the support in the number of 17 votes."

Many scanned the room, trying to count heads, and Blanchard knew he needed to be quick. "And to Miss McIntyre a total of...17

votes."

Supporters for both sides groaned.

"And shall ye cast the decision as to a winner?"

Blanchard couldn't see who spoke. "Had we put it into the regulatory procedures, aye, indeed I would. However, alas, no such provision was thought to be needed and so, no, I have no such authority."

Phemmie needed a victory and wasn't going home without it. "I see no problem, Mr. Blanchard". She spoke so all could hear. "All is well, for this result then shall mean that each of us shall write a letter, the content to be approved by the other, to the institution of our choice."

This met with grand applause, drowning out McLeod, who opposed the conclusion.

Phemmie could just make out, through the crowd, his quivering and downcast shoulders. She knew this battle was over, but not whether she'd gained nothing...or everything.

This story is part of a novel-in-progress.

75

Blow-ins

Come from away

Jeremy Akerman

He saw low mountain ranges like immense, slumbering prehistoric beasts, evanescent fields, blue-hazed woodlands and placid, meandering rivers. Into this lulling, luring place came Martin Gold, and long before he crossed the Canso Causeway he felt he had entered a land time had forgotten.

Frantic, slithering, silver streams flowed on either side and thick, storybook, cauliflower trees rolled steeply up to a roofless sky. Threading between romantically precipitous slopes he had almost gone off the road whilst craning to see the crests of the valley, and a truck coming from behind gave him a long, wailing, accusative, blast.

It was 1990, and Gold was here at the behest of his friend Dan, a Hollywood film director who wanted him to write a screenplay about Dan's hometown of Glace Bay, in the heart of the Cape Breton coal fields. It was to revolve around the area's turbulent, often violent history of industrial relations, particularly the bitter strike of 1925.

Gold had never heard of Cape Breton. Of the town, island, people and their history he knew only what Dan had told him.

After a restless night caused by dreams of walking woods and singing waterfalls, neon light relentlessly penetrating his motel room and a single mosquito, Gold rose very early and was on the road before sunrise.

As he was nosing the rental car around the outskirts of Port Hawkesbury, ninety miles away Lonnie MacPherson, pan-handler, ruffian, drunk was shuffling down Number Three Hill in Glace Bay, as he did many mornings. Picking out a church steeple here, a huddle of company houses there, a pale lemon yellow shaft of light from the sea's end darted across water and rooftops falling like a weightless blade across Lonnie's filthy, pockmarked, unshaven face. Lonnie blinked, rubbed his face with a gnarled and grubby hand, granted the nascent sun a disapproving scowl, then noisily relieved himself by the side of the road.

He spat and snarled at a small, sweetly-singing bird. "Frig off, ya little Christer!" His voice was dry as paper.

His pungent emission complete, he lumbered off towards the town by the sea.

In their own way, in their own places, Black Rory MacDonald, wife Margie, son Donnie and daughter Rita; Annie Pittman, Gorgeous Gloria MacKay, Little Marlene O'Brien and Bright Alec MacKinnon were respectively stirring, washing, shaving, dressing, eating, primping, smoking and yearning. The town was on the move.

In a softly glowing, somewhat intoxicating reverie, Gold wound his way along the gleaming Bras D'Or lakes, through tiny trim villages and scattered reserves, past old creaking farms, and by the time he found Glace Bay, the Melody Café was open for business. There, under Annie Pittman's censorious tutelage, Gloria and little Marlene executed their commandant's commandments.

When they saw him through the large window each of them, for her own reasons, wanted Martin Gold.

Thus, displaying her ample wares as unrestrained as law and Annie would allow, gorgeous, generous Gloria leaned over Gold as she served him eggs, toast and tea, cooing and brushing against him.

Eyes narrowed, Annie icily monitored this wanton rite and the instant Gloria had implemented her duties, she swiftly exercised her right of expropriation. Curtly dispatching Gloria to cleanse the windows, Annie slid her conscious buttocks into the booth and within minutes had learned his name and age, occupation, marital status, where he came from, and his business in Glace Bay.

It was she who told him about Bright Alec MacKinnon, so called, she said, because he had half his Grade 12—Grade 6. Alex, an amateur historian steeped in 'all that labour malarkey', would be able to steer Gold in the right directions. In New Aberdeen, locally known as Number Two, Alex lived with his aged mother Evangeline who, as a very young bride, had come from the French Shore 70 years before.

They lived next door to the MacDonalds who were friends as well as neighbours. Alex devoutly wished one of them could have been more than a friend, much more than a neighbour. Today as always, he leaned against the back fence, waiting for Rita MacDonald to put the cat out.

Today as always when shooing away the pussums, Rita would be draped in a shabby, shapeless, orphan of a garment which, as did all her clothes, concealed the sweet treasure Alex was certain lay beneath. Today as always, they would exchange civilities and Rita would go back inside, leaving him alone, yearning and desperate.

So it came to pass that Gold went to Number Two in search of Bright Alex, found him, and through him came to know Evangeline, the MacDonalds and little Ruby across the street, little Ruby who was dying from a rare bone disease. All of these, and other neighbours too, helped and befriended him with a naïve and ungrudging warmth he had never before experienced.

On many an evening over a boiled dinner, he sat with Ruby's parents, Angus and Carol, their sad colloquy being the inevitable, imminent demise of their lovely, cheeky child. On other occasions Gold joined the MacDonald table for salt cod, pork scrunchions and fried onions, whilst listening to terse, shrewd Rory and mercurial, loquacious, Donnie discussing sports and politics, and stealthily glancing at Rita who, all nerves like an apprehensive doe, darted her eyes away.

For several weeks Gold and Bright Alex were constant companions, as the latter regaled him with accounts of scabs, goons and pimps, armed soldiery and gunboats, heroes and traitors. Alex explained that the neighbourhoods in town took their names the collieries around which they had originally grown: Caledonia, Number Two, Number Six, Number Eleven, Reserve, the Hub, Dominion.

Alex told him that Glace Bay was a honeycomb of underground galleries as a result of more than a century of mining, and that dramatic subsidence was a regular occurrence. He explained that the coastline was frequently subject to erosion and showed Gold a stretch on North Street where an aggressively invasive sea had recently taken almost half the road.

Alex took Gold to the spot where William Davis had fallen dead in 1925, having been shot by the company police, took him underground at the Miners' Museum, and exposed him to the ribald, opinionated, orotund banter at the Pensioners' Union, where all the blood-curdling battles were fought anew and sometimes at greater length.

Thus it was that, over time, Gold came to love this strange and sluggish place. He was resolved not only to complete this project, but to come back to live here.

He had been seduced by the ineffably lovely scenery hereabouts, and by the lazy way of life in what to him seemed a curious backwater. Some of the women had also made this seduction tangible, corporeal.

The first to get him was Gloria, who waylaid him late one evening as he left the MacDonald house. She took him to her tiny attic in one of the big houses on Upper Main Street and fed him lemon gin, aptly describing it as "pants remover".

The next to have him was Annie, who, also late at night, grabbed him as he was passing the door of the Melody, dragged him inside and into the back room with the account books and cases of beans.

Then one night, Gold was stunned when he answered a knock on his hotel room door to discover, in a stupefying metamorphosis affected by anew outfit and a complete make-over, Rita Macdonald, who assailed him like one ravenous for nourishment.

Gold's Cape Breton idyll waned when, during an angry confrontation with Alex, the truth all came out. Alex angrily told him that not only was Annie Donnie's fiancée, but that Rita was the object of Alex's own deep-seated love.

"You bastard," Alex said. "I thought you were our friend, but you're just like all the others who come from away to exploit us and make fools of us!"

Guilty and well rebuked, Gold used his last few days to make modest amends. He had, in any event, completed his notes and had enough material so he could report back to Dan that there was indeed a movie to be made here.

There was little he could do for Gloria, but he bullied Donnie into setting a date for his marriage to Annie and he brought Alex and Rita together by telling them what each had always known but had lacked the courage to say to the other.

"Your Cheating Heart" was playing on the radio as he drove down Roost Street on his last look around.

Nobody knows what Lonnie MacPherson was doing on Campbell's Lane that day, but he lurched out into North Street as Gold's car came around the bend.

Gold swerved, flipped over the lip of the recent erosion, dropped like a stone on to the rocky beach and was dead within seconds.

Donnie MacDonald told his workmates in the colliery showers that Gold "came and went."

By the bay

eloise murray

Bill and Marcie Reynolds disembarked from the ferry in Digby, the GPS set for a destination less than an hour away. They were beginning a much-needed break after months of demanding work in stressful positions. Bill was the physician in charge of palliative care, and Marcie was head nurse in the neonatal unit, at a major hospital in Pennsylvania.

About a month earlier, chatting with Suzanne LeBlanc, head of long term care in the next building, they commented they had taken accrued vacation for an extended time off. She suggested they go to Nova Scotia. Furthermore, her mother had a summer house on the Bay of Fundy that was going to be empty, as her mother was coming to visit Suzanne for a month.

"We thought we might go to Maine."

"Maine is nice, but at this time of year, I doubt there's a place available near the shore for less than a king's ransom. Nova Scotia is not that much further."

"What would it cost to stay at your mother's place?"

"There would be no charge. My parents remodeled an old house with modern conveniences to share. One limitation: there is no WiFi."

The couple allowed that would be welcome as they needed peace and quiet. When they began musing about sandy beaches and swimming, Suzanne cautioned them about the rocky shoreline and the water being remarkably cold. They would need wet-suits. She added she had information about Nova Scotia and notes about the area that she'd bring tomorrow.

The boat had docked late in the afternoon and, as Suzanne, suggested they decided to have supper in Digby before going to their destination, with a plan to grab breakfast and shop for groceries tomorrow. Her notes directed them to a place for seafood.

Pulling up to a trailer, Marcie said, "No self-respecting foodie would never have chose this place. It looks like a greasy spoon."

But they were not disappointed; Bill allowed that his fried clams were the best ever. Her pan-fried scallops melted in her mouth.

That evening, sitting on the front deck of Suzanne's mother's house watching the sunset over the Bay, Marcie said, "I meant to tell you: breakfast is already here. There's eggs, a brown paper package that smells like bacon, homemade brown bread and dark roast coffee."

Bill sighed happily. Then he said, "I think I'll head for bed early. That was two long days of driving."

"Before you go, did you notice all the clotheslines with things blowing in the wind? That sure takes me back to being at my grandmother's house. I love the smell of clothes fresh off the line. Do you think we could have a clothesline in our development at home?"

"I think there is a regulation about that and the answer would be no."

"And another thing I wonder about is all the folk art in unexpected places. I saw a house with a twig or driftwood trellis with bright fish by the road. And I wonder where all those colorful gulls on people's porches and mailboxes come from. "

"I missed all that as I was concentrating on the road."

The next morning, shaking himself awake Bill was astonished that it was nine o'clock. He couldn't remember the last time he'd slept so late.

Marcie appeared as he was cooking breakfast. Taking freshly brewed coffee she went out to the deck to listen to the birds and the waves lapping on the shore.

As they were finishing breakfast there was a knock on the door. A tall, thin man in a plaid shirt, with a droopy moustache, stood there smiling.

"Morning. I'm Buzz. I look after this place. Guess Suzanne told you about me. If you need anything, my phone number is on the fridge."

"She did," Bill said. "Guess you're responsible for that great breakfast. We'd thought we'd have to go to McDonald's."

"That would mean a lot of driving."

Marcy said, "Who makes the bread? And where does the bacon come from?"

"Mary Bent sells bread from her home." Buzz scratched his head a moment. "That bacon's from a fella at the farmers' market in town on Saturdays. Smoked the old fashioned way. You can get it at the garage in town during the week."

Bill stifled a smile. "The garage: right."

"Do you like mushrooms?"

"Oh, yes," Marcy said. "Among our food favourites."

"Foragers keep the locations of their spots secret, but Suzanne said I could tell you where the chanterelles grow on the property."

"We've never had them. Are you sure they are safe to eat?"

"Been eating them my whole life."

As they made their way through the woods next to the house in search of chanterelles Buzz said, "Now, some people forage along the shore, but the only thing I know there that's edible is dulse. He can get some if you want to try it."

"Dulse...why not?" Bill said.

After putting the mushrooms in the kitchen as he was leaving Marcie asked Buzz, "What is going on with all those gulls on mail-boxes and porches? Is it a secret society or something?"

He laughed as if that was the best joke he'd heard in a long time. The prospect of a secret society where every one knew their neighbours just wasn't going to happen. Then he added, "Some old wo-man made those gulls from driftwood and painted them. She wouldn't take any money, but asked that if you got one that you make a donation to the upkeep of the local lighthouse. For that they got a tax receipt so it was a win/win."

When the lighthouse was decommissioned the community took over its care. Even though the fishermen used GPS, it was a wel-coming sight to them and others, gleaming in the night.

Buzz told them that on Saturday nights, at the community hall down the road, there were weekly jam sessions. If they had instru-ments, they could bring them. "They're always looking for singers, too." he said. "They even serve a lunch.

Bill and Marcie used to love live music, back before they got so busy, so they went to the community hall that Saturday. They weren't sure what kind of music it would be, but it might be fun.

That they were not locals was abundantly obvious. People smiled, a few said welcome. The person who sat by them apparently had noted their license plates and commented they'd come a long way for a song. before asking where they were staying.

When they told him, he said, "Oh, that place the come from away folks remodelled! Must have spent a fortune."

Bill quietly said, "I think the the owners' family arrived in 1645."

The man nodded, unfazed. "New comers."

He turned in his seat to face them. "So, do you sing or play?"

"I can barely play the radio," Bill said. "But my wife used to sing." Marcie had sung in a community choir until the schedules of two teenagers made it hard to get to practices.

At lunch break people were much friendlier. News had travelled fast, and the emcee came over to ask Marcie what she would like to sing.

"Oh, no," she said. "I haven't sung in public in years. I don't even have any music with me."

"Very few of these people are using music. Tell them the key and the song and I bet they will know it."

Marcie was first for the next set and sang "Amazing Grace". The crowd, who loved her rich contralto voice and the song, joined in.

At the end, someone called, "Encore!"

Blushing, Marcie said, "Maybe next week."

It really wasn't the kind of music event they used to attend, but the weeks they were there they were welcome regulars at the jam sessions, including bringing something to contribute to the lunch break.

When Buzz came by about three days later to mow the path to the shore, they asked where to get the best lobster roll.

"That would be the fish market in the cove. about ten minutes to the west. I know they're good because my wife is the cook!".

Arriving, they were delighted to see about fifteen fishing shacks, all painted bright colours. Bill took dozens of pictures before they went to what they had assumed was merely a market. They left saying they'd be back and carrying fresh scallops for supper. A really good lobster roll on the deck overlooking the colourful harbour and the bay didn't need any further ambience.

Without any discussion about it, the couple began to sleep in, take naps in the afternoon, go for walks along the road in the afternoons before having a glass of wine on the deck and then sharing cooking supper. It seemed like a routine they had once had.

They spent time reading books from the shelf, by local authors they'd never heard of, or simply sitting and watching the bay. Marcie often strolled along the shore, coming back each time with a few special rocks.

The farmers' market Buzz had mentioned when talking about Mary Bent's brown bread was not as expected; it was way better. There was live music, a wide range of craftspeople as well as vegetable and baked goods vendors, including some offering prepared food. They agreed to begin separately, choosing what they wanted and then do their food shopping.

When they met up, Marcie admitted she had taken things to the car, mostly gifts for family and friends.

Bill nodded. "I saw your bags when I was putting mine in the car."

They shopped for food and had a grilled sausage with sauerkraut as their lunch.

On the way home Marcie announced she'd purchased three small paintings.

"Good grief, why three?"

"One for each of our offices and one for the den at home. Two are sort of folksy and the other more realistic. They are all really well done depictions of that colourful cove by the fish market. You may choose the one for your office."

Bill told her about a conversation with a young man who had chanterelles for sale at a very high price. "I told him I was picking them every few days, and the guy was all about wondering where that place might be. I said my lips were sealed on that matter."

Then he added there was one thing he really wanted, but he wanted to run it by her. He'd been talking with a person who made shoes. He had long and very narrow feet making buying shoes difficult.

"Are these those ugly orthopaedic shoes?"

"Decidedly not," Bill said. "They would be classier than my favourite ones that I'm wearing right now. The cobbler would take a mould of my feet and send the shoes when they're ready."

"Bill, you spend a lot of time on your feet. These won't be cheap, but we can afford them. And if they have your mould, they can make others when you need them. Call him and make an appointment. Who knew it was still possible to get custom-made shoes?"

Bill nodded. "These shoes need new soles. I wonder if I can get them repaired."

Marcie grinned. "Ask Buzz."

She was right, Buzz knew exactly who could repair Bill's shoes. "You won't recognize them when they're done. In a good way."

The weeks went quickly. They were invited to a local community potluck event, went to breakfasts at the local fire hall on Saturdays and had lobsters picked up at the wharf. Cooking the first four for supper and then for a salad for lunch the next day prompted a debate about who would put them in the boiling water to steam. Bill lost. They agreed those lobsters meant they would never be happy with lobster at a restaurant. Occasionally they would take the car and go exploring recommended sights in the area, or just drive down a road to see where it went.

Their last week, on Friday afternoon they invited people they had met to a wine and cheese on the deck. It was a success, although local people had never met most of those who were from in town. Marcie's idea was that was what made any party interesting.

On the Monday morning they boarded the ferry to go home. Settling down at a table on the rear deck they agreed the vacation had changed how they saw some things. They had loved the walks before supper. On previous vacations they had rushed around seeing things to such an extent that coming home to go back to work was a rest.

Their diet had more fish and fresh vegetables. and far less pre-pared foods, something they wanted to continue at home.

"The whole experience makes me aware how we've been rush-ing home with an armload of stuff, having two glasses of wine and then throwing something from the grocery store freezer in the oven or microwave," Bill said. "We used to be foodies who shared cooking together."

"I think the big difference was we had connections to local people. Suzanne's notes pointed the way. Buzz certainly was a big help."

"Marcie, don't discount the fact your singing at those jam ses-sions let us meet a lot of people."

"Have you ever been in a place where you were made to feel so welcome? That first jam session, Mary Bent told me that on Thursdays she made meat and fruit turnovers as well as brown bread. It wasn't on a sales pitch; it was just so we would know. And what are we going to do without that brown bread for breakfast?"

"My epic day," Bill said, "was when I rented that sea kayak with a guide to paddle along the shore for about three hours. I learned so much about the area—not just the ecology, but also the history. Paul was so well informed.."

"But the next day you could barely get out of bed from the workout and being cramped in that little boat."

"It was worth it," Bill said with a laugh. "I was pleased he and his wife came to our wine and cheese."

"Bill, when did we last go to live music or entertainment of any kind? We haven't had people in for a meal in ages or even gone to a restaurant. We can't change our work responsibilities very much, but we sure can do a better job with the rest of our time."

"Guess we had to get away to realize that. When Suzanne told me that that place and those people could change how you see things, I had no idea what she meant."

Marcie was nearly asleep in the sunshine from the gentle rock-ing of the ferry when Bill nudged her to ask if she would clarify something. She knew from the tone of his voice she was about to be teased. She nodded.

"How many grocery bags of beach rocks did you put in the car and what you are going to do with them? If we stayed any longer we'd need a moving van to get home."

"I have plans for every one of them. For now they remind me of new friends, experiences we were not expecting and how much we need a reset in our lives."

Ginger ale and hostages

Rose Poirier

The end of a faded orange curtain waltzed around the broken window. I always thought of that colour when I thought of Bernice. She had what I called orange hair but everyone else said it was red.

She used to live next door. Before the house started sagging. If you tilted your head slightly, the house didn't lean at all, but when you got your head straight, the damage was obvious. No matter. Somebody'd bought it. They were here to look it over but hadn't moved in yet.

Standing there staring at it, I heard him coming. Joe at Johnnys, in his truck, rattling by, spewing plumes of dust and banging over the potholes. His trailer was the last one on the road and he had a massive satellite dish outside.

Sometimes, I wondered if I could take my father's tape measure up and see if it actually was bigger than the trailer. But I was a little scared of Joe's horse so that wasn't going to happen. I likely wouldn't have been allowed to go that far alone anyway.

Joe had the window rolled down and the Bee Gees blaring. I knew it was the Bee Gees because my big sister had bought the record, the one with the men with the shirts open down to their pants showing hairy chests and gold chains. I thought they were kind of gross. I rarely agreed with my father, but I did think a haircut would have made them look much better.

My legs started to itch. Grass or flies—I don't know. But I thought it was best to get out of the high weeds in the lane and back onto the road so I could walk home. I'd picked the lupines already—my mother had sent me here to get them for somebody's birthday bouquet. But I'd forgotten the can of Off and I was starting to get swarmed.

With the thought of my fresh stack of Archie comics inspiring me, I ran until I got to the bottom of our lane, lupines swinging from my hand, then trudged up the hill.

The smell of chicken haddie hit me before I even got to the screen door. I didn't like it as much as fried baloney and I had thought that my mother had quit frying haddie since she'd burned it when the American cousins came and whined in their nasal Bostonian accent, "What's that smellllllll?" Maybe I'd just eat the potatoes.

My brother was six years older than I was and barely noticed my existence on his way out the door. Nearly hit me with it. I didn't bother asking where he was going. Probably wouldn't tell me anyway. His 14 years were more like 24, at least in his mind. Because he had a banana bike and I didn't. I would never ask for one for myself. Figured I wasn't going to get a bike if money was tight or maybe I'd inherit his when he was finished with it. I'd rather read.

It was on this yellow and black bike that he rode down the lane the next morning. Before the panic set in. My mother had seen the new neighbours' car go by earlier—a white, boxy Volvo with a pile of stuff tied to the top of it. Well, sort of white. The dust was pretty bad this summer, so by the time it got the two miles past the end of the pavement, it was turning beige.

I don't think my mother had time to say anything to my brother. He was out like a shot. I figured he was checking out these new neighbours. The only ones, really. The next closest house on the other side was over a mile away. Then again, he may have gone to the store to get pop. Or to his buddy's place on the Shore Road. I'd heard my mother on the phone saying he had a girlfriend named Shanny or something. Someone's kid who was home from Ontario.

My parents normally would have gone to see the neighbours for themselves. They would have taken some biscuits as a cover for curiosity. But they'd just finished picking strawberries and had a pile of ice cream containers full of them that they wanted to freeze. Some went into the freezer quickly, and my mother stood by the sink trying to deal with the other ones. Griping about how my sister had to take everything in the field home and that there was more hay and stems than berries.

I waited until my mother had picked a full container clean and placed it behind her on the counter before loading up a bowl and adding my father's coffee cream and a few spoons of sugar. Took it the living room and started reading.

The sound of Joe's truck interrupted my fictional Archie and Veronica. This time it came up the lane and parked, Charlie Pride kissing his angel good morning before the truck door slammed.

"Did you see what's going on up there?" His voice booming despite a four-pack-a-day habit. "Friggin' hippies are gonna take over. They think their long-haired, drug-dealin' Satan-worshippin' ways are gonna work here, they got another thing comin'.'"

"Drug dealing?" I could hear my mother's voice go up an octave.

"What's this about Satan?" My father liked to talk over her when company came.

"Oh, we all know what they're like," Joe confirmed. "Lookin' for a place in the woods to hide whatever they're doin'. Well, they're not gettin' past me. I know exactly what's goin' on. I'm drivin' by there five times a day. And I'm gonna do it more now."

"Won't that take a bit of gas, Joe?" My mother suddenly re-membered what she called her manners: "And did you want tea? I can get you some berries and biscuits." No one set foot in the house without getting tea. Even the meter reading man.

"Ach, yes, tea'd be good. Tapa leat." The Gaelic came out as easily as the flecks of manure fell off the bottom of his work pants and onto the floor. My mother would curse about that later.

"Did you see them, Joe? I mean get a look at their faces?" My father said he could judge a man by his face. Never mentioned what he judged women by.

"Oh, you can't see their faces! They're covered with hair. Longer than Jesus'. Sandals, too, by God. I heard they're from California. Nothin' good comin' outta there. They ought to get the municipal-ity to stop this. Tommy the Fiddler would be turning over in his grave if he saw what was goin' on in the house he built with his own hands."

I had the Archie comic open but wasn't reading anymore. I pictured old Tommy, fiddle under one arm, slamming nails into wood with his bare fist. Didn't seem very sensible to me.

The talk went on for over an hour, my mother alternately questioning and defending the possible virtues of people we didn't yet know. My father focusing on the condition of the house and Joe adding issues one by one, like a bird building a nest.

He decided to stay for lunch and I wondered how he'd fit in his five or more trips driving by the neighbours if he were staying here all day.

The remaining berries were soggy when he left.

I had gone through three Archie Digests and two rounds of Oreo cookies with milk before my sister got dropped off from her summer job and asked where my brother was.

I shrugged and pointed out the window. "Somewhere on his bike."

Her brow knotted. Not that that was an unusual look. She marched into the pantry where my mother was starting to make supper on the hot plate because it was too hot to use the big wood range in the kitchen. Turns out we did have baloney in the fridge.

Fictional Betty was finally making inroads with comic-book Archie, so I had stopped paying much attention to the mumblings and rumblings of conversation in the kitchen. Then I heard the screen door slam and the car start up. By the time my mother called me to eat, thirty or forty minutes had passed since my father had gone to look and both my sister and mother were alternately staring out the window and scraping the Miracle Whip jar to get the last of what was stuck in the bottom.

My mother discussed things with my sister like an adult. Years later I finally let go of my resentment by figuring out she actually was an adult at that point. "You'd think he'd be back by now. I already called Jacky's to see if he was there but Dan Hector's wife said she hadn't seen hide nor hair of the yellow bike all day and Jacky was out on the boat, fishing lobster. Too young for that if you ask me."

"Did you try Norbert's? Or Rob's?" My sister knew all my

brother's friends and which ones might be more likely to show up in the court report in the weekly paper.

My mother nodded. "I bet he went that way." Tossing her chin in the direction of the old house with the new people. "Now, where the hell is your father? He should have been back from that house whether he found him or not. It's been over half an hour."

"Don't worry. I'll go check." My sister left her unwashed dishes in the sink—a sacrilegious thing for her—and took her new 10-speed out of the shed. I joined my mother at the window to watch her bike down the hill and turn left, the clock above the kitchen table edging toward 6 pm.

By 7 pm., I thought my mother was going to wear out the new circular dial on the phone. Round and round it went.

Finally, she grabbed her going-out sweater and said, "All right, that's it. Let's go see these people."

I had a vague unsettled feeling about going to see people without biscuits, but I put my sneakers on and sprayed myself liberally with Off as I wasn't ready to be chewed up by flies again and they were awful in the evening.

It only took us about 15 minutes to get there. I liked walking downhill.

As we approached the old house, we could see my parents' car parked in the overgrown lane with my sisters' bike resting against it. Right behind the dusty Volvo, no longer sporting the rooftop bags and boxes. One yellow rope still danged off it, though.

My mother gripped my hand. Getting closer, we spotted my brother's yellow bike right at the door.

I heard laughter and voices out the broken window, but I could tell by the force of my mother's rap on the door that she wasn't in a laughing mood.

The door squeaked open and a skinny man, taller than anyone I'd ever seen, stood smiling at us. Gleaming white teeth, deep tan and a head of dark curly hair. No beard. No ponytail. "Hello! You must be Mom and little sis! Come on in, please."

My mother was rarely speechless. She looked like someone had just popped a balloon in her face, but gamely stepped forward, still keeping a death grip on my hand.

In front of us were my sister, my father and my brother. No ropes. No handcuffs. No smoking drugs. Looking for all the world as if they belonged here, my father with a half-finished ginger ale in his hand, sitting on a cardboard box that obviously wasn't meant to support his weight.

The presumed wife of the man came forward. She stood almost at five feet with a smile broader than she was tall. Little round glasses like on my sister's John Denver record. "Welcome, welcome, I'm Sandra. and this is Terry. and I'm so glad you're here. We were worried that your son should have gone home, but he insisted he was fine and we fed him as best we could. He was a wonderful help to us unloading our gear and helping us set up. And then your husband helped, too! We can't thank you enough. Would you like some cookies? I'm afraid the only cold drink we have here is ginger ale."

That was it. If they offered food before my mother had a chance to sit down, my mother was disarmed. Flying the white flag. The standoff was over.

Years of cookies and biscuits traded hands as the clean-shaven, non-drug-selling, non-Satanic new neighbours repaired the window, straightened the house and convinced Joe that planting California artichokes was a fine idea.

The honeymoon garden

Gary Lovett

It was early in the morning when the ambulance drove through the tiny fishing village on its way to the hospital on the eastern shore. The red light was flashing, which caught the attention of almost everyone whose modest homes were clustered along the twisting, coastal highway.

Tongues began to wag almost immediately. The phones started to ring. Before long the party lines had sorted out the matter. A young man and his girlfriend had ridden their motorcycle into the woods after missing a turn. The young man had died at the scene and the girl was in critical condition. She would be stabilized and transferred to the Victoria General Hospital in Halifax.

There was some truth in the rumours. There was a motorcycle accident. A drunk driver had forced the oncoming motorcycle into the ditch when he pulled out to pass a school bus. The bike had slid down an embankment, carrying the two riders to the bottom. The girl had managed to get her leg up, which left her bruised but mostly unhurt. Her boyfriend had fractured his leg below the knee and burned his arm on the exhaust pipe. It was not a pretty sight, but it was not fatal.

The girl was riding in the ambulance with her boyfriend. She would be examined and released. Her boyfriend was admitted into the local, one-story hospital. He was x-rayed and placed in a cast from the thigh to his foot.

His girlfriend found a rooming house to stay in for the two weeks he spent in hospital. It was a quiet home run by a small, wiry woman whose husband had been killed in a logging accident years before. She took her meals at the rooming house because they were included in the twenty dollar a week fee.

She and her boyfriend were from Ontario. They had spent the summer touring Newfoundland and the Maritime provinces. They were on their way to Halifax, where they would work for the winter and then head for Europe. They would have probably sold the motorcycle before they left.

Money was tight. He called his parents.

She spent a lot of time at the hospital. It was too hot in the rooming house, where the woman prepared the food on a giant wood stove that made the kitchen intolerable. It was cool in the hospital. Fluctuations between extreme heat of the rooming house and the coolness within the red-brick hospital are how she remembered that time.

That was many years ago now.

~

Her guitar had broken in the accident. People told her a local artisan might be able to help.

"Can you fix it?" she asked in his workshop near the rooming house.

"I am Claude," he said and gently took the guitar from her hands.

He resourcefully repaired it with the mounting rod from a broken mirror on the motorcycle. Glued and clamped, it had sat in his shop for three days.

When she was not at the hospital, she busied herself in Claude's workshop, sweeping and placing lengths of planed wood into stacks along a wall while watching her new friend meticulously tap joinery into place. He didn't seem to mind her presence in the shop. She was mystified by his attention to detail.

Her boyfriend was released from the hospital and his parents loaded him into a car to take him back to Ontario. She was sad to see him go. They had been together for a couple of years and he was a great travelling companion, but she couldn't let go of her longing to see the world. Not yet.

She went to the shop to pick up the guitar. "How much do I owe you?" she asked after sitting the guitar on her knee and tuning it.

"Don't owe me a thing," he said. "You give the shop a good cleaning. Tit for tat."

She began to strum and hum along. Blackbird. Fly.

He was watching her fingers form the chords and for the first time she noticed his intensely blue eyes. *I think I'd like to know him better,* she thought.

She found a buyer for the motorcycle and was thinking of heading to the city to find a job. Some waitressing work where the tips were good would have her on a plane to France in three months, she figured.

But first she had to visit Sheldon. He was a somewhat loony old man who had shared the hospital room with her boyfriend. She had promised to come with her guitar and play him a tune.

She settled in and started playing Danny Boy, with which he seemed very familiar.

A nurse's aid came in pushing a cart. She waited till the song was over. "That was beautiful, Miss. Mister Parker, would you like a snack? I have cookies, cheese and crackers, or jello."

"I'd like a piece of p-pa-pa- pie," he replied, struggling with the words.

Blushing. "Oh Mister Parker, please slow down a bit. Which would you like?"

"I said I want a piece of p-pa-pa-pa-pie!"

She put some cookies on his tray, turned and pushed the cart out of the room, muttering as she left, "No pie as always."

Swinging around with the guitar, the girl began to play You Can't Always Get What You Want. It was hard to keep a straight face as Sheldon rubbed his whiskered chin, false teeth on a side table and a puzzled look on his face. *Where do we go from here?* she thought.

When the small hospital converted to long-term care many years later, she began to volunteer there a few days a week. She always brought her guitar and was easily coaxed into a sing-along in the lounge. This involved more hand-clapping then singing on the residents' part, but she enjoyed the old, familiar songs. Songs her father had sung to her when she was a child.

She sat near the parking lot on a bench and smoked a cigarette. It had been a long time since she had smoked. Her hand shook and as the smoke filled her lungs she became a little lightheaded and felt nauseated. She stomped on the cigarette and wondered what had possessed her to ask the duty nurse for a smoke.

She was angry at her boyfriend for leaving her here alone. "Get rid of the bike and you'll be okay," he had said.

She couldn't remember his name.

She hadn't heard a word from him all these years. So much time had passed by and never a word. *What was his name?*.

She was in the room her boyfriend had been in many years ago, talking to an elderly woman, when her mind started drifting, wondering why she had never heard from that boy again. Maybe the father crashed the car on the way home. Perhaps.

She had never felt the need to know. *Why now?*

She had gone to the city and worked there for the winter. She sent Claude a letter with her address and an 'if you're ever in the city....' type invitation.

After a few weeks, Claude began to come visit on weekends. At first, he would arrive in the morning and, after a day in the parks and maybe lunch in a cozy, warm restaurant, he would give her a big bear hug and then drive away. She enjoyed his company, the way he talked, the light touch of his hand on her arm as they crossed the street, and she knew she was falling in love.

After a month or so, she held onto him and said, "Please stay. I don't want you to go."

Her bachelor apartment became their sanctuary and their lovemaking showed a wild side of Claude unlike his slow, precise cabinetry work in the shop. In the mornings there they would watch the sun fill the room with brilliant light and eat rolls and drink coffee and orange juice till the noonday gun from Citadel Hill punctuated the intimate conversations they shared.

Spring came, and in May she moved back down the shore. She and Claude were married in a small ceremony in the backyard. They postponed a honeymoon to put in their first vegetable garden.

She tilled Claude's ashes into the soil in the garden after a car accident took his life. They had two children and five grandchildren who helped put in the garden that year, unaware that it had become a memorial garden as well. That summer the garden flourished and they celebrated its bounty together at Thanksgiving.

But as fall deepened she found it hard to concentrate. She still played the guitar, but sometimes had to start over because she had lost her way. The old folks in the hospital didn't mind. They would resume their clapping and try to remember the words so they could sing along.

One night she got out of bed and went out to the shop. It was untouched since the accident. She found bins full of bits of hardwood squirrelled away under tables. Claude had saved them to create fanciful inlay around drawer handles and decorative trim.

She swept up and sprinkled the sawdust in the garden as the sun started to rise over the cove.

She found his worn book full of drawings and plans. She pulled the big carpenter's pencil from the binding. She inhaled the woody smell that was a part of him. She wrote on the front page:

You made everything beautiful

Then she went inside to make the coffee.

The Blairs

John MacEachern

Shawna and Carl Blair were senior partner and managing director, respectively, of Blair, Blair, Cogswell and Blair LLP, possibly the most prestigious law firm in all of Canada, with offices in Toronto, Vancouver, Ottawa, New York and London. Shawna and Carl were both patrons of the Canadian Opera Company, The National Ballet and the Toronto Symphony. They were on numerous Boards of Directors of both Canadian and international companies and were members of the Granite Club, the Badminton Racket Club and the Royal Canadian Yacht Club.

It's not like they enjoyed the ballet, opera or even classical music, but it was the contacts during the intermissions where they found new clients while discussing the attributes and nuances of different Chardonnays or Pinots Noir.

Their son Gordon ran the Ottawa division, as he was very much involved in the political game and was very astute at supporting three different political parties at once. Shawna and Carl wintered in their large home in a gated community in Naples, Florida, where Carl played golf every other day at the championship course while Shawna enjoyed her martinis with friends around the pool at the club.

When in Toronto they seldom ate at home, but rather had a regular table at either Winston's or Le Provençal. They were also very big fans of sushi, so usually every Friday night, if they weren't out of town or at Roy Thompson Hall, they would treat themselves to dinner at Toronto's HiroSashimiSushi, often advertised as serving the finest sushi in North America.

One night, after dinner at Winston's, they arrived home to their penthouse condominium and put their feet up with a nightcap to watch The National. Shawna had a frosty martini which Carl had carefully stirred for her so as not to bruise the gin. He settled down with a dram of Bruichladdich, Isle of Islay single malt scotch, neat.

During the first commercial break, an ad came on for Nova Scotia. Carl put his arm around Shawna and suggested they walk on the wild side and fly down to Nova Scotia to see where the wind would take them.

"Oh my God," Shawna said. "What would I wear? Those people wear jeans down there."

"You've got jeans. What's the problem with that?"

"Carl, they're eight hundred dollar Gucci jeans. I'd stick out like a sore thumb. Furthermore theirs are all worn and faded."

"Well," he said, "we could consider it a business trip and look at opening an office in Halifax."

"Now that you put it that way and we can write off the entire trip, I'm in."

Carl made reservations, first class on Air Canada to Stanfield International and reserved a late-model Lincoln to pick up at the airport. Soon they found themselves heading down the Annapolis Valley.

They stopped in Annapolis Royal, where they found a beautifully restored Victorian bed and breakfast. Their hostess, Cicely Crump, told them about the King's Theatre, where there was a live performance of ten minute shorts. They particularly enjoyed one called "Speed Dating at Elderberry Manor".

The following day, after a beautiful breakfast featuring homemade scones with local preserves, they headed out towards Digby, which they had heard was famous for its scallops. As they approached Digby they saw "vacancy" on the Bayview Bed and Breakfast road sign.

They quickly pulled in and headed up a long laneway with wild lupines on either side of the road, until they reached the top of the hill where there was a very large home overlooking the Annapolis. They could see the town of Digby in the distance.

Connie Bent showed them what she called "the Bridal Suite",

with a king-size four-poster bed, a private ensuite and a large slid-ing-glass door which led out to a lovely veranda with a magnificent view of the bay.

"As well as breakfast, I offer afternoon tea to anyone who is in-terested. This way, if anyone wants to know of what to see and what to do, I'm there to answer their questions."

Shawna and Carl decided to go down for tea, and Carl asked the name of a good restaurant known for scallops. Shawna wanted to know where she might find a cozy sweater as she was feeling a little cool from the breeze from the water

"Carla's has the finest scallops you'll ever find. Her husband is a scallop fisherman, so you know they're fresh off the boat. And just before that you will see Frenchy's where you will find just about any clothing you need, dearie."

Shawna was so excited to know that there was a cute little Paris-ienne boutique way down here in Digby. *Frenchy's, how quaint. I love the name,* she thought.

Aloud she said, "Why don't we go shopping at Frenchy's and then go out for a nice leisurely meal at Carla's for some scallops. We can see what else they might have on the menu, perhaps steak tartar or veal scallopini."

They decided to make it an early night and soon headed into Digby. The first thing they saw was the large sign saying "Frenchy's", on a building not at all what Shawna had imagined. They opened the door and saw a large room filled with bins brim-ming over with used clothing.

"Let's go. I'm out of here. This is certainly not the cute little boutique I had imagined." Shawna said.

"Just a minute," Carl said, "Let's just see what's in here". He headed over to a bin marked "Women's Sweaters."

Shawna was most uncomfortable and looked around to see if anyone was watching.

Carl finally held up a beautiful, pastel-yellow cashmere sweater and said, "This is perfect. It looks like it's just your size and is def-initely your colour. It doesn't even look like it's been used." He checked the label and said, "It's a Brunelle Cucinelli, if that means anything, and it's only three bucks."

"Let me see that," Shawna said. She grabbed the sweater out of Carl's hand.

"My God it is. That pink one I have at home is a Brunelle Cucinelli and I paid well over three thousand at Holt Renfrew."

She held the sweater up to herself and said, "Okay, I'll take it, but don't you dare tell anyone back at the club or I'll kill you."

They found a pair of Levi's jeans for Shawna and a Blue Jays jacket for Carl, and the total of the bill was thirteen-fifty plus tax.

Shawna, quite pleased with herself, said, "Now I'm ready for a good dinner. I trust the scallops will be fresh. If not, there's probably a lot of other things on the menu. I'm also ready for a good glass of Chardonnay."

It was only a few hundred feet down the road when they saw the sign "Carla's Take-Out". "No, no way am I interested in take out, and that's that," Shawna said.

"Here, you stay in the car and I'll go in and see."

Carl soon came out and motioned for her to come into the restaurant. "They have tables inside," he said.

Carl went to the counter and ordered two large plates of scallops and a small one of fried clams, as Mrs. Bent had recommended their clams and they had never had fried clams before. When the scallops came to the table Shawna put the first one into her mouth and started to eat it. Her eyes widened as wide as her grin as she continued to chew it.

"I have never, ever, tasted anything that good."

Carl tried his and agreed, and then they dove into the shared plate of clams. The same reaction: "Unbelievable," Carl said. "You'll never find anything that good anywhere in Toronto. I'm shocked."

During their breakfast, Connie asked them where they were headed. They said they might try to go down towards Yarmouth.

"Well, if you're going that far, you might as well go to Wedgeport, the southernmost town in Nova Scotia. They're having their Tuna Festival this weekend, which is always fun. If you're interested I'll call my cousin Muriel and see if she has any rooms left in her B&B."

They agreed and Muriel told Connie that she had just had a cancellation, so the room was theirs if they want it. So they reserved it at the South Point Inn B&B and headed out to Wedgeport.

After a two hour drive they finally found Muriel Bent's South Point Inn and were taken to another beautiful room with a great view of the harbour. Muriel explained to the Blairs about the tuna festival, where the fishermen would catch their tuna and bring the huge fish in to be weighed. There were buyers from Japan. The fish were gutted, packed in ice, put into refrigerated trucks and rushed to the airport to be shipped to Japan. Canadian tuna was very much revered in Japanese sushi restaurants.

Carl and Shawna drove to the edge of town, where a golf cart shuttle took them to the bleachers. They sat there for at least two hours, watching the weigh ins. They were fascinated.

Carl, on his way to the Johnny-on-the-Spot, saw a large tent and asked someone what it was for.

"It's a sushi tent," the man said, "so everyone can enjoy some."

When he got back to the bleachers he told Shawna, knowing their shared love for sushi, and they immediately went to the tent. At the entrance a young woman greeted them and sold them two five-dollar tickets. Each ticket was for five tuna sushi on Japanese sticky rice and five pieces of raw tuna sashimi.

They sat down and immediately a young college student brought their meals, along with some wasabi, soy sauce and ginger. At the end of the tent they could see Japanese chefs creating dozens of meals for the patrons.

They looked at each other and said at the same time, "Hiro should see this." They laughed, and Carl went up and got two more tickets.

He said to the lady selling the tickets, "Who gets the money from this?"

She said, "Everything, but the tent, is donated and we are all volunteers, so after the tent costs are covered, this year's money is going to renovate the Fire hall."

Carl pulled out his wallet and gave the lady an additional fifty dollars, "Please put this towards the Fire hall." He went back to the table to get a second plate for each of them.

Shawna and Carl had only two days left in Nova Scotia but decided that they needed another feed of scallops and clams at Carla's and were able to book another night at Bayview Inn before catching their flight back to Toronto the following day.

When they arrived home they made reservations at Winston's. The Maître d', Jacques, greeted them at the door and mentioned to Shawna that she was looking particularly attractive that evening. She was wearing her new pastel-yellow Brunelle Cucinelli cashmere.

They looked at the menu and saw that there were fresh Digby Scallops on special on the menu, so Carl decided to try them. A plate of three, very large, pan seared scallops with a ring of seven green peas surrounding them was put in front of him. Shawna looked at him and chuckled, "Is this what they call Nouvelle Cuisine?"

He reached out and held her hand and said, "I think we have to reevaluate our lives."

"I agree."

Not in everyone's garden

Grace Keddy

Another late winter, early spring snowstorm. Nothing unusual and nothing more annoying. They never seem to last long. Poor man's fertilizer my family called it. A very true statement considering the rich, nitrogen-filled flakes that covered plowed ground and dormant.

My father and brothers, all three of them, were out with the tractor, shovels and strong backs, clearing the wet, heavy snow from driveway and vehicles. My car being one of them.

The house was warm, heated with a wood furnace that was filled on a regular basis only due to my mother's prompting one of us three girls to go to the cellar to fill or check the fire.

We would open the heavy, cast-iron door and move the burning coals or remaining junks of wood to make room for another huge piece of hard wood. Mother would know that the chore was done on two counts: one was the sound of the heavy furnace door clanging loudly and sending a vibration through the kitchen floor. Second, there was usually a poof of smoke coming through the floor grate when the door to the furnace closed.

The cellar was a mud floor, huge boulders of granite for the walls. Rows of wood dwindled throughout the winter, a remainder of preserves lined shelves, enough to carry the family through until the next crop was ready to harvest, jam or pickle.

Everyone was busy, as was the normal condition of a farm household. There was a job for each and the jobs had to be completed for the farm to run smoothly. It was easier that way.

My mind was in the two-hour drive back to Halifax. I had packed, hoping the roads were in dryer condition after one more day of plowing and salting. The main roads were not a huge concern. It was the mountain and cursed back roads that were always the last to see a machine from Department of Highways. There was a celebration to see a machine after a week of snow filled-roads preventing traffic.

My visits home depended on weather forecasts during the winter months. I didn't want to get trapped and risk losing my job.

City people didn't understand the rural workings of road clearing. There was always a risk that the forecast would be wrong and a flash storm would come across the bay, causing a surprise snowstorm.

The snow started sometime during the night. Came in on the tide and lasted for over twenty four hours.

Life continued. Meals had to be made to feed the nine people in the house, working up appetites from snow removal or looking after animals or other jobs that made up the day's obligations.

Lunch had been over for a while, the clean-up completed. Preparations for supper were in the works. Typical huge pot of baked beans was in the oven, potatoes were being peeled, nothing was left to the last minute, nothing was instant.

There was sound of someone shuffling playing cards: my youngest sister begging for a game of Crazy Eights. With a lull of household chores, there was time for a quick game.

These were days before computers, before multi-channel television. Entertainment was reading, checkers, card games or the occasional visitor to bring the latest gossip. We relished, appreciated those visits, and everyone was excited to see guests. Tea was always brewing on the stove, and dad would sometimes bring out his stash of rye if the guest was one who needed a reward.

There was always enough food to share, enough room at the table for another place setting. If not, the youngest of the family took their plates to the kitchen table to make room for the guests. No one left hungry or, in some cases, sober, except by choice.

The sun was warm coming through the kitchen windows. I shuffled the cards and started dealing out, eight for her eight for me. Another sister chimed in to have a hand dealt out for her. Another sister was sent to check the furnace, complaining that it was always her turn. It wasn't but we all noted she was the best at keeping score at just who had checked it last.

We could barely see my father and brothers, the drifts of snow had blown in around the lower part of the windows. There were piles of shovelled snow blocking the view of most of the vehicles. The tractor was running but not moving. Dad was probably waiting for one of the boys to move one of the vehicles in the yard.

The dogs were barking and I could hear one of my brothers telling them to be quiet. That wasn't normal. They only barked at strangers and they were familiar with the neighbours.

Mom had stopped mid-stream of her task to look out at the yard. She was standing on her toes to get a better view.

"Can you see what's going on out there?" She nodded at me.

"No the drifts are too high. The boys were probably teasing one of the dogs."

I went back to playing, it was my turn and I had a couple of eights in my hand.

My sister came up from the cellar, closing the hatch with a bang that caused my mother to jump and glare at her. We all let it drop. Mom wasn't paying attention to her, but to the barking of the dogs.

"There is someone out there talking to dad," a sister announced. She had a better view from the porch window.

Mom sidestepped from the sink and took a peek out the side of the window, a look of puzzlement on her face. "I didn't hear a truck and I can't see who that is."

She came back to the sink to finish up her task, deciding it was more important than her curiosity.

I continued to look at my cards and spoke over my hand. "You can't hear anything over that tractor. Dad will probably bring whoever it is in to warm up."

I won my hand and waited for my little sister to shuffle, not an easy feat when you are five years old; but she mastered it quite well.

The racket had moved from the yard, the tractor had shut off, there were loud voices and lots of them out in the porch.

The door opened with dad saying, "Got anything to make a sandwich out of? These guys are hungry. Where's my rye?"

Which was code for dad trusted whoever it was and he would start telling his army stories. He was only in for three or four years, but from the stories he told, over and over, he sounded like a career man and had forty years service. We had all heard the stories over and over and could recite them word for word.

My father, three brothers and four grown men of various sizes came into our warm farm kitchen. Mom went into super mode, slicing homemade bread. There was always bologna and slices of beef or cheese in the fridge. She was making school lunches for five kids and work lunches for her and dad, so the fridge was always stocked.

The glasses were lined up, five matching ones that came out of a bag of dry cereal or from a gas station promotion. I remember the Centennial ones that we were never allowed to use. *They might be worth something someday.*

No ice, no cola. It was rye and water or rye and ginger ale if there was a bottle in the house. They were in luck: a bottle had been stashed away for an emergency just like this one.

The gents started peeling off outer wear. The garbage bags inside of their boots was original. We only ever used bread bags when a rubber boot had a hole in it.

"They were up to the lake, got caught in that blizzard." Dad passed around the generously-poured drinks. "Put that to ya, it will warm ya up. Something to eat is on its way."

Mom piled the sandwiches on a platter, passed out some smaller plates. The four men each reached for a sandwich big enough to fill their hand. I couldn't help but think it was going to help cut the taste of the rye.

The mystery was unveiling itself. These men were here trying to open a cottage they had bought at the local lake. The road to the lake was impassible for their vehicles and they had run out of wood for the stove and gas for the generator. No power, no phones, no heat, the four decided to start walking until they saw someone to help them.

They had been walking in thigh high snow for about three miles.

We hadn't changed over to kilometres as yet.

They were sweating from walking, hungry, frustrated and now relieved. Dad had said he would go with the tractor and my brothers to assist in the dig out. Something I'm sure my brothers were thrilled to hear. More shovelling.

Filled with fluids and my mother's sandwiches, the eight of them left, all piled on the tractor. It looked much like a clown circus act. Seven of them clinging to anything they could hold on to, my father driving, all of them plowing through the snow-filled road.

Three hours later, it was chore time and my mother went out to see if she could hear the tractor coming back. If not, we would all have to bundle up and go to the barn to feed, water, and bed the animals for the night.

Not only did she hear the tractor, but she saw a large yellow snowplough and two half-ton trucks.

The boys went to the barn with the four gentlemen in close pursuit, offering their help. The least they could, do they said. A payment for the assistance they received.

My father came in shaking his head, a huge grin on his face.

"What happened?" My mother asked, passing him a mug of hot tea.

My father sat with his feet on their normal perch, the open oven door. "Ya know, we may be farmers and not too sophisticated, but be damned would I walk three miles in deep snow when I had two snowmobiles on the back of my truck."

My father always had a rumble of a giggle. It would start in his stomach and work its way up until it was a contagious belly laugh.

"They claimed they had left the keys to the machines in the city. I guess they didn't see the pull cords. Common sense doesn't grow in everyone's garden. I don't think they'll stay for supper. The plough has gone through and the young fellow jumped on the back of their truck and showed them how to touch the wires and pull the cord. Just in case it ever happens again."

Connections

Making tracks

Jan Fancy Hull

I like to welcome visitors from the city to my home in the country. But why is the first thing out of their mouths always, "Gosh, it must be cold here in the winter. Do you get a lot of snow?"

Even in summer, they say this.

They drive an hour on the highway, turn inland for another fifteen minutes on a twisty-turny, potholed, bumpy, two-lane paved road, and then turn onto a short stretch of dirt road. When they reach my yard, they often have the urgent look of those who can't hold their double-doubles for another minute. They just didn't think it was so far. They ask if we store our provisions in a root cellar to get us through the winter. We get our groceries in town, same as everyone.

It's gorgeous here. The trees, the lake, the quiet, the clean air, the open spaces...are all worth the drive.

Anyway, that's not what I wanted to tell you. Sorry for the rant, there. I do have a story about snow, though.

Do you remember that winter a couple years back, how it started out cold and cold and cold, but no snow, and people were whining that we wouldn't have a white Christmas? Commuters don't complain about no snow, though we do have something to say about road maintenance. Anyway, the ground was bare and frozen hard that year as Christmas approached.

So, the guy who was living here then wasn't interested in Christmas, or much of anything as far as I could tell. I put some candles in the windows, but mister said if your neighbours can't see your house, who would more lights be for? I thought they could be for us, but he didn't want to bother.

A church down the road was holding a Christmas concert, and I decided to go. I'm not a churchgoer, but I hoped that seeing decorations and hearing children sing carols would do me good. The forecast was for snow flurries, but not a big storm, and the concert wouldn't be that long anyway.

I took the car because it's easier on gas than the truck. He stayed home.

"How late will you be, d'you think?" he asked me, twice. "I want to know when to start worrying about you on the road." So sweet.

I'm glad I went. The kids performed like little stars, and "Silent Night" always gets me in the feels. Everyone in the church was smiling and friendly and it felt so nice to be there.

We all laughed when Santa showed up—except for one little fella who burst into tears and his mama had to go on stage to pick him up and take him back to her pew.

Wouldn't it be great when things get overwhelming, I thought, if someone would just come and wrap their arms around you and carry you right off the stage like that?

Outside, after the concert, was magical. Big flakes were floating down, a perfect Christmas card scene.

Of course, as soon as I left the parking lot where the bright lights lit up everything, it wasn't so romantic. The road was pitch dark except for my headlights making tunnels of light in the snow. It seemed like more than a snow flurry to me.

The distance home was what, ten kay? Seemed a lot more. I didn't dare go over fifty, windshield wipers flapping hard.

Whoever's tire tracks I was following had turned into their driveway halfway to my place, and I almost followed them in. After that, I had to find my own way, though the snow wasn't all that deep. Good tires under you and a steady hand on the wheel are all you need. And patience. God knows I've driven in worse lots of times.

But by the time I got to my road—by memory as much as by sight—I was almost rigid from holding my breath. That's how quickly the magic can disappear.

Streetlights would be great, but I was the only car on the road, judging by no tracks; not a good reason to hang bright lights on every other pole out this way. That's what visitors should really ask about: does it get dark here at night? You bet it does, and street lights would only dim the stars and bother the birds, so we do without.

Anyway, I made it home safe, just a bit wired.

I got out of the car and stood there for a moment, breathing deeply. It was a silent night, the real deal. The snow was swirling down fast. You could see the big wet flakes melting on the vehicles, and hear them landing on the ground. Yeah, that's a thing. In the country-quiet, you can hear dry leaves hitting the ground in the fall, and snowflakes landing in winter. I love it.

I thought back to the warm glow of the concert, the bright-eyed innocence of the kids. I'd take my own babies there one day, if things go that way. I'm glad I went. Merry Christmas to me.

Inside the house, mister was stoking the fire.

"Did you let the fire go out?" I asked. It had become his major evening entertainment.

"Musta fell asleep, yeah."

I poured a glass of eggnog, added a good splash of brandy, and sat down to wait for the questions you'd expect, like how was the concert or how was the road. Didn't happen. He was so preoccupied with the fire, jumping up to poke it every two minutes, it hardly had a chance to catch.

So I did what you do: I talked, about the road and the snow and the little kids. The conversation was mostly me, with a few grunts from him as usual. He eventually got a huge blaze going and then went to bed. I had another nog.

The snow stopped overnight but tracks of vehicles that drove on it before the plow and salt truck came by were packed solid. It made for treacherous driving the next morning, but at least we could see the road.

We had a white Christmas and a white winter, but no whiter than anywhere else. It might look like more here, because we leave most of it right where it falls. In the city, they cart it all away because it's a nuisance. Here, it's scenery.

It was a cold winter, too, especially inside the house. We were eager for spring, for signs of a warmer, better life. I was, at least. I couldn't figure out what he was eager for.

Wherever you are in Nova Scotia, the end of winter and beginning of spring are pretty miserable, weather-wise. Also, in the country, when the first warm breezes blow across the remaining cold snow and ice, we can get some very thick, very local fog.

So, this one March Saturday was foggy like that, but the warm breeze was melting the snow off the field very quickly. I went out to the mini-barn to check on my summer tires, hoping they were good enough for another commuting season. It's a rite of spring, like looking for the green tips of crocuses, which I also checked for.

On my way back to the house, I happened to glance at the boggy field between our house and our neighbour's property. We can't see her house because of a big alder grove in the swampy area between us.

The snow in the field was going-gone, uncovering last year's brown weeds. What caught my eye was a pair of icy white car or truck tracks running from our yard and across the field toward the alders. I wondered what had made these tracks. We can't drive over the field because it's usually too soft.

It was misty and I had only my sweater on, but I walked over for a better look, my boots squishing in the matted grass.

The tracks went beyond the alders and directly into the neighbour's yard. I stood and stared, as the mist changed to drizzle, trying to understand what I was looking at. Vehicle tracks, yes, but what did they mean?

The fog was clearing as the last of the snow melted from the field, and my mind was clearing, too. Funny how you can know what something is even though you've never seen it before.

Soaking wet now, I walked back to the house along the disappearing ice tracks and knocked on our back door. Pounded on it, actually. I could hear him talking on the phone inside.

He came to the door and gaped at me standing there, dripping. "What the hell?" he said. "What's—?"

"Come out," I said.

"It's raining," he said.

"Now," I said. "Right now."

I stepped off the doorstep and began walking back to the tracks. I heard him clumping along in his rubber boots to catch up with me.

I stopped in the middle of the field, where the tracks were still visible for all to see.

"Have you lost your mind?" he said. "What are we doing out here?"

"Good question. What are we doing? What made these tracks, hey?"

"What tracks? How should I know? Snowdrifts? I dunno. Maybe somebody drove their Skidoo over here."

"They don't make Skidoos that wide, pal. Not with tires, either."

You know, until I'd seen those tracks leading to her house, I never really knew what was up with him. I'd had my suspicions, of course. But in that awful moment, once I saw the tip of the iceberg, so to speak, I knew the whole iceberg.

"I have a better theory," I said. "Maybe somebody drove his truck over here last winter when the marsh was frozen hard. Maybe he —maybe you just couldn't resist sneaking a visit to the neighbour-lady when I was out that first night it snowed, remember that? Sure you do. Maybe you drove across the field to see her because—because you couldn't risk going out on the road and leaving tracks in the snow that I'd see and ask questions about when I came home."

"I don't know what you're talking about."

"Yes, you do. Want to walk with me and see where these tracks go? I just did. Yeah, let's go and visit your lady-friend, maybe have a nice cup of tea with her. Would you like that? Or would I be in the way? I probably would be. You bet I would."

I thought I was remarkably well-controlled, considering. "You're nuts," he said. "She just phoned. She saw you standing out in the rain, staring at her house."

"Aw, she called you, did she? Was she concerned about me? That'd be so nice. Oh, maybe I frightened her? I hope so."

"Please, let's go back to the house. You're—"

"You know what else, now? That night, that same night when I went to the concert at the church, and left you here because you wanted to stay home in front of the fire, and then I drove home in the blinding snow? When I got out of the car, I watched the pretty snowflakes falling and melting on both vehicles, which I saw but didn't see at the time, but now I'm wondering, why would snowflakes melt on the truck when it hadn't been started up all day? Why was the truck warm, hey? And why did the fire go out if you'd been home all evening?"

"Come on, you're just—"

"The fire was out because you were out, mister. Don't you dare BS me. It's all falling into place now, just like snowflakes. Oh, you're right, it's damn cold out here in the rain. I'm sorry. Tell you what. I'm going back in the house now. It's my turn to be alone for a while. I don't think you really want to be alone, or with me, so you damn well know where you can go."

I pointed toward the alder grove.

"I can see you know the way."

I turned and trudged home. When I reached the doorstep I turned and looked back. His boots were sinking in the bog with each step as he rounded the turn by the alders. The icy tracks had disappeared.

If I'd gone out to check my summer tires ten minutes later, I'd never have seen what I saw, and I would've had to resolve the winter of our discontent some other way.

I agree with visitors: it gets cold here in the winter, and yup, it snows. It warms up and everything melts in the spring, too.

But, I tell them, you have to be looking at just the right time to see what it reveals.

Hope springs eternal

Michelle Wamboldt

Everybody calls him Maverick, after a car he loved in another life. That was over fifty years ago. His real name was Roy. Is Roy.

He remembers being married once. Briefly. He can't recall her name, or her face. If he really concentrates, he can close his eyes and feel the cool soft flesh of her bare breasts on his cheeks. He can smell lilacs. That was nice. He remembers that.

Nora sometimes feels her life got turned upside down and she never really recovered. She sits in a hard little chair and looks out the window. She sees the neighbour's garage. Rotting wood and fading paint. There is a tree. It makes her feel lucky. She watches it change.

The seasons pass and her son keeps her in the room. They don't want the dog to become too attached to Nora. It's best you stay in the room, Mom. Just throughout the day. They really love that dog.

Nora gets to use the kitchen. Sometimes she pets the dog when they are at work. What they don't know won't kill them.

Maverick and Nora met at the Tim Hortons. She walks there most days. Maverick just started going. His truck is working again, so he can drive to town. When Nora asked if she could share a table with Maverick, he said he wasn't so good with women. She didn't think he was so bad.

They started sitting together every day. They talked a little. She liked his eyes. He drove her home one day. He picked her up some groceries the next week. He asked if she thought they may have sex sometime. She didn't think so.

Maverick took Nora to his house. The bumpy road went far into the woods. No electricity. No running water. She said it could use a woman's touch.

He agreed. He let her go in every room and look at whatever she wanted. He made her tea. His old dog lay at her feet. She told him he was lucky to have a place for himself. He laughed.

He took her home and watched her shuffle up the long brick walk to the big house with cedar shingles and potted plants. Her son hiding behind a window curtain.

Nora didn't see Maverick at the Tim Hortons for an entire week. She worried.

Finally, he appeared. His truck broke again.

She nodded. She told him she had a mini stroke and he took her hand. It was soft and wrinkled. He thought it felt nice.

I'm okay now, she said.

Maybe you can come for another visit out to my place?

She said that would be nice.

Maybe we could have sex this time?

She didn't think so.

He nodded.

He sipped his coffee and held her hand.

Nora looked at Maverick's fingernails. They were black from grease and dirt. She smiled.

Graffiti rhapsody

Lindsey Harrington

They had blasted along the mountain's base to make way for the new highway. People still called it that, even though it was built twenty years ago. The result was a tall, jagged rock wall you hugged with your car as your drove along. Yellow hazard signs warned of falling rocks.

A rainbow of graffiti scaled the wall, mostly block letters and dicks rebellious teenagers had scrawled. Except for one recurring piece, her 23-year-old boyfriend's contribution: 'Krista n' Jonny forever' in gaudy orange. It repeated at one-kilometre intervals the entire length of her commute—seven times.

Whenever she drove by one, she made a face like she had eaten something off. Each time, she instinctively felt the outline of the ring in her pocket.

She told her mother she was going for supplies before her shift with the VON.

Town was a sleepy seaside hamlet with a general store, a post office, and not much else. It stood on a spit of land between the ocean and a ridge of mountains—no room for growth. But if she ever felt claustrophobic, she turned to the ocean and imagined all the things on the other side of it. All the possibilities that existed outside her small world.

In primary school, her teacher had asked the class to draw pictures of where they wanted to live when they grew up. All six students, aside from Krista, drew the picturesque town. Crude renderings of towering mountains, rocky beaches, and houses, weatherworn but cozy. Pencil strokes of smoke swirling from the chimneys in miniature.

She had found a piece of poster board and drew a world map. She traced all the countries and labelled all the seas. There were many she never heard of before, Red and Dead, Aegean and Baltic, not just the harsh blue-black Atlantic beating the coast relentlessly.

"I don't think you understood the assignment, sweetie," her teacher whispered. But Krista had understood perfectly.

The map was now laid away with her other drawings, and her college applications, in the attic. She hadn't picked up a pencil or paintbrush in years. The irony was not lost on her that all her classmates had left, and she was the one who remained.

The snowbanks along the highway were melting. Their remnants were canvasses for Mother Nature's gritty abstract art, dead grass and gravel sprayed across their surface. *This one is about the messiness of life, and this one, its meaninglessness*, Krista joked to herself.

Their runoff streaked the road with temporary waterways. She wanted to float away on one.

As she pulled into town, she saw snowmen on lawns disintegrating. They lost limbs and noses as they fell apart. Sheets of ice were breaking up with one another in the harbour.

She passed another garish orange proclamation and her face grimaced. Her hand went to her pocket.

At first, she had thought it was sweet, albeit it a little immature. But that's what drew Krista to Jonny to begin with. He thought everything was possible and worried little about what others thought. She was the opposite, obsessing over the life that was passing her by while she rotted away here, wasting her youth caring for the old.

But her mother needed her, the clients needed her. What would they all think and say if she abandoned them?

The flaming words had begun to suffocate her. All the ladies at the shop teased her, and the fisherman on the dock elbowed one another as she walked by. Even her mother playfully asked if that Jonny fella was going to make an honest woman of her. It became a dog pissing on its territory in her mind.

Her sister, Gail, had asked what sins Jonny was atoning for with the obscene gesture. Krista never told her about the ring burning a hole in her pocket.

"Real love's not like that," Gail said as she cut carrots into coins with more force than necessary. "It's not fireworks and roses. It's hard work bartered for relative comfort."

"Sounds like a trip to the dentist."

She saw the last piece of Jonny's group of seven and eased onto the brakes. She pulled the car over and grabbed her backpack, the contents rattling as she shifted it onto her shoulder. She didn't have a lot of time; her shift started soon.

"Always rushing, never accomplishing nothing," she muttered to the rock wall.

Not watching her footing, she stepped on a chicken bone flung on the shoulder of the road, rolling her ankle.

When they had first started dating, she and Jonny would drive the hour to the airport, picking up a bucket of KFC en route. He would park his truck in a dirt lot next to the tarmac. They'd eat cold chicken and watch the planes taking off and landing. They threw the bones out the window and made bets on the crows fighting over them as the sun set and the radio hummed.

The planes were so loud, they sounded like skyscrapers emerging from the ground, fully formed.

"If you could go anywhere in the world, where would you go?" she'd asked.

"I like to watch the planes, but at the end of the day I want to drive back home," he'd answered.

"Just pretend," she pleaded.

"S'pose I'd charter a plane to take me back home," he laughed.

Krista rolled her eyes. But she knew she'd never leave either. Even this venture to the airport was on the cusp of impossibility. They would need to leave soon so she could help her mother with her bedtime routine.

"You know, witches throw bones to look into the future. Maybe this will tell us." She flung a half-eaten drumstick over Jonny and out the driver's side window.

A crow picked it up midair and flew off.

He kissed her then, urgent and pleading. He tasted like greasy chicken and coleslaw when what she wanted was a steak.

It was there he had proposed three months ago, the ring nestled between wings of the Colonel's chicken. She told him she'd have to think about it. They hadn't been back to watch the airplanes since.

People always accused her of thinking herself too good for the town, and everyone and everything in it. One night, when she was a teenager, she had poised herself on a ledge of the rock wall, her trigger finger hovering over the nozzle of a spray can. She was about to unleash a stream of aerosol onto the rock face, a crowd of classmates cheering her on below. It was a rite of passage in their small corner of the world.

But she lowered the can and made her way down off the ledge, keeping her head high. She had stalked off down the unlit highway alone, her classmates' jeers fading behind her.

Soon that ritual would be a thing of the past. The council had issued a memo that there would be a crackdown on vandalism along the 304, claiming it was hurting the town's tourism.

It was the talk of the meadow, where everyone 15-30 gathered to drink and smoke weed.

"It's not vandalism it's art." Jonny hauled deeply on a joint and held the smoke in his lungs. He passed it to his left before exhaling the plume.

"Sure, Jonny, your three-foot blue dick is art, alright!" someone quipped back, and everyone laughed.

Krista surveyed Jonny's latest Picasso, their names linked together, high up on the wall. How the hell am I getting up there? She dreaded the embarrassment of another failure.

It wasn't that she was too good for the town or anyone in it. It was that she didn't belong there. Her life was waiting for her elsewhere.

Lately, she had faced interrogations from a string of interchangeable aunts with short perms and beer-bellied husbands. "You know no one is perfect," they lectured when Krista shrugged off their questions about Jonny.

It had happened again last night, and her mother had surprised her. After the company was gone, and the mugs were drying on the sideboard, she was helping her mother to bed. Her mother braced herself on Krista's shoulder as she navigated herself under the covers.

"Don't listen to them, Krista," she had wheezed. "You do what makes you happy."

Krista thwacked through the thicket of scrappy alders growing out of the rock wall's base. Her shoes filled up with slushy snow, the branches grazed her arms. She looked for something to grab hold of, to pull herself up, and something to balance on once she got up there.

She eyed a small ridge and vaulted up, grabbing the ledge just in time. The rocks gave way underneath her feet. She held on, white-knuckled. How had Jonny managed this, seven times?

She scrambled up to the next landing, which was sturdier. She caught her breath and found herself face to face with the magnum opus. The orange letters, each two feet tall, broadcasting Jonny's bragging rights to the town. She rifled through her backpack and extracted the spray can of white paint, ready to redact Jonny's un-authorized claim.

Krista held the paint can out, her arm extended and flexed, her finger braced over the nozzle. Sweat beaded her brow although it wasn't cold out. She could hear the chants from her high school classmates, but when she looked over her shoulder, she was all alone.

The unanticipated view of town surprised her. The rocky beaches and weather-worn cozy homes, the granite-hued smoke swirling from the miniature chimneys just like those in her class-mates' childhood drawings. When was the last time she had looked at it, instead of past it?

The arm gripping the spray can fell. She turned completely to see the full view. Her right hand reflexively stroked the ring in her pocket.

Taking a deep breath, Krista took in the beauty of her town be-fore her, the graffiti glowing sunset orange behind her.

Clothesline aesthetics

Melissa Armstrong

Elanor and Mildred had been neighbours for the past 30 years. Elanor's home was a quaint, two-bedroom bungalow that she and her husband had built themselves, on land they had received from her husband's uncle. They hadn't wanted anything fancy as their priority was landscaping and building gardens.

Elanor kept her small home tidy, but most of the time she, her husband and son spent their time in their gardens. They planted vegetable gardens and even had chickens at one time. The pride of their yard were the various berry bushes, Elanor loved her blueberry bushes the most. She gave many pies and muffins to friends and family from the abundance of fruit. When Elanor's granddaughter visited she would often sit amongst the bushes, eating to her heart's content as she listened to music.

Mildred, her husband and three children had lived with Mildred's parents in the two-story home her mother had grown up in. Mildred's children had grown and moved away, settling in different parts of the country. Mildred was not much for the outdoors. She preferred spending her time indoors quilting or knitting.

Both women were now widowed and lived alone. Although they didn't share much in common, they both loved to hang their laundry out on their clothes lines. There was no greater smell than making a bed with fresh-off-the-line bed linens.

Mildred and Elanor had a clear view of each other's clothing when it hung on their respective lines. You could see Elanor's from the road. This bothered Mildred a great deal, especially in summer when Elanor's granddaughter came to stay, as Amelia had a habit of hanging clothes any which way.

Somehow the knowledge on hanging clothes in the appropriate manner was passed down from generation to generation. The rules are as follows:

1) All towels are to be hung by size, starting from largest to smallest, making sure any overhang over the clothesline is equal.
2) When hanging washcloths, one pin is to be shared with the following washcloth. The same rule applies in dish towels.
3) All shirts are hung together, pinned upside down, as well as all pants but, the pants are to be hung by the waistband.
4) Socks are paired together and pinned by the toe.
5) Bed sheets are hung near one another, then pillow cases.
6) If your line is visible to those passing by, your delicates are not to be hung outside.
7) If it's not visible, then you can, but they are hung as the last things so they can be removed first.
8) Clothes are not to be left hung overnight, unless they are hung late in the evening and are promptly removed first thing in the morning. One would not want to let others think you were lazy or that you were not well enough to tend to your clothesline.
9) Like colours are to be hung together.

Mildred was very strict on these rules even though her line was not visible. Elanor, on the other hand, was not quite as keen at keeping to the unspoken rules. There was the occasional mixing of order of sizes, shirts hung by the shoulder, even socks mixed amongst bed sheets. Mildred found it irresponsible but simply looked away.

In summer, when Elanor's granddaughter came to stay, Mildred kept a watchful eye on the clothes line. There was more traffic going by, sightseeing in summer, especially city folks. Individuals who didn't have the luxury of hanging their clothes out and getting that fresh scent. Mildred felt it was important to have the clothes lines visibly pleasing to those who passed by.

One day, when Elanor was away grocery shopping and her granddaughter, Amelia, was out hanging her laundry, which included her bathing suit, Mildred marched over to assist the young girl hang them appropriately.

"Let's hang that bathing costume closer to the end, so you can retrieve it faster in case you are up for swimming suddenly," she said, pegging clothes in a steady rhythm.

"Ooookay," Amelia said annoyed.

~

To Mildred's disappointment her instructions did not stay with Amelia. A few days later Amelia hung a load of towels haphazardly in various sizes and even manners. She hung some smaller towels by their length rather than their width.

Mildred sat in her rocking chair, fanning herself as she stared out at the mess Amelia had made. This was a Saturday. She knew Elanor and Amelia were soon to head out to the farmers' market.

Mildred sat impatiently staring out her window, waiting for the two to leave. She had been rocking in her chair so vigorously she was making herself queasy.

At 11 am Elanor and Amelia left for their outing. Mildred waited another ten minutes before executing her plan. Then she went out to her own clothesline and removed her clean laundry so as to not look suspicious, as many people on her street walked or rode bikes past her and Elanor's homes. It was common to see Elanor out there, and people would wave or stop for a quick chat, but it was unusual for Mildred to be out any length of time.

After placing her own basket of clean, dry laundry on her back deck she made her way across the yard up the steps to Elanor's back patio and began to remove the mis-hung clothes from the line. Moving fast, Mildred unpinned towel after towel. It was in fact a great day to hang laundry out as there was a slight breeze with the occasional gust of wind.

A large towel near the end of the hung laundry got closer to Mildred as she pulled the clothesline; a gust of wind wrapped the towel up and over the line. Mildred was familiar with the method of pulling on the line slightly and wiggling it at the same time to help the towel fall back in place. Another gust of wind pushed the towel to wrap itself again around the line.

"Had they been hung correctly the first time, this wouldn't happen" Mildred said out loud to no one but herself.

Mildred continued her pull and wiggle method, not noticing that the pole holding the line at the opposite end of the yard was also doing a wiggle dance. She was beginning to sweat as she tried to get the towel free.

In frustration she planted her foot firmly on the rungs of the patio railing and her back against the house and pulled as hard as she could. The towel came flying towards her, bringing along the line as the pole fell crashing into Elanor's blueberry bushes.

Mildred panicked at the sight of the downed pole and towels mixed among the blueberry bushes. Grabbing the basket of clean clothes she headed to the pole and removed the rest of the towels from the downed line. Then she made her way across the yard to her home as fast as she could with the heavy basket of damp and now-dirty towels. She threw the dirty towels in her washing machine.

Mildred knew that her neighbours were likely to return before long. As soon as the towels made their final spin cycle, Mildred headed out to her own clothes line and began to hang Elanor's basket of towels. She was grateful she had removed her own wash from the clothesline before she had planned her adventure.

Finally finished, Mildred sat in her rocking chair to enjoy an iced tea after all the work she had done this afternoon. She was taking one last sip when she saw Elanor's car pulling into the driveway.

Elanor and Amelia were busy taking the things they had bought out of the car, when Mildred came by with a well rehearsed speech about the clothesline.

"I've seen it happen before," she said. "A few strong gusts of wind can knock down the best line."

"Did the towels all fly away?" Amelia said.

"Oh, no. I gave them a quick wash and hung them out." She gestured to her own yard. "And there they are, neat and tidy, like ducks in a row."

Elanor said, "That was so kind of you, Mildred."

Mildred found herself blushing.

"But it's odd," Elanor continued. "It seems like just a light breeze."

"This was earlier," Mildred said quickly. "You had barely left, and, um, over the pole went."

"That's never happened before," Elanor said.

Mildred could not help herself. "Of course, if the towels had been hung in the correct fashion, the line might not have come down at all."

"There's a correct fashion?" Amelia said.

Mildred swallowed her lecture on correct fashion. "If you can come by after supper, dear, to pick up your grandmother's laundry, it should be ready for you."

At 6 pm, when Amelia still hadn't come to take the laundry off the line, Mildred was getting impatient. She didn't want clothes left on her line overnight, especially when they weren't even her own.

A whole hour later Amelia came over with a blueberry pie. "My grandmother said I could wait to take the clothes off the line in the morning since the evening dampness will have set in" Amelia had a sly smirk when she said this.

"Thank you for informing me," Mildred said stiffly. "That will be fine. You will come first thing tomorrow?"

Amelia was already on her way back to Elanor's. "See ya," she called over her shoulder.

All night Mildred tossed and turned, wondering if Amelia would have them off the line in the morning or if she would have to do it herself.

At 7 am Mildred sat in her rocking chair, sipping her coffee and staring out her window at the laundry. At 7:45 she couldn't take it any longer and headed outside.

Mildred usually enjoyed taking her time folding clothes as she went, but this morning she removed them as fast as she could and pitched them into the basket as if they were hot. She made her way up the patio stairs to Elanor's back door to deliver the clean laundry. She didn't look at the down clothes line pole knowing that was all her fault.

Before she was able to knock on the door, Elanor opened it.

"Hello," Mildred said with a strained smile. "I thought Amelia may be sleeping in and thought you may need your towels."

"Thank you for bringing them over. Amelia in fact is still sleeping. Would you like a blueberry muffin and a cup of tea?"

Mildred wanted to return home, but after a teetering pause said, "Thank you. That would be very nice."

They headed inside Elanor's kitchen, where the smell of sugar and cinnamon filled the air.

Elanor began to tell Mildred of their outing to the farm market yesterday. Mildred was trying to keep interested in Elanor's story, but it wasn't until Elanor shared that she had seen Helen, who lived a few houses up the road from them, at the market that Mildred became acutely focused on the story.

Helen went for a walk every day, rain or shine. Mildred knew Helen's daughters had recently bought her one of those fancy phones that did everything, including taking pictures. Helen liked walking to the beach and taking pictures of the ocean, rocks, and even the seagulls.

Mildred became anxious as she feared where Helen's and Elanor's encounter might have gone. Her fears were confirmed.

"So Helen showed me some pictures of this house yesterday. And there you were, on our patio."

"Uh..." Mildred said.

"You had a foot on the railing and you were trying to tug the towels free. Helen said you looked like you were reeling in a shark."

"There was a wind," Mildred said faintly. "That's why the towels were all tangled."

"Oh, I know," Elanor said. "Just not quite the tornado you described."

Mildred stared at her muffin, trying to think of a way to escape.

"That pole must have been ready to go," Eleanor said. "It was no match for you."

Mildred let out a deep sigh. "They weren't hung right and I just wanted to fix them."

Elanor roared with laughter. "I know what you were doing." She doubled over as she laughed.

Mildred looked embarrassed and irritated.

"I can only have my clothesline fixed next weekend," Elanor said through her laughter. "Until then I plan to use your clothesline."

Mildred was in no position to protest. Elanor was only asking to use her line, not have her pay for the repairs. Mildred nodded her head in agreement.

For the next week Elanor and Amelia came to Mildred's clothesline to hang clothes. They hung them in whichever manner they chose, which infuriated Mildred, but she simply watched from her window and waved with a forced smile on her face. Once the week was over and Elanor had her new clothesline erected, Mildred was relieved to not have to endure the haphazard clothes on her line any longer.

Elanor still didn't follow clothesline etiquette as closely as Mildred did but she did make an effort to try. When Mildred was unable to hang her own clothes after having injured her arm, Elanor came once a week to do Mildred's laundry and hang it out on her line. And she followed all the rules exactly as Mildred would.

A sequestered spot

Carolyn MacIsaac

Over the past week, Eric had watched, from his porch overlooking the harbour, as a young woman arrived at the end of the cul-de-sac across from his property. She had carried a kayak in the back of her white SUV. From a distance, with her blond hair tied up in a pony-tail, she looked like a tiny young girl barely old enough to drive.

He was impressed watching her as she handled the kayak with ease. Within minutes, she had it in the water and was rowing up stream.

Most days, Eric would see her return within two hours or, if he was busy, would take notice later on in the day that her car was gone. But as he watched today, two hours passed, then three, until it had been four hours she'd been out there.

Eric didn't know the girl, had never even seen her up close, but he was worried. The wind had picked up, and some dark clouds hinted that a thunderstorm was brewing.

On impulse, Eric pulled on a tee-shirt, grabbed a ball cap and headed towards the water himself. Around the bend from where the girl put in, Eric had a small wharf his grandfather had built on the property. There was an old boat tethered there, with a small motor, that his grandfather had used for fishing.

Eric was well-muscled. The credit went to his pipe-fitting job in Fort McMurray. After a couple of pulls, the boat started, and Eric headed upstream in the direction the girl had gone.

It didn't take more than five minutes to go the same distance the kayak would have taken an hour to travel. Around the second bend in the river, Eric held his breath as he saw her blue kayak pulled up on shore. There was no sign of her. He let the motor stall as he scanned the water.

Then his eyes caught a glimpse of smoke, and he spotted a small tent behind a tree just ten feet from the water's edge.

Three things happened at once. First, Eric realized that the girl was safe and simply planning to spend the night tenting. Intending to beat it out of there quickly, he tried to restart the motor without success.

Second, the girl stood up acknowledging him.

Third, the heavens opened up, releasing a huge downpour.

Within seconds they were both soaked and neither seemed to know what to do about the situation.

~

Dana was happy to have a week off work. She had just graduated that spring with a nursing degree, and as much as she was thankful to have landed a full-time job in a nursing home, as the new girl she got the worst shifts. All of her friends were at work and, since no one was available to spend time with her, every morning, after her parents left for work, she packed up her kayak and headed to where the river merged with the harbour. It was her favourite thing to do.

Her week was coming to an end, so on this particular day she gathered up her brother's small pup tent, a small ice chest filled with food, a camping barbecue, and some bedding.

After the SUV was packed, she dragged the kayak to the back of it and cautiously lifted one end to the edge of the trunk, then pushed it in until only about a foot of the kayak hung out the back. Finally, she threw in a small rubber boat that belonged to her brother. After attaching a red cloth to the end of the kayak where it would hang out of the trunk, she headed away for the night.

When she arrived at the shore, she waded into the water with the kayak, then tied the little rubber boat behind it. She was on her way, bringing provisions to the spot where she planned to spend the night.

Dana put up the tent, had a swim, read for an hour, and then gathered twigs to start a fire. Supper would be hot dogs, potato chips, and s'mores. It wasn't calling for rain, but there were some dark clouds in the sky. Did she hear thunder?

Just then, she was surprised to hear, and then see a small boat round the corner. It looked like a row boat with a motor.

At first, she crouched down, hoping the man wouldn't see her and be on his way, but then the heavens opened up.

It began to pour, and she stood up wanting to run to the tent. Instead, she stood glued to the spot as the owner of the boat got out and hauled it to shore. He was tall, very tanned and his blond hair was dark and glued to his head.

"Sorry about that," he said. "I can't get it started. I don't mean to invade your space, but I'll have to leave the boat here and walk back through the woods to get oars."

"Why here?" she said.

He didn't know if he should tell her the truth. But standing there looking like a drenched rat, she didn't look too scary. "I live in the old cabin where you put your kayak in. When I saw how long you were out, I decided to check in case you had run into trouble."

"I have my phone with me if I need help."

He was shivering. Hesitating for only a moment, she made an impulsive decision. "You may as well try to get warmed by the fire before you go."

It had stopped raining as quickly as it started. She went into the tent and came back with a sweatshirt for herself and handed him the one towel she had brought with her. Eric was digging around the coals to get the fire blazing.

The silence was overpowering. "So...you live in the house at the end of the road where I park. Do you live there all year round?"

He smiled at her, and his smile warmed her more than the fire. "I've lived in Toronto all my life. But my mother, she grew up right here in Nova Scotia, in the cabin. It wasn't always in such bad shape, at least I don't think so. Mom hated it here, and when she turned 18, she left for Toronto and never looked back."

Eric was silent for a bit, and Dana got up and put two hot dogs on two sticks. She handed one to Eric. He turned the hot dog slowly over the glowing coals.

Then he began again. "I was only here once when my grand-father was alive. The whole family came to visit one summer. We weren't here ten minutes and my mom and sisters wanted to go to a hotel. I stayed here with my grandfather for two nights. I slept in the tiny bedroom on a cot, and every morning I sat on the wharf with my grandfather, and we fished. It was the best vacation I ever had. Gramps didn't talk much. I can't explain it—we just connected. Three days later I headed back to Toronto with my parents and sisters. Life went on and I never gave Nova Scotia another thought."

Dana handed him a bun and a tiny package of ketchup she had saved from McDonalds. She had only brought two hot dogs with her, but she had a large bag of potato chips. She poured half on a napkin for herself and handed him the bag. She had several cans of pop and water with her so she offered him a choice. He picked a cream soda.

Neither seemed to realize it was getting pretty dark for a guy who planned to hike through the dense woods.

"How did you end up here then?" she asked.

"Gramps passed away last winter. My sister Glenna wanted his car, but other than that he had nothing. They were going to let the place go for taxes. I recognized that the house had no value, but it was sitting on a million-dollar property. I bought my family out for a song. By that time, I was working in the oil fields in Alberta. I work out there three months and then get a month's vacation. This is my second time coming here for a month."

"It sure is a beautiful spot," Dana said softly. "Do you like s'mores? You know you can't hike through the woods this time of night. Can I trust you to take my kayak home and come back in the morning with oars for your boat?"

"Yes, and yes," he said, and there was that beautiful smile again.

They ate the s'mores, and Eric asked about Dana. He found out she was older than he'd originally guessed. Twenty-three in fact, and she was a nurse, living with her parents and her brother not more than a five-minute drive away.

"I should go," he finally said, as the fire was dying down.

"I hate to see you go in the dark. Do you think we could share the tent? I mean…you know."

"I'm not trying to take advantage of you, Dana, if that's what you're thinking."

"Oh no, I didn't mean that. It's just the tent is small, and I only have one pillow and blanket."

"It's okay," he said. "I'm going now." He stood up to leave.

"Please stay," she said. "We'll make it work."

They sat out talking until well after midnight and then got in the tent together. They stayed as far apart as possible. Dana felt safe with him, although the next day she would be appalled at knowing she had allowed a stranger to spend the night in her tent. No one could ever know about it.

While Dana slept, Eric lay awake wondering about the coincidence of their meeting. He could smell a mixture of sea salt, pine, and her. She was beautiful. She smelled beautiful. Even with her long blond hair soaking wet, she was the prettiest woman he had ever seen.

Eric didn't have time for relationships. Since he was away three months at a time, he figured no woman would want to wait patiently at home for him. And now that he was here in Nova Scotia, he pretty well kept to himself.

He fell asleep close to daybreak, and woke up to the smell of coffee and the sound of bacon sizzling.

Eric climbed the hill to relieve himself and then went into the water to wash up. The sun was shining. It was going to be a hot day.

Dana had boiled water and poured it through a napkin that held ground coffee into a Styrofoam cup. She used a tinfoil pan to fry bacon and eggs, enough for only one each, and one biscuit each.

She had become shy overnight and cursed herself for being so careless. Things could have gone badly.

Dana was the one to leave, Eric having told her where she'd find his oars.

After Eric finished taking down the tent, he had lots of time to think. She was a nurse. He had nothing to offer her. He would not likely ever see her again.

Dana was back in a little over two hours with the oars, and they headed back at the same time. Her kayak sliced through the water, faster than his row boat, until she was out of sight.

By the time Eric got to the house, her car was gone. They hadn't said goodbye. He didn't even know her last name, but he couldn't get her out of his mind.

Dana brought her kayak again the next day. Eric watched her come and then leave two hours later. Did she glance his way at all? Then she stopped coming. He figured she must be working days.

Eric's time to go back out west was coming soon. Fall was coming, so he boarded things up in the house the best he could. He made a trip to town for a haircut. Sometimes, he drove around hoping to spot Dana's vehicle, but there were too many white SUVs, and he didn't even know the make.

He did spot a sign for an outside church picnic at the old Log Church in Loch Broom. There would be Celtic music and everyone was welcome. Eric decided to go in one last hope of seeing Dana. He shaved for the first time in a month, put on long khaki pants and wore his brown Doc Martins.

At the church yard he walked around. A few people spoke to him. He didn't see Dana.

There was a woman at a table with literature who looked a bit like her but her hair was different. He waited about ten minutes until no one was around her table, and then he sauntered over.

"Dana?"

She answered, "Yes," as she was looking up, and then, "Oh, Eric?"

"Yes, it's me, cleaned up a little. I wasn't sure you'd recognize me. It's nice to run into you. How have you been?"

"Hello. Good," she answered, "and busy."

He nodded.

They both were at a loss for words until Dana broke the silence. "If you're still around at four o'clock, I'll be finished here, and if you're interested, I could tell you a little bit more about the Scottish history these pamphlets are about."

"Yeah, I'll be here."

Another man approached the table so Eric turned and walked away. He spent the next 90 minutes reading the inscriptions on the monuments and looking inside the old log church.

He learned that the first settlers, coming on the ship *Betsy*, had arrived in Pictou County in 1767. In 1773, more settlers arrived on the ship *Hector*. Eric had seen the replica of the *Hector* on the Pictou waterfront. In the 1700s there were no roads, so the river was the settlers' way of travel.

By the late 1700s the settlers were looking for a minister. They had built the log church in 1787. Dr. James MacGregor preached there in both English and Gaelic. The original log church had been replaced in 1973 with the replica he was seeing this day.

Long before four o'clock, nervous and anxious, Eric was standing about ten feet away from Dana's table. He watched as a woman came to relieve her.

It wasn't long before Dana was standing in front of him, looking more beautiful than ever in a long, flowing, flowered sundress.

Dana, not sure if she would ever see Eric again, and not sure if she wanted to, decided that she had to see if there was something between them. He had obviously waited for her.

She started the conversation by asking him if he had gone through the church and taken note of the uncomfortable wooden pews, and did he notice there was a ladder to reach the loft?

They chatted for a few minutes, then Eric stopped and turned towards her. "Will you go out to supper with me?"

"Yes, I'd love to. When—tonight?"

"I leave in three days, so it could be tonight, or if you'd rather tomorrow or the next day."

"I'm starved now. How about you?"

"I was just thinking I'd need something to eat soon. Do you need to go home first?"

"No, unless you think I should change. If you like, I can leave my car here, and you can drive me back for it after supper."

"You look great. I was thinking somewhere in New Glasgow. Do you have a preference for chicken, fish, Chinese food?" His voice trailed off. "Or something else?"

"It all sounds good. You choose."

"How about Chinese food at Ming's, then? I think they have a buffet today."

The meal was delicious. The place wasn't too crowded and Dana found she was relaxed around Eric again. They talked about anything and everything.

Eric drove the long way back through Abercrombie and Pictou. Just before they reached the road to the log church, Dana said she would love to see his home. She didn't want the day to end or to say good-bye to him just yet.

"It's kind of a mess with all the windows boarded up and my stuff packed. I'd love to show it to you, though, maybe get your ideas for renovating it."

The small house sat on a large lawn that went right down to the water. Eric pulled the car up near the front porch.

They got out and looked at several small flower beds. Black-eyed Susans in bloom crowded out any weeds. Rose bushes still had red and pink roses on them. There was another pretty purple flower Dana didn't recognize.

Dana gestured to a couple of Adirondack chairs near the water. "It would be really nice to have a picnic there."

"Next summer." Eric responded.

It was a promise he meant to keep, but he did wonder if Dana would want to by then. She had told him the night they met that she didn't have a boyfriend, but that could change. He hadn't planned to come back until spring, but he did have a month off at Christmas. With any encouragement from Dana, he would definitely come to Nova Scotia any chance he got.

Inside, the old house was pretty rustic. Eric told her about his plans to remove a wall in order to open up the kitchen to the living room. Dana mentioned how nice it would be to have patio doors opening onto a deck facing the water.

Then she said, "When do you plan to come back?"

Eric hesitated. Now would be his chance to see if she felt the same about him as he did about her.

"I have a month off at Christmas, then April and again in August.

Dana, I don't mean to be pushy, but time is short. Would you ever be interested in dating a guy who leaves for three months at a time?"

Dana had been hoping he'd make a move. She had her family nearby, so it wouldn't be like she was completely alone when Eric was gone, and one month with Eric was worth more than four months with any other guy she'd ever met. "Oh, yes, Eric, I'd be very interested in dating a guy who leaves for three months at a time, and then comes back to spend a month with me."

Eric's smile grew even wider. He pulled her in for a hug, his heart warming after the lonely season he'd been through. They fit together perfectly.

His cabin finally felt like home.

Postcards from Hey-May

Tracy Matheson

When the aroma of fresh blueberry lemon loaf (Nan's favourite) sailed through the house, I knew it was a beach night.

I'd skip with a puff of joy barrelling from behind me down to the basement bathroom, where I'd pull bathing suits from the back of the door, flinging them on the floor till I found mine. I'd be ready at least two hours early.

Where I come from, summer smells like warm blueberries, salty wild roses, fire-roasted hot dogs, and watermelon. With all the surrounding farms, others might say it smelled like fresh shit, but this never overpowered my olfactory memories of joyful summer evenings at the seashore.

Dad would fill the truck bed with chairs, blankets, firewood, and instruments. Mom took care of the cooler she carefully packed with delicious things.

We'd all squeeze in—cheeks to cheeks (top and bottom).

Right on cue, one of us would holler, "Who farted?" or, "Ewwww squish over!"

Nan always called shotgun, but we all knew it was hers except for Marty, our goofy golden retriever, who would jump in her lap. Nan would complain his nails were too long, and he drooled too much. Nevertheless, she was happy to share her regal position as the copilot.

With the tanned, toned legs of a deer Mom would friskily leap in the back of Dad's old but clean as a whistle truck. I loved watching her move. Her supple body floated with cheerful confidence. She reminded me of rolling seaside waves under a peach sky.

Her sun-spun hair always had streaks of crystal white that

sparkled in the sunlight. She told us the angels put them there.

I'd scramble up into the back of the truck and take a standing ovation beside Donald at the crossbar I could barely reach. We probably looked like a postcard a tourist might pick up at the 5¢ to a $1 store on their way through town.

Without fail, Mom made me sit on the floor.

I would protest, "Why? Do I got to?"

Knowing what she would say, I mouthed the words with her: "Because if you fell out, Hannah-May, I would cry. You would spill over the dusty ground like my favourite string of pearls slipped from my neck, each pearl scattering too fast to see where they rolled: lost forever."

"Not fair. Why can Donnie stand up?" She never worried about him.

"Cause if he fell out, he'd roll like a dirty potato and still be good enough for the table."

I did what Mom told me to do.

We all knew who the boss was, but we never questioned if she loved any of us more than the other. Mom had a way of divvying out six dishes loaded with love, just served in different ways.

~

We lived 16 minutes and 28 seconds from the beach. I timed it: I chewed each fingernail for 90 seconds, giving myself seconds at the end, to ask dad if we were almost there yet, shimmying my way closest to the tailgate so I could be the first one-off.

I got my unwavering commitment to exactness from dad, and now I drive the truck.

The neighbours would wave when we rolled on by and thank us for whatever song we were singing. Keeping tune, we waved merrily, except when Chase stepped on my fingers and I shoved him over.

Then Simon would cry, and somehow Bill would end up responsible.

Everyone knew when the Gillis family arrived at the beach. The gulls alerted the surf commander: The sea urchins are here!

We were loud, but our lullaby melodies made up for any obnoxious character eccentricities.

Friends and families would wander over to say hi. Mom taught me sharing was a gift. She told me always to come prepared with extras. She sure did! Bags of chips, thermoses of tea, three bologna sandwiches for Mr. Sampson, and pretty printed napkins were handed out to everyone. Her voice sang. "Come on, Alice, there is more than enough."

The loaves always seemed to multiply. She pulled them from the picnic basket like blueberries from a bush. I'm sure she baked a half dozen or more. Often still warm from the oven, the syrupy glaze was sticky over fingers and dripped down our chins. The laughter brewed a strong medicine called community.

~

Evenings at the beach were bliss. Kids played, kicking up sand. Shades of pastel sherbet layered the horizon. As the last glimpse of sun nodded a goodbye, stars bejewelled the sky and a synchronized moment of silence took hold of each heart.

One by one exhales from the day played a song that stays inside you forever. Cozy sweaters got layered on. Before long, the instruments got fired up, lively tunes circled in the air.

I preferred grown-up conversations and loved to listen to the world around me. Dad called me a wordsmith sent from the heavens. He'd tell anyone who'd listen, *she's an old soul wrapped in ink-stained pages.*

I guess being the family songwriter sort of was my destiny.

~

The dusk-covered summer evening that I remember best was when Earl came into our lives.

We were at the beach for my 12th birthday. Never wanting to hurt any feelings, I remembered to make everyone feel intelligent, but Earl was the smartest person I have ever met.

I heard Dad call out, "Hey Earl, over here."

To us he said, "He's new in town—a quiet guy, but funny. I got a good feeling about him."

Dad and Mom taught us to appreciate differences and see the good. Earl seemed lonely, but for someone so lonely, happy all the same.

He started spending summers in our area. His hefty height matched well with his wide-angled shoulders and a sprawling kind smile that crookedly balanced between his bright green eyes. He had soft, fluffy hair that shone like the snowflake obsidian I carried in my pocket.

Meeting a person like Earl is like getting assigned a soul-passion mentor, special delivery from beyond.

Earl was a professor at a fancy university. More than that, he was a writer and my friend. Fancy is what I called his job.

I never called him by his given name, instead, I referred to him as Professor Grey, while he called me, "Hey-May!" It had a joyful tone. I heard, *Hannah-May, you can do anything.*

He reminded me of soft wool mixed with granite. Most people don't like the colour grey or anything that involves a grey area, but I adore it.

Professor Grey noticed my attention to detail and the stories I'd tell. He let me read all his books, even left one with me until the following summer.

I cried when he left the first season. He wiped my tears away and told me we were only postcards apart. Earl cheered on my inner storyteller.

For my 13th birthday, he gave me a leather-bound journal and a hand-turned pen. He told me the wood came from a special place where he grew up. Land is sacred but where you make family is where you're from.

He had a friend that stayed with him. At first, I thought maybe he was his brother. Either way, Tom spent most of his time in bed at the cottage.

By the end of the third summer, I knew Earl and Tommy were

more than just friends.

I knew Tom was sick, and they loved each other like a bee loves a flower. I never asked, and Earl never told me.

In '77 Earl took the year off to care for Tom. They moved to the cottage. I'd go there more than I went to school. Earl wrote, and I wrote alongside him.

That year, one of my short stories won a prize.

I kept them company. We'd move Tommy to the front porch. He liked the ocean view. We'd sit and sip sweet tea.

When Tom died, I didn't know what would happen. I worried Earl would stop coming.

Earl started travelling a lot for work, but he never stopped coming for summers. Our beloved postcard tradition lasted 33 years.

His collection came from far-off, exciting places. I started taking photos and made them into cards which he seemed to enjoy. I'd write him a poem about the photograph.

I did some travelling, but not as much as I had thought I would. After the boys left and dad was gone, I knew Mom was lonely, so I stuck close to home.

On quiet summer evenings, I'd help Mom in the truck. We'd sing and drive 16 minutes and 28 seconds to the beach.

We usually just sat in the truck, licking ice cream, watching the tide tell stories.

The stories added up to years of ending.

Mom passed away quietly in her sleep, the night after one of our trips to the beach. She had a cone of Wild Blueberry.

When the time came to clear her clothes from closets and drawers, I found a gift bag tucked far back in the corner of her closet with a beach scene. Delicate tissue embossed in gold seashells cascaded from the top like clouds. Inside was her favourite outfit: faded denim shorts that held her shape and a cloud-white muslin blouse printed with a wild strawberry pattern.

I remember when she made it. It was the first thing she made with the new sewing machine Dad gave her for Christmas '72. He couldn't understand why she'd sew blouses in the dead of winter when the snow-drifted driveway kept us housebound for days, and even with the woodstove goin' you never forgot the sweeping wind chill of -30 would freeze you faster than ice cubes in a tray.

In her serious tone but with an inside smile, she said, "Sewin' summer things keeps my insides warm, John. Really, do I need to explain everything?"

The worn-in pleated shorts dad always told her to toss out had a postcard sticking out of the pocket. On it was a photograph, one I'd taken of Mom in the sunset. Her strawberry blouse blowing in the sea breeze caught in mid-bite of her famous loaf—sweet glaze glistening on her chin.

Written on the card: "Wear these in tall sea grass and think of me. You're as elegant as a string of pearls and hearty as any potato crop. I'm proud of you, Hannah-May."

I wept and felt her smile seeded in my heart.

~

Earl passed away the same year.

A few years before, he had thanked me for being his family. His will was well-divided amongst things he cared about: scholarships for writers, donations to several charities, and his books and cottage to me.

In the study, I found his weathered grey satchel, busting with postcards, and a storage container full to the brim with more.

The note on it read:

> To my favourite writer - thank you for being my understanding assistant. Please honour our friendship by turning these cards into a book. We're only pages away. Keep me posted.

I spent several months at the cottage rummaging, reading, and crying over the postcards. I'd wear Mom's outfit and sit on the front porch watching the sun, listening to families farther down the beach, laughing, and singing familiar songs. Maybe one I wrote.

The smooth surface of obsidian rolled between my fingers to

comfort me.

The best song is the hymn you hear if you listen closely to the setting sun and the speckled blanket of stars hugging the ocean.

And a goodnight hush in the rolling waves.

In loving memory:
The Gillis Family and Professor Grey

Isabel

Carolyn Nicholson

Like many of my nursing school chums, I was returning by train to my hometown from Halifax for the weekend. My parents were there to meet me and load my suitcase in the trunk of the car. Then we started off for the few miles from the train station to our house.

"Anything new since I was home last?"

"No, not really," my father said.

"Well," my mother said, then paused.

"Do we really have to talk about that again?" my father said.

"Don't you think she'd want to know? It is about her cousin, after all."

"Which cousin?" I said.

"Isabel."

"I suppose it's about her education or about boys, or both."

I knew her parents wanted Isabel to 'take a course' so she could support herself, at least until she got married. She didn't have a line-up of boys wanting to date her; not because she wasn't pretty but because she was smart, very smart, always winning highest grades and honours. She was the perfect candidate to go to university.

"Well, I guess both," my mother said. "She has a beau and is spending all her time with him, to her parents' consternation."

"I would have thought they would be pleased that she had a boy-friend. Is it someone I know?"

"I don't think so, dear. His name is Henry Upchuck, or something like that."

"That doesn't sound Scottish." All our relatives were Scottish or Irish, with a little English to round things out.

"It certainly is not," my father said tersely.

"What does he do for a living?"

"Can we change the subject, please? Your mother and her sister have spent the last month discussing nothing else. You'd think the girl was doing something entirely unusual. Let's hear about how you're doing at nursing school."

"Okay. I think I'm doing fine, not the top of the class, but respectably close. I'm enjoying the course in Anatomy and Physiology and soon we're going to start Microbiology. Pathophysiology is for next year. We spend quite a bit of each week on the nursing stations learning how to do all the practical work—bed baths, catheters, blood pressure, all that stuff."

"I'm glad you're liking it, dear," my mother said. "I always wanted to be a nurse, but my parents wouldn't hear of it."

"Why not?"

"They thought it was too low-class. Young ladies learned to knit and sew and take household arts so they could provide a comfortable home for their husbands and children."

"What if they didn't get married?"

"Well, then, they could work in a store or be a nanny for little children, that sort of thing."

"Doesn't sound like you could make much money doing such work."

"That's right. So, every young lady needed to put all her effort into finding a suitable husband who could support her and her children. I certainly heard all kinds of horror stories about women marrying unsuitable men—men who couldn't hold a job, or were into alcohol, or ran around with other women. We all felt sorry for those women and proud that we had good husbands."

"Well, I'm glad that times have changed. Now, girls can get a good education and learn a profession and make their own money."

"But," my father said, "surely you plan to find a husband and get married? Your mother and I want to have grandchildren to spoil, and you're our only child."

"What if I was to become Director of Nurses in a Halifax hospital? Would you be proud of me then?"

"If that's what you want, dear," my mother said. "But surely you're going to give us a few grandchildren. All our friends talk about theirs and show us pictures, and they get to go to the children's concerts and graduations."

My father wasn't saying anything, but I could see he had his lips pursed and a bit of a scowl on his face. I decided to drop the whole matter, if possible. "Isn't this the weekend for the blueberry festival?"

"Yes, and I forgot to tell you we have tickets to go to the pancake supper this evening. Hope you're hungry. You know how big their servings of pancakes with blueberry sauce are."

The thought of the supper was enough to cheer up the atmosphere, and we were all in a good mood as my father carried my suitcase to my bedroom so I could 'freshen up' before we headed off to the church hall.

The hall was crowded, and I got to say hi to many of my cousins and friends from high school. Each girl told me proudly about her boyfriend and where she was working in some local business. Some were waitresses, some clerks in stores, some already married with babies. If you didn't have a boyfriend, husband, or children to share stories about, the conversations were quite short. No one seemed impressed by my nursing-school stories.

My parents took pains to talk about the upcoming weddings, and about those who were married and pregnant. I didn't say much, as I knew the pressure was on for me to meet their expectations, nursing school or no nursing school.

Of course, the next morning I headed over to Isabel's house. I really like that house: two stories with a gable roof, painted pale lilac with green trim. It looked so elegant, surrounded by a green lawn that sported a couple of red maple trees and flowering rhododendron bushes.

Isabel was on the front step playing her guitar and singing to herself, looking radiantly happy.

"Hi, Isabel. What're you up to?"

"Hi, cousin. Let's go up to my room so we can talk."

We both felt that we were now adults and that our parents took too great an interest in our 'private' lives.

"I hear you have a boyfriend. How's that going?"

"Oh, Caroline, I'm so smitten. He is just the most wonderful person. I'm sure you'll think so, too."

"How do your parents feel? Have they met him?"

Her face darkened a little. "They haven't even met him and already they're not approving."

"Whyever not?"

"They think I spend way too much time with him. But I don't think they'd worry about that if they really approved of him. They want me to get an education, maybe become a teacher."

"You'd be such an excellent teacher, Isabel. You're so smart and you really like children."

"Thanks, but I don't know for sure what I want yet. Lots of the girls are engaged or married and Alice already has one child, and another on the way."

"There's lots of time to take some training and get married later," I said. "But I support you, whatever you decide. Parents always think they know best. We're not children who still need their advice."

"Look, here's his picture. Henry Herbert Upchuck. Isn't he handsome?"

He was handsome: tall, dark hair and eyes, rather athletic looking.

"Isabel, he's gorgeous. I bet you two look great together; he with his dark good looks and you with your strawberry blonde hair and blue eyes."

She nodded as she continued to stare at the photograph. She did remember to ask a few questions about my nursing course before I gave her a kiss good-bye and headed home.

I determined not to say anything to my parents, as they and Isabel's parents were way too involved in her personal life.

The next time I came back for a visit, things had not improved. Our mothers were talking about 'the situation'. Then Isabel called and invited me to come along on a visit to Henry's parents at their cottage at 'the lake'.

Lots of people in town had cottages at the lake and I had been there before. The cottages weren't anything special, the kind of places where no one cares if you come inside in a wet bathing suit or with sand on your feet. Kitchens were minimal, as people did most of the cooking on outside barbecues. You could get Cracker Jacks treats and marshmallows for roasting at the tiny general store, and the kids went there every day as part of the lake routine. So, going to the lake on a nice sunny day in July seemed like a good outing.

Isabel's mother was driving, with my mother in the passenger seat. Isabel and I were in the back seat. I could feel the tension from the two mothers, but Isabel was in seventh heaven: smiling and happy as usual.

She gave directions and soon we were out of town. After about ten miles, she told her mother to turn into the next driveway.

There was a very shabby house surrounded by scrub grass. A dog barked at the end of his chain. Very shortly an older woman with frizzy permed hair, probably this Henry's mother, wearing less than stylish clothes even for going to the lake, came out of the house with two children, a boy, and a girl—he about eleven and she younger, I thought. Both wore shorts and tee-shirts. *But where was Henry's father?*

The woman nodded at us and got into the other car with the children. We were evidently to follow them to the cottage. I had the funniest feeling at this point, but Isabel was still smiling, so I tried to quell my uneasiness.

We hadn't travelled long until we came to a turn-off onto a dirt road and then a right turn onto another, and finally into the long grass beside the shabbiest cottage I had ever seen at the lake. Now, I was really wishing I could just go home. Things just didn't feel right.

We all got out of our car as the woman and the two children got out of theirs.

"Well," the woman said, "let's go in and get a cold drink and have a nice chat."

At that, the boy ran off down the lane, and the girl ran ahead into the cottage.

Isabel seemed oblivious to the tension, and the two mothers chatted stiffly but politely with Henry's mother. I just sat in a worn-out old rocking chair, trying to avoid the strange-tasting lemonade, and listened to what was and wasn't being said. Henry's father had a bit of a drinking problem, we learned—not directly, but by inference phrased as 'he's under the weather so we left him at home'—and the children were those of her daughter, who had recently moved to Boston to be with her new boyfriend. The shy little girl was Kathy and the boy, her brother, was Danny. I could see the disapproving looks on Isabel's mother's face, reinforced by her quick glances at my mother.

I wondered where Danny was and why no one was checking one him. Cathy was playing with a worn-out toy on the dirty carpet, talking softly to the cloth doll with button eyes and red yarn hair.

I just wanted to go home.

Then the warped aluminum screen door slammed open and a young man I recognized from Isabel's picture strode into the room. Henry took one look at us and asked, "Who are these women and why are they here?"

He didn't say hello, and before his mother could introduce us, he turned to Isabel and said, "What are you doing wearing that blouse? I told you it's too revealing."

"It's such a hot day, Henry, I thought it would be cooler. Besides, there's no one here but us." She offered him a bright smile.

Henry turned on his heel and stamped out of the cottage, slamming the door behind him.

I was no longer on Isabel's side. Now I knew why the parents were concerned. Now *I* was concerned.

The visit wended its weary way through the afternoon, and I could barely stop myself from giving a cry of glee when it came time to take our leave.

That evening I asked my mother what was going on; what was the whole story.

"You know the saying, 'the apple doesn't fall far from the tree.'"

I nodded. *A good reason for concern.* "And what else?"

"Well, he didn't finish high school."

"He wasn't able to?"

"No, the principal reprimanded him for some sort of behaviour and, instead of amending his ways, he told the principal off and quit going to school. I think he's smart enough. And he is good looking, I'll give him that."

Before I went back to Halifax, I visited Isabel. "Cousin, I'm worried on your behalf. If I'm hearing right, Henry hasn't finished high school, and I can see he seems to have a chip on his shoulder. I was shocked by how rude he was to us and how he talked to you, as though you didn't have perfectly good sense about how to dress."

"Well," she said bitterly, "I see you've been listening to your mother—who's getting all her information from my mother. I thought you said you'd support me in my decisions."

"I would, Isabel dear, but I can't get over what I saw with my own eyes. I only want the best for you."

"Then I'm telling you that Henry is the best for me. And if you can't support our relationship, then I don't think we can be friends."

"I've never heard you talk like this. I'm not just your friend, I'm your cousin. Our mothers are sisters. You would throw away everything for a boy you just barely met? A boy who isn't going to be able to support you if you get married—or support your children, for that matter?"

"I think you've said enough. Henry and I are going to get married, and you won't be invited to the wedding."

I turned on my heel and left with tears streaming down my face.

Two months later I heard that Isabel and Henry were married by a justice of the peace, with only her mother and his mother as witnesses. I had another great cry.

Many years passed. I heard that Isabel had twin boys and that they were living in Henry's parents' old home. On my rare visits home, I contrived to avoid seeing her as I wouldn't know what to say. My parents never spoke of Isabel. Occasionally, our cousins would share a tiny bit of information, but it seemed that none of the extended family were in contact with her. That made me incredibly sad, as I loved her dearly.

Then came the shocking news that Henry had died in a car accident. The newspaper report said the coroner found his blood alcohol level was so high that it must have been the cause of the crash. Fortunately, no one else was killed or injured.

It's now or never, I thought.

I took a few days off work, shared my plan with Iain and the girls and drove to the church from which Henry would be buried. The whole way I wondered, *Will she be happy to see me? Or will she ignore me in front of his friends and relatives? Should I just go right over and give her a hug or wait in the background for her to notice me?* I tried to shake off the anxiety and focus on my driving.

I parked the car in the packed lot and decided to go in through the church hall door. After taking a deep breath I opened the door.

Isabel was there with the boys, talking to a couple I didn't know. She excused herself and came over as soon as she saw me, and hugged me. "Cousin, I'm so glad you've come. I've missed you so. Here, here are my sons, Alexander and Allister."

"The twins!" I said and smiled.

The boys smiled, with less sadness than I might have expected. Isabel herself didn't seem in the depths of grief.

"Cousin," I said, "it does my heart good to have you back in my life. What lovely sons you have—so handsome and well-mannered."

"I have to go and greet my other guests, but we'll get together tomorrow, for sure." She smiled her wonderful Isabel smile.

After the service, Henry's family walked behind his casket to the spot where the grave had been dug. I went with them to support Isabel and her sons.

When Isabel and I got together the next day, I watched as her parents were so warm and supportive of their grandsons.

"Guess what, Caroline," Isabel said. "I've enrolled in university. Going to get my Bachelor of Education."

I gave her a big hug. "Any school would be lucky to have you, cousin. I'm thrilled."

"How are your husband and children?"

"They're well. Iain has a practice with several other doctors, and the kids are going to a private school in Halifax. My parents are so happy to be grandparents, and the girls love coming back home to be fussed over."

"And you're the Director of Nursing at the big hospital, just as you always wanted?"

"Yes. It's not an easy job, but I want our patients to have nothing but the best care, and that's satisfying."

Isabel nodded. "And now we'll be able to see each other often, since I'm going to Mount Saint Vincent University."

"We will, indeed, cousin. We'll just pick up where we left off and go from there."

She smiled her Isabel smile. All was right with the world.

The working life

A dip after work

Leah Benvie Hamilton

Tom has been in the stifling hay field most of the day. He pulls their old '64 Chev into the parking lot at the river park. He recognizes his brother-in-law Glen's car among the others that are there and slides in beside it. It is the bunch of old school buddies that often hang out together, some driving their own cars, others the cars of their parents.

It's the first time Tom's come to the park after work and he isn't sure what he's doing here. He only knows that a swim will feel good, that the desire for one propelled him to turn the car in this direction when he left the farm instead of going home.

Home is so final at the end of a work day, the bumpy road up the long hill feeling as if it comes to an end outside of everything.

They'd finished haying early tonight, everyone on the crew having pushed it all day. They finished up and headed off in different directions, hoping to find some fun on a Friday evening.

If he makes it home by dark or soon after, Evie won't know he didn't come straight from work. Not that he's doing anything wrong. It's the wounded look on her face he wants to spare himself. The look he sees when he comes home late or when he goes out, leaving her alone with the baby for the evening. Or times they go to her mom's for a visit and he leaves, as he mostly does, to do some socializing, look up some weed. As if he's not coming back, for Christ's sake.

She is not able to join him, as she once had, in the things they used to do together. She's become unbearably responsible.

As soon as summer hit, he could barely hack it anymore. Evie and her friends playing house. The domesticity. It isn't enough for him.

And it isn't that he doesn't love her. Most of the time he can't believe it's really happening—Evie, the property, a home, his being part of something so intricate. Fatherhood. Owen. Their very own baby, so beautiful and small, so totally dependent on them both.

He knows it's a really big deal. That's just it; it's too big a deal. Sometimes he has to get away from it, spread his wings a little or else he'll go completely crazy, disappear or something.

He opens his door, careful not to hit Glen's newly-washed black Mustang. His swim shorts are under his haying pants and he slips off the dusty jeans, tossing them into the back seat.

From the parking lot he can't see the water or the river bank, but he can hear the shouting and the laughing, the coaxing and the banter. He can hear names being called out.

"Glen! Over here!" a girl's voice shouts.

There is an echoing holler and a splashing sound as somebody hits the water after letting go of the rope tied to the big maple branch that hangs out over the swimming hole.

He grabs the blue-and-yellow towel with the faded red letters proclaiming "SURF'S UP!" off the passenger seat. It's an old passing present from grade ten he's hung onto and keeps in the car in case the haying crew takes a dip in the brook at noon.

Tom approaches slowly, with the slight discomfort of one who is entering a party that has already begun. He steps through the split between alder and chokecherry bushes where people enter the sandy beach beside the swimming hole.

A few guys and girls are scattered in the water, splashing and horsing around. Voices bounce off the trees on the other side, resounding in the languid, mosquito-filled air. Up the grassy bank, purses and sandals and packs of cigarettes lay here and there on spread-out towels, some inhabited, others empty, their barely-clothed owners swimming, or standing, smoking and talking, taking a break from the river.

Tom makes his way toward Glen. "Water nice?"

"Yup. Drop down for a swim?" Glen says.

"Yeah. Long fuckin' day."

"Evie home?"

"Uh huh."

"Comin' in, then?"

"Sure."

Tom drops his towel and follows Glen down to the water.

"Is it dry around?"

"Not bad, need some?"

"Nah, I'm okay for now. Just wonderin'."

They wade in quickly. Girls take their time getting in, make a production if they want. Guys figure they have to go straight in without a fuss, cold or not.

Tom and Glen swim, leisurely, without talking, to the other side, turn and swim back, Tom putting his feet down a fair distance away from the half a dozen teenagers who are still frolicking in the water. They ignore Tom. He's five years older than they are and out of the loop. Glen's attention is on a couple of the girls who have begun splashing him as he returns with Tom.

Tom turns in the opposite direction, moves away from them all, stands and rests his arms on the surface, looking downstream, where the sun will be setting in an hour or so. He draws a long, deep breath. He stands for a time taking in the definitive line of horizon, the soft, baby-blue sky, cut in pieces with the zigzag of dissipating jet trails. There is sadness in him that won't let go. Around him, darning needles grab their prey, darting and circling like dancers near the glassy surface of the river, a magical haze hanging over it, the water warm and still, its currents deep and mysterious.

Something touches his leg and he turns, startled. A girl has come close to him, swimming, has brushed his leg with her hand.

"Whoops!" she says easily, her laugh tinkling in the cooling air.

She swims a wide circle around him and, embarrassed for a moment, he turns to keep her in his view. She is directly in front of him now, and swims toward him, shielded from the view of the others by Tom's body.

Suddenly, she goes from her belly to her back, her toes pointing at his torso, her feet kicking and making the water ripple slightly near his groin. She rests there in a float, her bare, hard belly just under the surface, neat, blue-striped breasts in bikini cups poking out of the water just a little. She rests there until the current has carried her a few yards downstream and then she flips onto her belly again and swims toward him, this time stopping and treading water before touching his leg lightly.

"Let's go to the other side," she says, her eyes staying with his for a few seconds. Confident he will come with her, she turns facing the opposite bank, kicking her feet and swimming away from him.

"Uh, sure," Tom says and slips into the water, catching up and swimming beside her, keeping time with her strokes as they head in the direction of the other bank.

Out of earshot of the others, she says, "Can I buy a joint from you?"

"Uh, sure, I guess."

"Let me know when you leave. I'll meet you at your car, okay?"

"Okay," he says.

They reach the other side and turn. She swims back, more distant from him this time, back to the swimming hole, then splits from him, laughing with her friends, her tanned and sparkling back toward him, wet with water.

He wades out, whisks his towel off the grassy bank and begins drying himself. The air feels chilly to him now but he's refreshed, that moment of having been targeted, even if only for a joint, awakening something in him.

He sits, watching them, coveting their revelry, their freedom, the simplicity of their play. He can still feel the brush of her hand on his leg, the electricity in that startling moment when she swam toward him, holding his eyes with hers, keeping his attention, defying him to reject her lead to swim to the other side.

"Glen!" he says, seeing that his brother-in-law is within earshot. "What time is it?"

"Almost nine," Glen says, glancing at his watch. "Ten to."

"I've gotta get going," Tom says, so that she can hear. It suddenly feels late. And it's a good twenty minutes to home.

She has made the swim across again with a friend, a girl with short, curly hair. Her own dark blonde hair is long, wet curls down her back, darkened a bit by the wetness of the water. They are back now and he glances her way, wanting to catch her eye.

She sees him, fixing him with her grey-blue eyes as before, and he nods his head discreetly, turns and walks up the bank, disappearing through the opening in the bushes.

"Be back in a minute," she says to her friend and wades out, scooping up Tom's faded, blue-and-yellow towel from the bank, throwing it around her shoulders and running up the path to the parking place.

Tom is opening his car door. He sits in the driver's seat facing out with his feet on the ground, reaches across and opens the glove compartment, removing a small plastic bag containing three joints. She steps into the space made by the open door. He takes out a joint and hands it to her.

"How much?" she says, sweetly.

"Two bucks, I guess." he says.

"I'll give it to Glen sometime, 'kay? Got a light?"

He pushes in the car lighter. They wait without speaking. The lighter pops. He removes it and passes it to her awkwardly, their fingers touching, each trying not to get burned. She puts the joint to her lips and holds the lighter up to it, draws a few short puffs, passing the lighter back to him while taking a draw, a big one, sucking it in and holding it.

She extends her arm, with the joint, out to him. He takes it, placing his lips where hers had been and draws on it, then passes it back to her. Back and forth it goes until it is done, the ritual drawing them together while the smoke lasts.

When it gets too short to hold, she burns her fingers and laughs, drops it on the ground and steps on it, grinding it into the smooth, dry mud with her bare foot. She removes the towel from her shoulders and hands it to him, and then, as if that's all there is to it, she turns, throwing her head back over her shoulder.

"See ya!" she says and is gone back through the split in the bushes at the edge of the river.

Tom sits holding the towel, the car door still open, watching the place where she has disappeared. For a few moments he sits there, believing that he will see her again, that the petite figure in the blue-striped bikini will emerge like a siren at dusk, reappear to thank him for the smoke. He pauses a little longer, then shuts the door slowly and turns the key.

Tom pulls the car onto the main road and heads toward home. By the time he gets there the lamps will be lit and the soft glow of the light in the windows will pull him back into his life with Evie and Owen.

In the rear-view mirror the jet trails have turned a vibrant, un-reliable pink, picked up temporarily from the sun, now setting on the horizon.

He refuses to feel guilty. After all, it was only a joint. He will enter the house with his shorts still damp; he will say they had a dip after work.

Fruit of the ancients

William Dockrill

Here, lemons are tan and leathery, iceberg lettuce baseball-sized and white, bananas either brown and mushy or black and viscid. The island does without watermelon, eggplant, bean sprouts, star fruit, escarole and a great deal else. Soft fruits and vegetables don't travel so far, so well. Like today's romaine he tried to revive with cold water. Joey knows only the Doctor's wife will want any, and only at a discount. He will throw the rest away.

Joey Moon unloads the mainland produce truck. This is one of the assistant manager's jobs, one he's been doing for sixteen years at the town's only grocery store. At forty one, still in his home town and not a fisherman, he is happy to have a steady job, though it's mostly lifting and stacking. He feels lucky he does not work at the fish plant as his wife Judy must.

"Storehouses of Nutrition," Joey intones with each fifty pound sack of carrots he shoulders into the cooler. "Caesar time!" he exclaims with each bedraggled romaine he lifts from waxed cardboard cartons and plunges into a tub of ice water.

These phrases grace the produce department display cards and accompany pictures of produce in the weekly sales flyers. As long as Joey has worked here, carrots have been storehouses of nutrition and romaine lettuce has been linked with the puzzling phrase "Caesar time!" At Joey's house a salad is iceberg lettuce, never-ripe tomatoes and cucumbers drenched in pickling vinegar and flecked with salt and pepper. That a salad could contain raw egg, salty fish, cheese, and mustard is beyond him.

At 10:00, a break. Joey, short, slope-shouldered with a magnificent head of Irish-red hair, slips into his store softball jacket and out the loading door. Two short blocks away, in front of the fish plant, he meets Judy.

She stands with the other women from the line: hair-netted, blood-and-fish-oil-slick aprons reaching to the bulbous toes of high black rubber boots. When Joey arrives they school across the street to the convenience store.

Cigarettes, lotto tickets, Pepsi, potato chips and wieners: there is little else available in the tiny store. When fishing season arrives the plant stays open long hours, the women stand on wet concrete floors in a damp chill, hands cold in thin rubber gloves, noses red and running. There's hourly money and production bonuses. The fishery being the way it is cutters drive themselves. It is a race to get enough earnings for decent winter UI and enough cash to get from the end of fishing season to the first cheques.

Often, then, breakfast or lunch or dinner becomes another cigarette, another Lune Moon, another Pepsi, another couple of wieners. These last are sold cold, without condiment or bun. It is common to see pale grey-pink wieners tucked into breast pockets of the cutters smocks like pens or cigars. Fat and salt and nicotine and caffeine work their wonders and the cutters go on, weeks after week.

Joey and Judy Moon hold hands as they cross the street. He gives her a peck on the cheek and smells fish. Even at night after Judy bathes the smell clings. They joke and tell each other they don't mind. But they never eat fish at home. Usually it's sausages, corned beef or hamburg meat.

Each now buys salt and vinegar chips, a Pepsi and two wieners. Neither smoke anymore. It is a luxury they can no longer afford, though they pretend to each other they've quit because it was bad for them.

"Think of the money we're saving," they tell each other.

The truth is they can't save anything and never have. Judy's only paid work is cutting fish; it is uncertain at best and most years it is a struggle to get enough weeks for unemployment. Joey's $5.50 an hour doesn't go far and raises at the grocery store come in fifteen cent-an-hour increments. Their mobile home is nearly paid for and falling apart.

Joey and Judy don't have kids. Her relatives don't understand. Judy is one of seven kids herself and her married sisters and brothers are awash in children. Joey has lazy sperm, the Doctor explained to them. Joey takes this as a personal failing and broods on it.

He and Judy, the still-thin slip of a woman he married twenty five years before, don't make love much anymore. For her it is a relief; her legs kill her after standing all day on concrete; she has shin splints. Joey's got a pinched nerve in a vertebra high up in his spine that almost paralyzes his neck and shoulders. It's worse on produce day after all the unloading.

He hasn't said anything to Judy or the store manager. When he sits very straight in a pressed-back chair it's not too bad. But he is always a little tense, waiting for the pain when he moves his arms up too fast. He just doesn't feel sexy. And then there's the herring smell.

Swigging soda, smoking, crinkling chip bags, betting lucky numbers, gossiping, the women and Joey take their morning work break. One of the fishermen who sells to the plant stomps in with five bucks, gets lottery tickets and leaves, trailing cigarette smoke.

Everybody knows him. He won a hundred thousand a few years ago. Treated the town to its first Canada Day fireworks. Bought a new truck one day and lost it the next in a drunken clam digging disaster. Drove out on the low tide sandbar, dug til the water started coming. Got the four wheel drive stuck. Burnt out the clutch. Ran to shore for help. The sea rolled in. No insurance, of course. Couldn't get any after he lost his license for the fourth and final time: lifetime suspension for drunk driving.

He stayed loaded while the money lasted, lent to anyone who asked and just couldn't remember who they were when he needed it back. People still thank him for the fireworks at the Legion and down on the wharf and at the liquor store, though you can see him grind his teeth when they do.

Joey checks his watch, kisses Judy and hurries back to the store. Waiting for him are three pallets of potatoes, five hundred pounds of onions, cartons of oranges and apples and one small box made of what Joey thinks could be balsa wood. Lurid purple and fuchsia and electric yellow is the label, but the picture of what is inside lacks definition; it is just a blurred red oblong.

Joey Moon saves the box for last, for after he's made an end-aisle display of fifty pound bags of potatoes, stacking them chest high, re-bagging the onions into two and five pound sizes, mounding the oranges in the centre aisle bin and arranging the apples, already wrinkled and bruised. He considers re-bagging the apples, turning the bruised sections inward, but does not, rushing in order to make time to explore the box.

Once, mistakenly, a case of Japanese pears arrived in a shipment. Joey was astonished; not only did each fruit sit in its own nest, as an egg does in its carton, but each pear also was enclosed in an open-meshed plastic sleeve so that one piece of fruit would not touch its neighbours. Joey admired all things Japanese from that moment on.

Of course no one, not even the Doctor's wife, would buy the pears and Joey had to throw them away. He kept the plastic sleeves, imagining he would use them to store Christmas ornaments. After a time, he threw the sleeves away as well.

Joey pries the top off the box, this box that looks like the one the pears came in. He sees red-skinned fruit with a funny end where they must have been attached to whatever it was they grew on. He replaces the cover and crosses the storeroom to the stack of the week's leftover flyers. He flips to the produce page.

Along with specials that include carrots, potatoes and romaine is a notation about imported from Guatemala (he has never seen the word and doesn't pronounce it to himself, he has no idea what it might be) Pomegranates. Above the price—$3.99 each—is "Fruit of the Ancients."

He returns to the box, lifts the cover and stares. He is confused by the name, by these things he's never seen before. And with "Ancients" come rapid images of flowing robes and shepherds staves and long-bearded prophets and sacrificing lambs and sons to a God long on revenge and punishment. From Bible classes thirty years before come impressions of deserts and wandering and slavery and plagues and lions dens and the Angel of Death.

He picks up a fruit and, guilty and excited, hides it in the workbench clutter. Joey takes the box out front and arranges the display. At closing time he conceals the pomegranate in his jacket pocket.

Judy gets home to find Joey sitting at the kitchen table with something in front of him on the vinyl tablecloth.

"What's that, anyway?" she says as she takes from a parka pocket a much-creased and grease-spotted bag. From it she takes two wieners, a half-empty bag of chips and two fingers of Pepsi in a plastic bottle.

Joey holds the pomegranate up for her inspection as she crosses the kitchen, removing her coat. She looks over her shoulder.

"It's...it's..." He is embarrassed, sensing something ridiculous. "...Fruit of the Ancients." This in a rush, to get past the feeling that he doesn't know what the thing really is.

She plugs in the frying pan which sits in permanent place on the counter top next to the sink and moves to the round-shouldered refrigerator, opening the door. "Fruit of the...what did you say?" she says, her voice echoing from the fridge as she gets the sausages.

"Ancients." Joey says again. "But they're really called poem-granites." He is sure that's how you say it.

She stands now at the sink, cleaning vegetables. "How do you eat them?" she says, cutting an eye from a softening potato.

Joey, with the pomegranate in front of him and a steak knife in one hand, says, "First, you cut it open." He saws the fruit in half.

He is unprepared for the burgundy pool on the vinyl. He looks up at Judy, who has filled a blue ceramic pot with water and is placing it on the stove's big front burner which she has turned on HIGH.

She looks, cries "Have you cut yourself?" and comes to him.

She sees it is juice right away and returns to her peeling.

Joey pokes at the pomegranate with the knife, dislodging a spill of seeds. He takes one between thumb and forefinger and holds it up to the ceiling light. He thinks that this Guatemala (he only imagines the word in his mind, sees it rather than hears it) must be in Japan; only the Japanese could be responsible for something so amazing.

It's another strange fruit, a crimson liquid held in a clear membrane with a tiny pale seed at the centre.

Into boiling water Judy drops potato, turnip, carrot and half a cabbage that must be cooked today or thrown out. Sausages sizzle and leak grease in the pan, filling the kitchen with their aroma. "Put that away; we're having dinner soon," she says.

And while the vegetables boil in water saltier than the sea, Joey considers the seeds in front of him, rubies scattered across the white tablecloth.

Drive-thru Christmas

James O. Weeks

There wasn't anything special about the fat man's order; he always ate that much. What set that night apart was the fact it was Christmas Eve, and I, for one, didn't want to spend it selling doughnuts and coffee to people who didn't have any place better to be.

Madeline and her senior fitness class had eaten lunch and headed home to family gatherings or church. Archie and the older gents had been in for early breakfast, and had long since left to spend the day with their grandkids. But there I was, under the bright red name shining away into the cloudy evening sky, just waiting for closing time.

I should have known I was in for a strange night when I took over for Brenda at the takeout window. She was on early break to call her husband. I didn't know what was going on, but they were having some kind of trouble. Anyway, I slipped on the headset and clipped the transmitter to my belt.

"Merry Christmas," I said. "May I take your order?"

"I'm stuck at the stoplight," a deep, syrupy voice said. I somehow knew she was blonde. "But I'm thinking about being with you in front of the fireplace."

"May I take your order?" I said. "Hello?" I felt like an idiot. I hated talking into that little microphone.

Her voice seemed to be growing fainter. I leaned forward and looked back to the ordering box. I wasn't surprised to see the drive was empty. Somehow I'd picked up a mobile telephone transmission. It happened to Brenda a lot.

"Merry Christmas," I called softly into the microphone, a farewell gesture.

"Same to you," a husky male voice said.

I leaned forward and saw the pickup truck.

"And gimme two turkey sandwiches, two large fries, and two large coffees, black."

"Please pull forward to the window," I said.

I put the sandwich order in, got the fries, and poured the coffees. I took them to the window, got the man's money, and gave him change, just as his hot sandwiches were ready. Where was that blonde going?

"That was quick," the man said. "Thanks."

"Merry Christmas," I said again, watching him pull out. Then Brenda was back, her eyes swollen and teary.

"Thanks," she said.

"You okay?" I said, unclipping the radio that started it all.

"Oh yeah" she said. "It's just Angus. He lost his job at the radio station last week, and he's feeling pretty beat up by it all."

"Doesn't make for a great holiday," I said. "Any chance of a new job?"

"I can't get him to get out and look. He knew the station was losing money and all, but he feels like he did something wrong. He was maintenance, you know."

"Well," I said, heading back to my normal spot on the counter, "he can always come here."

We laughed, but not too hard. Neither of us planned to make this a career. I'm only twenty-three, and selling doughnuts and coffee loses its thrill after a year or two. But what choice do I have? My parents aren't rich, and I want to be a journalist, which usually requires a university degree. So I'm in school, taking one course at a time, and working my butt off. I drive to school in the mornings and do my homework, then come here at four. I dream of seeing my byline in the Chronicle-Herald, but until a good story comes along or I graduate, here I am.

"Let's get the cups refilled while it's quiet."

It had been too pleasant. Odetta, our manager, had been in the back, counting coffee cartons. Now she was here, a little deaf, shouting out instructions.

"I did that already, Odetta," I said. Dealing with her would be so much easier if she would look before firing off orders, but she followed the management handbook's schedule, whether it was needed or not.

"Let's look sharp, people," she barked. "This may be Christmas Eve, but we're still open for business."

She was about to say more, but the door opened and a customer came in. Odetta moved over to inspect the takeout area.

"May I help you?" I asked. *A lobsterman*, I thought. He was wearing jeans, two sweatshirts, and heavy rubber boots.

"Yeah. I'd like two hamburgers, large fries, and a large coffee, black. For here." He glanced behind me at the menu sign. "No cheese on those burgers," he said.

"Right," I said, punching in his order. He handed me a twenty and I gave him his change. "No cheese."

"I hate that stuff," he said. "I always have hated it. Cheese."

"Right," I said. I got out a tray, put a placemat on it, and went for his coffee.

"I won't touch any of it," he said, putting away his wallet and shaking his head. "All those cow products are poison to your system. Cheese, milk, eggs. I'm strictly meat and potatoes."

"That's smart," I said, putting his burgers on the tray.

"Even yogurt," the man said. He picked up his tray. "They won't tell you, but it has milk in it, too. It's printed right there on the label. It's poison, just like all those cow products."

I knew Chuck and Rick, who were cooking, would love this conversation, and I almost had a chance to go back and to tell them about it. But just as the lobsterman reached a table and put his tray down, a woman came through the door.

She stood just inside, looking around for someone. She was maybe fifty, wearing slacks and a parka, with graying blonde hair. But what stood out was her split lip, and her right eye, which was nearly swollen shut.

I guess she didn't see anyone she knew. So she turned and took a seat at the table closest to the door.

"Odetta," I said, going over to the takeout window. "That lady's hurt. Maybe we should get her some help. Either she was in a crash or someone hit her."

"What do I do?" Odetta whispered. "Should I talk to her?"

This wasn't in her manager's guide, I guessed.

Just then an older woman walked in wearing a suit and longer overcoat. She spied the blonde woman at once and went straight to her. She put her hand on the woman's shoulder, spoke to her quietly, then headed to the counter.

"May I help you?" I said.

"Yes," she said. "Two large double doubles and a cup of ice, please. The lady over there has a split lip."

"No problem," I said, pouring the coffee. "Is she okay?"

"Her face hurts," the woman said as she gave me money. "Her husband beat her up this afternoon, and she finally got up the nerve to walk out. So I'm taking her over to the Haven Sanctuary at the hospital. We're a new shelter for abused women and children."

I gave her a plastic bag for the ice, and she headed back to the table.

"Christmas Eve and he beat her up," Odetta said quietly. "That just isn't right."

The door opened and the fat man came in with his nephew. They were becoming regulars, stopping in for dinner every week or so. The fat man was old, and weighed close to three hundred. My dad is big at two sixty, but this man was just plain huge.

He walked slowly and with a cane, and his nephew had to help him into a booth. Then the nephew, a wiry man of about forty, came over to order.

"Two double cheeseburgers, two large fries, and a chocolate shake, for here," he said.

"Anything else, sir?" I asked.

"Yes. For myself I'd like a chicken sandwich and a small black coffee."

It was no surprise; the old man ate that way every time they came in. I got the food together and gave it to the nephew.

"That just isn't a healthy meal," Odetta said. "All those fries."

"He isn't going to die young," I said.

I hadn't seen him come in, but suddenly I realized I was being watched. A tall, muscular man in a wool parka stood just inside the door, looking around. He was clearly upset, and then I remembered the woman with the split lip.

"Uh-oh," I said.

Odetta had already reached for her phone when the man looked at us and smiled.

"Angus," Brenda said, coming past us. "Be right back."

She hurried over to him, gave him a hug, and steered him to an empty booth.

"Is it snowing yet?" Chuck called from the back.

"Not yet," Odetta said. "You have the grille cleaned yet?"

She headed back to keep the troops in line, while I wiped the counter for about the tenth time that hour.

"Excuse me," the nephew was at the register. "Can someone help me? Uncle Chris can't get out of the booth."

"Odetta," I called as I went around the counter.

He was wedged tight. He'd gone through both burgers and most of the fries, and that had done the trick. The problem was that, despite his bulk, Uncle Chris was about eighty. His arms were frail and brittle, so we didn't dare pull too hard. Even his hands felt fragile.

"I have to go," he said.

"We'll get you out," I said, looking under the table.

"No, I mean I have to go soon!" he said.

"What's that? Speak up a little." Odetta said.

He glared at her. "I'm stuck in the booth, and I have to go to the washroom."

"Should I call the fire department?" Odetta said. "Otherwise we may be here until tomorrow."

"Christmas?" Uncle Chris said. "I don't want to stay here all night. And I don't want to miss Christmas dinner with my family."

"No worries," the woman from the shelter said. "They'll have you out in no time flat."

"Need a hand?" Angus was beside me, his dark eyes now concerned and gentle. He sat down on the edge of the bench beside Uncle Chris. "You live near here?"

"Part of the year," Uncle Chris said. "And I want to go home. I have to change."

"I knew it."

Everyone turned to see the lobsterman standing on the bench at his booth, looking down at us.

"You ate cheese with those burgers. That poison will kill you dead."

"I'm not dying," Uncle Chris said. "I'm just stuck, and it's Christmas Eve."

"Let's all calm down now," Odetta said.

"Hey dude, it's snowing."

I turned and saw Chuck and Rick at the counter, grinning.

"I have to get out of here," Uncle Chris said. "I'm Santa Claus."

"Whoa," Rick said. "And he came in here to eat."

"He means he's being Santa at the hospital tonight," his nephew said. "He's not the real Santa Claus."

"Ask them about cheese at the hospital," the lobsterman said. "They'll tell you it plugs your veins."

Everyone turned again to look at him.

"Hey! What's in that cup?"

"It's a chocolate shake," the nephew said. I noticed he was wringing his hands.

"A milkshake?" The lobsterman jumped down and ran across the room. "That's what did it. Poison in a cup! Death with sugar in it."

"That's enough." Odetta waved her arms and everyone turned to look at her. "Don't you be blaming our shakes for this accident. We serve low fat in every shake."

"Low fat," Angus whispered to Uncle Chris. "That'll teach you to go on a diet at Christmas."

"Some diet," the fat man chuckled.

Then he began to laugh out loud. He leaned back and guffawed, just as Angus flexed hard, put his arm around the fat man's shoulders and pulled. The seat back groaned, and Uncle Chris came sliding out, supported by Angus.

"Thank you, young man," Uncle Chris said, shaking hands with Angus. "It looks like I get to be Santa tonight after all." He turned and hurried to the men's room.

Angus was waiting when he came out a minute later. "If you run across a job in that bag of yours tonight, you know where to find me," Angus said. He was smiling about the job now. It would be okay.

"I might be able to help," the woman from the centre said. "We need someone to be a driver and do a bit of maintenance."

"Now, wait," Odetta said. "I think we could come up with an offer here, too."

"My God," Angus said. "This is gonna be a good Christmas after all."

"I have to fly," Uncle Chris said. "I wish you all a very Happy Christmas."

He paused and looked at the lobsterman. "You're right to scold me," he said."I ought to be eating tofu. It has no cow in it."

"You're okay, Santa," the lobsterman said. "Merry Christmas."

Uncle Chris nodded to his nephew, grabbed his cane, and started for the door. I jumped ahead and opened it for him, looking out at the snow.

"We're closing early, people," Odetta said. "It's Christmas Eve."

Uncle Chris winked at me as he passed and ventured into the snowy night. Then he turned and met my eyes. "Get typing, young man. See what you make of it all. I've done my part, you know."

The large red sign above us blinked off then, and I could see beyond the parking lot to strings of twinkling coloured lights decorating homes and stores just down the street. I heard laughter behind me in the restaurant and felt it flow out and surround me in a rush of warmth and dizziness.

"Goodnight," his voice called. "Merry Christmas."

And then the wind picked up a swirl of snow, and the holiday night was upon me.

Goin' down the road

Tara G. Harris

The spring tide had chosen tonight as the peak of the elver run, turning their work into an all night operation. Darkness reduced them to shafts of light blazing from headlamps stationed up and down the river. Below the bridge, commercial fishers handled billowing dip nets while the research team emptied their traps further upstream.

Adrian's supervisor, Kit, had warned him that the few, thready, sperm-shaped elvers coming up the river a month ago would become clots of jellied masses with numbers that clogged the traps. He found it hard to imagine, but as the days went by, the run of elvers swelled until it overwhelmed their small team of researchers. Tonight, the team had pitched tents on the side of the river to catch some sleep between the night run and the next, which would come in on tomorrow's tide.

He could tell by the beam of light from her headlamp that Kit was looking downriver toward the fishers. The height of darkness had passed, and she was watching for Jim's lanky outline.

Adrian had been grateful for Jim's help when he started working on the project. He knew exactly where to place the traps and how often they would need to be emptied. When Jim was on the river with the commercial operation, he always checked their gear, too.

As the spring wore on, Adrian realized there was something more than Jim's naturally helpful nature at work. He and Kit had long talks as they stood beside the river, watching elvers make their way through the slow water at the edges.

"They do it all backwards, you know," he explained to her one day. "You're supposed to spawn in your nice, safe home river, have the young grow up there, and then go out to the ocean. No one lays their eggs in the ocean and lets their offspring find their own way back to the safety of the river."

"On the other hand," Kit argued, "lots of people go south for the honeymoon, so maybe the Sargasso Sea calls to them like the thought of a destination wedding."

"True," he agreed, "but you've got to get the youngsters back home to safety. You can't just turn them loose in the ocean and hope for the best."

"These have done okay," she said, pointing to the glass eels swimming through her reflection in the water.

Adrian was elbow deep in an icy bucket of elvers and river water, and only half listening to the pretend argument they were using as an excuse to flirt. Out of the corner of his eye, he could see Kit, drowning in her oversized wool sweater, and Jim, bulked up in layers beneath his red and black checked shirt. Their rubber boots were almost toe-to-toe as the insistent elvers made their way steadily up the river.

"I don't know about that," Jim continued. "The ones I catch are getting on a plane for Asia to grow up in tanks until they are big enough to be eaten, and the ones you catch—well, what you do is like an alien abduction. They get taken up by strange creatures, probed, and set loose. They're never the same after that, you know."

"We collect data to ensure sustainable harvesting," Kit shot back defensively.

"I hope no one is getting us ready for sustainable harvest," he joked.

Adrian liked Kit and he liked Jim. Kit was team lead and had single-minded dedication to the success of the research. Jim was fun and his extra help made the work go faster. He often tweaked the traps or carried buckets of elvers up to the field lab.

"Got some more million dollar babies," he would declare as he settled a bucket on the deck outside the lab door. Then he would be off to take care of his next job.

Adrian stood in the river, looking downstream in the direction

Kit's headlamp was pointing. Small bits of foam floated aimlessly in the air. He hesitated, then straightened his back. The weight of the bucket of elvers pulled his arms tight as he set off up the trail. He was sure Kit's thoughts had been overtaken by a quiet calculation of how much time she would have between the peak of the run and the end of the season.

"As soon as we're done fishin', I'm goin' down the road," Jim had announced that evening as they unloaded gear.

"What?" Kit asked, pulling her waders and life jacket out of the back of her vintage Civic hatchback.

She was already wearing her headlamp and Jim squinted his eyes, caught in the intense beam. "Goin' down the road—you know, like Pete and Joey in that old movie they used to keep showing on the CBC. My cousin has a good job in Alberta, and he says the recruitment manager would hire me in a flash."

Adrian could feel Kit's mind stirring for words. There was a pause, and then, "Who's going to get your grandmother's firewood if you go to Alberta?"

Jim looked sideways and winked at Adrian, who now understood why Jim had hired him to help move firewood this spring when he could have easily handled the job himself.

"I can't just sit around here doing nothing until next season. Besides, half the people I know are already out there."

"My uncle went out to the oil patch before I was born and never came back," Adrian said. He knew immediately from the unwavering stare of Kit's headlamp that it was exactly the wrong thing to say.

The light over the field lab's deck flicked with the assault of insects as Adrian left his bucket of elvers with Ben and Mia, who were weighing and measuring. "I'm crossing over to check the west side trap," he said and began walking toward the highway.

The river was too deep in the middle to wade across, so they used the bridge, crossing with empty buckets one way and full buckets the other way. In the daytime, traffic rolled along beside them. Drivers distractedly gazed over the edge, caught up in a classic maritime view of the mouth of the river opening into the ocean, blissfully unaware of the infrastructure disintegrating underneath. Adrian had been surprised to see the bridge's iron rods sticking out, exposed, and the cement crumbles lying in the riverbed. Kit said the bridge was on a government list somewhere, waiting for repair.

"Are you making the Tim's run soon?" Adrian shouted from the top of the bridge down to Jim, who was knee deep in the river. The grip of dark was giving in to dusty light and Adrian knew it would soon be time.

"Yeah," he heard Jim reply over the rushing water. "She opens in half an hour. The boss is paying tonight—said to get coffee and Boston Creams for everyone, even you science nerds."

Working on the project would be a lot less fun next year without Jim around, but Adrian understood. His uncle had offered him a place to stay if he wanted to go out and look for work. He hoped it wouldn't come to that, but living with his parents was getting old and it was unlikely he'd be able to afford his own place anytime soon.

Adrian was on his way back across the bridge with a full bucket of elvers when he heard the horn and saw the lights. They felt like they were coming straight at him, forcing him to jump sideways.

When his eyes opened, he was eye level with the shoulder of the bridge and the horizon was filled with rubber boots and lights from headlamps. The contents of the bucket had spilled and a highway of shiny elvers followed the water over the edge, back to the river below.

"It was the fucking yoga bus," he heard Jim yell with exasperation.

"What?" he whispered, feeling the grit between his teeth.

"You almost got run over by the yoga bus! Every morning the resort takes people out to do yoga on the beach at sunrise."

Kit arrived and grabbed Adrian by the arm. "Is anything broken? Do we need to call an ambulance?"

"I think I'm okay," he said, wobbling to his feet like a newborn deer. "I don't think it hit me. It just squeezed me up against the guard rail, and I fell."

"The driver must have been half asleep at the wheel," she said.

Kit helped Adrian to his tent. Jim delivered coffee and Boston Creams, and they had a laugh about the rogue yoga bus.

As the nighttime operation died down, he could hear their voices outside his tent. Jim talked about big money in Alberta, and Kit talked about the terribly cold winters.

"You should come out, too," Jim said.

The bubbling of the river covered Kit's response. Conversation faded until Adrian could only hear the flow of water against the migrating masses.

Tax audit

Thibault Jacquot-Paratte

Buford Glenn Burns hadn't had a job in over ten years.

The last job he had held was a simple janitor's job in Truro. He didn't mind the work, though minimum wage wasn't much for the amount of work that he had to do; or, more specifically, it wasn't much to live on, period. One day when he was taking out trash bags, one of them ripped open—it had been damaged by a tin can lid—and he had had to pick up all the loose garbage. He then noticed quite a few unsorted bottles in what had spilled.

Mindful to sort the trash, he put them in a plastic recycling bin. Right then, he counted that in just about a minute, he had picked out 15 plastic bottles, one of them being a large Pepsi bottle worth 10 cents if you claimed the deposit.

I make just about ten bucks an hour, he thought. *If I can gather 20 of these a minute for 10 minutes...*

The idea looked silly, but the next day, at work, play-acting so as not to tip-off his colleagues, he went on some rant about recycling, and sorted out every trash bag. Some colleagues though it was great he was taking *An Inconvenient Truth* so seriously; others thought it was degrading, and disgusting, to go through everybody's garbage.

In time his boss told him to stop doing it. Buford stated he would rather be dismissed, which he was.

If his colleagues thought it an act of *green rebellion* (in which some joined by donating money to The David Suzuki Foundation, Greenpeace, Sierra Club or Sea Shepherd), the truth was that Buford had, in reality, proven what he had wanted to prove.

He took to learning the ways of locks, and scouting locations.

He was lucky that his home near Kennetcook was far from neither Truro nor Halifax. After a few visits to Wolfville, he deemed that university dorms were worth a weekly trip; campus security was a myth in the dead of night, and dorms like Crowell Tower would be full of empty two-fours.

In Halifax, he managed to make skeleton keys for the garage doors of a large number of condo buildings. Those near the Waegwoltic or the Public Gardens were the ones that really paid off—the wealthier the estate, the less the residents cared about bottle returns.

Usually, in those buildings, it would be effortless: before he would even get to the dumpsters, cases of beer bottles or wine bottles would be waiting, stacked in the trash room. Inside the dumpsters, he could often count 20-30 bottles per trash bag, happy about those bags being transparent.

Between midnight and six a.m. on weekdays, there would never be anyone around; he could take up all the room and empty out the dumpster. He always left the area clean when he left—they'd never know he was there. A single apartment building could yield $15-40 a night, and he would do four or five a night on his usual route.

Every night, he would come home with his pickup truck and its trailer packed full. Most often, he even had to resign himself to leaving some behind.

The guys at the eco-depot came to know him by name. "Jeez, Buford, where do you find so many?" they'd ask him.

"Don't you ever wonder about all the stuff people just toss out?" he replied.

Buford began to get scared around 2017 when Greta Thunberg was all over the news, telling people who pollute they should be ashamed of themselves. He wasn't ashamed of himself—hell, if he could sort out and wash tin cans, plastic containers, and all the other waste he saw every night, and get the same price the government gave him for bottles in return, he'd be all over that deal. He'd be recycling king! There would be no more trash in the whole of Nova Scotia, if he could recycle it all!

He felt lots of sympathy for the girl—he could see around the

Bay of Fundy how fast the coastline was eroding in some places, and all the trash that washed up on shore; he heard that on the Magdalen islands, they had lost about 20 meters of coast in some spots, and he had also heard Nova Scotia might become an island because of rising sea levels.

That being said, he also feared that environmentally conscious people might be the end of his business. What if no more bottles would come?

As if life hadn't had enough irony yet, he did not find fewer bottles, but more. Not only were there more, but they were, for the most part, bottles of beer, rum, vodka cocktails, or wine—bottles worth double the standard. "Looks like they're dealing with climate anxiety in a wholly different way," he concluded.

When the Canadian Revenue Agency decided to audit him, Buford laughed. "If they're only coming now, no wonder so many billionaires get away with tax evasion."

It seemed unlikely, the CRA stated, that Buford could be unemployed for a decade and still have paid off his mortgage, put money into a pension plan, and invested in a Tax Free Savings Account.

Quite frankly, the CRA agent sent to audit Buford was really afraid it would be another one of those unfriendly and menacing dope fiends. He had seen his share of those aggressive looking hicks who didn't have any excuses as to why they declared zero revenue in their income tax returns, but obviously had lots of cash (new cars, new 4X4s, new TVs and computers...). Usually they would stand, jaws clenched, and state, "I don't know," in response to every question, or would come up with bogus excuses: "Those four-wheelers? They were a gift from my cousin. That new Chevy? That was a gift from my uncle."

Nova Scotia was sadly full of those people; the ones who grew crops of weed in their out-of-the-way yards, the ones who smuggled cocaine for the fishermen, the ones who cooked "E", amphetamines, acid, or other crap for all the campuses around, from St. Anne's to St. FX and Cape Breton University. Worst thing was, as a tax representative, he really didn't care how they made their money—that was the police's business. Couldn't they just, at least, declare their revenues so that he wouldn't have to deal with them?

Buford Burns' house didn't fit the 'dealer' profile, though. It was a small, ordinary house in the woods. It wasn't big by any standards, and could even have done with a paint job. The garage seemed like it was a mess, the driveway's pavement was cracked and full of potholes. Maybe he was one of those small-time fiends who only sold his home-grown stock cheap for lack of knowledge in today's market prices?

What shocked the CRA agent the most was the warm greeting Buford gave him. The front door of the house led into the kitchen, where large plastic boxes had been piled up.

"As I mentioned over the phone, all the money I have, I earn from bottle returns, which are non-taxable," Buford explained. "I kept all the receipts I've gotten since I started earning my living this way; the boxes are labelled by date. I realize many of them might be faded by now, which is why I also scanned them. There are thousands of them, though, so I'm not too sure how I can send them all to CRA. Can I just give you this hard drive?"

During the time of the audit, Buford had been stressed—what if something would go wrong? He couldn't find a job now, after being unemployed for so long. Could he lie on his CV that he had been self-employed? Claim that he had managed a private trash sorting firm?

Fortunately, "This certainly is a unique situation," explained the CRA agent.

Bufford passed his audit, and was even still entitled to his HST/service tax refund. He's got his fingers crossed for people not to start recycling, so that he can remain unemployed for another decade.

When Buford reads the paper, he laughs at seeing the slow rise of the minimum wage. "Maybe some day, they'll earn as much as me!"

For the love of sap

Annette Muise

The sun shone through the window, waking Jack from his sleep. Through the open window he could see the orange glow waking up the forest.

He stretched his tired muscles and looked over at his wife, Grace, lying next to him, still fast asleep. After over 25 years of marriage he still never got tired of watching her. She was just as beautiful today as the day he had met her.

He quietly climbed out of bed, pulled on his clothes and opened the door. The cool morning air hit him, and a chill ran through his body. Although the sun was shining, the crisp winter morning air was still enough to surprise you.

As Jack breathed in the air, he could smell the coming of spring. It was as if he could smell the forest waking up and, maybe it was his imagination, but he could swear he could smell the sap rising in the trees.

Jack stretched once more, and walked the few steps off the deck, to the attached building. Here was where the magic happened. Large openings on each wall allowed you to see the beauty of the forest while being warm and secure. A feeling he experienced every day during February and March of each year.

Walking through the doorway, Jack looked around. In front of him was a large wood stove with square pots lining the top. Rows of buckets sat on a long wooden bench, and a stainless steel holding tank sat in the corner. Beyond that, a few cords of wood were piled to the ceiling.

He walked over to the wood pile, gathered some logs in his arms and began building a fire in the wood stove. Before long the fire was roaring and the heat in the building was rising.

Jack began to pour buckets of what appeared to be water into the pots on the stove. Soon the sweet smell of maple syrup filled the air.

He had been sapping in Yarmouth for many years. With each year, his production grew. He had grown up sapping, but only after he took over the ridge did he have a full appreciation of the process.

As he sat drinking his steaming cup of coffee, he thought back to his first year of sapping on his own. In the beginning, Jack had put a tap in each tree, hung a bucket, and spent hours each day walking the maple ridge and lugging buckets to the stove to be boiled. It was a labour of love, but one that grew tiring. Over the years he had installed plastic lines between trees that let the sap flow into a holding tank.

This year, as he sat warming himself by the fire, he saw the ridge full of lines, and two large holding tanks. The methods had changed, but the experience only got better with time.

The creak of the camp door shook Jack from his memories. Grace, eyes still full of sleep, walked slowly toward him. She wore his faded hoodie and it hung almost to her knees.

"Good morning, love," she said as she leaned down and kissed him. After all these years they were even more in love than on their wedding day.

She went to the wood stove where the pot of coffee was warming and poured herself a cup. They sat in silence for a while, enjoying the solitude that only the forest could bring. This morning, with birds chirping around them, the smell of wood smoke rising in the air, their love was ever-present.

After enjoying her coffee, Grace started to make breakfast. There was never a shortage of food at the sugar shack, which was just the way they liked it. With the wood stove always hot there were snacks and meals warming all day long.

This morning she mixed the pancake batter and ladled it into the cast iron pan at the back of the wood stove. Soon, not only the smell of syrup filled the air but a delicious breakfast to start their day as well.

When the pancakes were ready, she laid them on plates and drizzled the fresh syrup they had finished the day before. They never tired of that taste.

Later in the day, after boiling many gallons of sap, they put on their coats and grabbed some buckets. As they hiked up the hill to the top of the ridge they could feel their sore muscles with each step.

Despite all the lines they had installed over the years, they continued to use buckets on some trees. They did this partly to keep the tradition alive for themselves and for the younger generation. Many times children would visit, and they always enjoyed the task of collecting the buckets. Although most sap might be spilled or drunk in the process, it was worth it.

As they reached their first tap, they looked into the bucket. There wasn't much sap in it, but they poured it into their carrying buckets and continued on.

When they were almost done, buckets much heavier with the weight of the sap, Jack spotted something sticking up from the ground. From a distance it just looked like a twig, but something about it intrigued him.

Setting his bucket down and stretching out his tired arms, he walked over to it. As he bent down and touched the object, the icy metal stung his already cold fingers. He tugged on the object, and the realization of what it was came crashing down on him. Years of memories came flooding back, for in his hand he held a cast-iron tap, one his grandfather would have used on this ridge many years before.

Jack was transported back to memories of his childhood. He and his father used to come to this ridge for most of the sapping season. He would help drill taps, hang buckets, lug buckets, and, as he got older, help keep the fire going.

He remembered one day in particular. He was only nine years old. He was staying at the ridge with his grandfather as his parents had gone away for the weekend. The sap hadn't flowed much the day before so there was not as much boiling to do.

After a few rounds of cards in the sugar shack, his grandfather suggested they go gather firewood from the forest. They worked all day cutting and lugging trees. Some trees had fallen in a recent wind storm, while others they felled in order to give the maple trees more room.

When neither could work anymore, they sat down on an old log. His grandfather reached into his metal lunch box and pulled out some chicken sandwiches and hot cocoa. The smell of the hot cocoa had drifted up to Jack's nose, and his belly growled in response. Never before had a sandwich and hot cocoa tasted so good.

His grandfather had said, "That's one of the many rewards of the great outdoors, and especially this ridge. Everything smells and tastes so much better."

Grace's voice shook Jack out of this memory. Standing there on the ridge, he was sure he could smell hot cocoa.

He missed his grandfather. He had been gone almost ten years now. On days like today, he longed to sit by the wood stove, the steam rising from the sap, and hear the stories of long ago. Much of the reason he continued to sap year after year was the connection he felt to his grandfather while on this ridge.

He showed Grace the tap and placed it carefully in his coat pocket. He knew just where he would put this treasure when they got back to camp.

After they had emptied all the buckets and placed them back on the trees, they began the long walk back to the sugar shack. With muscles even more tired, and the light of the day beginning to dim, they made their way slowly back. They had to move carefully for there were fallen trees, rocks, and sticks lining their path.

The orange and red glow on the horizon was breathtaking. No matter how many nights they spent here, they still felt the magic each time they saw the sun rise and set.

After making it back, and putting the buckets down, they went to the fire to warm up. The night air was creeping back in and they could feel the chill in their bones. Jack loaded more logs into the fire, to keep the sap boiling and to keep them warm.

Hours later, after their bellies were full, Grace decided to head to bed. She kissed Jack goodnight and headed in to the camp, ready to get into her flannel pajamas. She enjoyed being at the sugar shack, but after a long day she was ready to go in and curl up in bed with a good book.

Alone in the sugar shack, sitting on the rocking chair, Jack listened to the crackle of the fire. Hours before he had put on his slippers and sweater, and the chill of earlier was long gone.

With the fire stoked, the sap boiling away, and the sound of the peepers in the distance, his body began to relax. Moments later he was fast asleep. Many nights he slept by the fire like this, only to wake hours later and creep quietly into the camp, so as not to wake Grace.

Hours later, after the fire had burned down and the chill had returned, a sound woke Jack. Only the moon lit the sugar shack. Feeling that something wasn't right, he stayed very still, listening.

There was definitely a rustling sound, and he would have sworn he heard a grunt. Something was moving in the shadows of the forest, but what he did not know.

Very carefully, so as not to make a sound, Jack rose from his chair. His shotgun was hanging on the wall just a few feet away. Unsure of what he was dealing with, he knew he had to take his time and be quiet, going unnoticed.

After what seemed like an eternity, he made it to his gun. He reached up, and just as he was about to take it off the wall, a sound behind him made his blood run cold. He froze, knowing that whatever had been rustling outside had now entered the sugar shack and was only a few feet away.

He turned slowly, not taking his hand off his shotgun. There in front of him, on the other side of the wood stove, was a black bear. Steam rising in the air from the sap blurred his vision slightly, but there was no mistaking it. He was alone with a bear. A bear that was clearly looking for something to eat. A bear that was looking at him.

Jack had heard stories of bears in these woods, but he had never seen one, or even any signs for that matter. He knew that sometimes bears would walk off on their own, but other times you had to encourage them with bear spray or a warning shot. Very rarely, deadly force was needed.

He thought of his wife, asleep inside the camp. He thought of his children, all grown up but still so many more memories to be made. Memories flashed through his mind. His wedding day, the days his children were born, first days of school, teaching them to drive.

In that split second he knew he had to act quickly. He tightened his grip on the gun.

So far, the bear was just sniffing around the wood stove. Jack knew the smell of the maple syrup was what had attracted him.

He slowly lowered the gun off the wall and got his finger on the trigger. At this movement, the bear looked up and began to move to the front of the wood stove, getting much closer to Jack.

It was now or never. He pointed the gun out the open door, way to the left of the bear, and fired the shot.

The sound echoed in Jack's ears. He got ready to take another shot if need be, this one meant to kill.

The bear, startled, backed up, knocking over a table. Dishes and food clattered to the floor. The bear looked at Jack one last time before quickly padding out of the sugar shack and into the darkness of the forest. He was gone.

Moments later Grace came rushing out of the camp, shotgun held in a tight grip in her arms. She saw Jack standing by the wood stove, frozen in his place. She could see the tension in his posture but there was a relief in his eyes.

She scanned the sugar shack and forest, looking for any sign of danger.

Finally able to speak, Jack told her about the bear.

Grace stood in disbelief as he recounted all the details. Once she knew they were okay, she ran to him and wrapped her arms tightly around him. She held on to Jack, her heart pounding wildly, keeping a similar rhythm to his own.

As they crawled into bed together a few minutes later, Grace snuggled into Jack's arms. For the rest of the night they never let go of each other.

Hours later, the sun shone through the window, waking Jack from his sleep. Through the open window he could see the orange glow waking up the forest.

He stretched his tired muscles and looked at Grace lying next to him, still sleeping. He quietly got out of bed, pulled on his clothes and opened the door. The cool morning air hit him and a chill ran through his body. But this morning the chill was not just from the air, but from the encounter just hours before.

He still saw beauty when he looked into the forest and out over the ridge, but now he was aware of the dangers lurking there. He had always instilled a love and respect in his children for all living things, and was thankful a warning shot was all that was needed.

During that sapping season, and the many that followed, he still fell asleep many nights by the fire. But when he did, his shotgun was always right next to his chair. He would live with nature, and still be in awe of it, but never again would he take a chance on safety.

199

Transitions

Baby grand

Grace Keating

You start out on Monday, like any other day and you head to the office. Mondays mean long, weekend-stories from your co-workers instead of the shorter, previous-evening, conversations. You're not prepared for anything to be much different. You've had this job for three and a half years and you've been in this city for five.

You miss home, you call once a month on the last Sunday, except for the Sundays you can't, but they're rare. Your mom fills you in on family, foes and friends, and you tell her how you miss home and how you've been.

This particular Monday morning you're ready to start. You have a coffee, granola and yogurt. Toss on a few fresh berries, a treat you allow. Reminds you of the field by the ocean, picking berries in the salty air.

You puff a little make-up on your cheeks, Cinnamon Kiss on your lips. Cinnamon Kiss, your weekend purchase. Nothing too red, nothing too deep, nothing too coy, just right for the office.

You step out the door to the grey of the city. A cold grey that always catches you off guard. Not the warm grey of ocean skies, not the warm grey of the bark on your grove of white pines, but a cold grey, unique to cement. You're still in the warm ocean breeze with the smell of fresh berries on your fingers.

You drink it all in, walk with the waves as you sidestep cracks on the sidewalk. You take transit to the office. One bus, one subway, one more bus and you're there. Twenty-six minutes.

Twenty-six minutes, another two on the stairs, around a corner through three doorways, coat off, scarf off, computer on. You start. Like any other Monday at your office. You process files and respond to emails. Sticky this and sticky that.

It's in the kitchen, when you get your coffee and you hear Scott and his weekend story. It hits you hard, so hard you almost have to sit. You almost drop your mug. You want to appear unaffected, that things are the same, but there's been a subtle change.

You feel heat in your cheeks and on your neck and you turn toward the wall. You know you're a deep red and surprisingly, you question your choice of Cinnamon Kiss, maybe something softer, something more pink would've been better.

You head back to your desk, tic, tic, tic...tap, tap. Sliding your mouse this way and that and all the while you're thinking of Scott and his story. It takes you home to the big white house by the ocean. Along the beach, across the road, the tails of the kite your brother flies, ripple in the wind.

You tic, tic, tic and tap, tap and float your fingers across the ivories. Music lives through you. Black and white keys, bubbles and jellyfish leap and splash to the rhythm of waves as they crash and slide home on the rocks.

You make a mess of the typing on your computer and you take a rare second-morning-coffee-break.

The kitchen is deserted. Everyone is at their desks, processing. Working. You hadn't spoken, you hadn't told the rest of the story.

You'd passed a giggle from your lips, like your co-workers, but you hadn't known how to make the bridge from the setting of Scott's story to the office. From the beginning of the story, the part he couldn't know. The part of the story that had been lost, years earlier, in the front room of that big old house, that looked out to the sea.

It wasn't that you'd been embarrassed, nor shocked. It had been more of a story out of context. One you hadn't wanted to tell. You hadn't wanted to bring your Nova Scotia home into the office. Your life from Nova Scotia didn't work in the city, it didn't work in the cold grey of an ordered office. So you hadn't told anyone the rest of the story. There was no way to bridge that gap.

Back at your desk, nothing happens. You play with stickies. Line up colours and re-arrange. Three rows of five. A long row of fifteen.

Zig-zag. Straight. Circled. Pinks cascading, blue in blocks, yellow in a row. You pull them apart and re-order. Three rows of five. One of fifteen. You try your special pen, but you can't get away from the world Scott has taken you to.

You can't stop the decision you've made and you're not even sure you've made one. Scott and his story took you home and now that you're there, you can't be where you are. You know you're confused. Everything ties you to your father, your mother, your brother, the house by the ocean. Wind in grey skies. Wild waves. Bright sun and you in the room with your baby grand.

As simple as that and as complicated as that, you want to go home. Real home.

In the evening, back in your apartment, you daydream. You're sitting on the grass, looking for a four-leaf clover, you're eleven or just-turned-twelve and your mom calls you in to help your brother and your dad.

You know what has to happen, you've been told. Months earlier, you'd seen something you weren't supposed to see, letters from some collection agency, hired by the piano company. All tied together with butcher's string and stored in a Peek Frean cookie tin.

Your dad had grumbled and grumbled and all your relatives and friends knew the code. Let the phone ring once, hang up, and call again. It signalled a friendly call. Your dad had finally come up with a plan and you were all in on it.

The whole of the story, the part Scott couldn't know, started when you were maybe five or six. You were in the shopping mall one Saturday morning. Your mother and brother had gone off to purchase a suit and you were adventuring with your dad. You'd been enticed to a shop window, just the way it was meant to happen. It's mid-summer. The cool of the mall was a welcome respite from the heat.

"What do you say, Queenie, would you like to play the piano? Look at this beauty and, look, you can buy it on time. Forty-eight equal payments and they'll deliver it right to our house. What do you say?"

The salesman tells your dad, "Why, she's a natural-born talent," as they sign the papers.

A few weeks later, a big van came and dropped off a baby grand piano. Baby grand in a big van.

That first night, you couldn't sleep. You snuck yourself awake, avoiding the creak on the landing. Yes, it was there, in the big side-room with the windows that face to the ocean. The stars and the moon and the silence of the night played the promise of its first notes. The man had said you were a natural-born talent. You knew he was right; you felt it.

And the day on the grass when your mother called you in to help. You'd been put on labelling duty. Every type of screw tagged with a piece of masking tape. Number this and number that to a diagram your brother drew and every screw and bit dropped in a Player's tobacco tin. Strings all coiled tight and taped together, and numbered too. All the while, your dad cursed the finance company, cursed the man from the shopping mall, cursed the small print on long forms. No interest for forty-eight months, but they tacked it all on at the end. Cheaters. The cheaters. He'd cursed the twelve dollars he'd had to spend to purchase the special screwdriver he'd needed to properly remove the strings. He cursed the half-hour trip to the next town to buy it, and the half-hour return trip home.

Big boxes packed, small boxes packed.

"Queenie, I'll make it up to you. We just can't keep your baby grand. You all right? You'll be all right. We'll get the upright from Gramma's house. She said she wants you to have it. I should'a known there was a catch."

You're on a plane sitting beside a man who has a flower shop in Halifax. You tell him you're moving home and he knows. He'd been there himself, years earlier. Flowers, weddings and design work-shops, that's how he made it work. Not rich, he tells you, but enough. It only has to be enough.

You tell him about Scott and his weekend story, how he'd gone to a jazz bar with a group of friends. How the piano player had told how he came to have such a magnificent piano. He'd worked for a moving company. Years earlier, mind. And tucked in the corner, on a few packing crates, were boxes labelled, one of six, two of six, and so on.

It took him a year, but he finally asked, "What's with these boxes?"

"You can have 'em. Someone couldn't make the payments. A piano, I think. The company doesn't want it back. You play, don't you? Take 'em."

Your flower man on the plane laughs and you laugh with him, a fellow Maritimer. You're on your way home.

Dracula's dotage

Bob Bent

I was not supposed to grow old. Vampires do not grow old. But, alas, old age has come to me, with its regrets, its restrictions, its infirmities.

It is entirely the fault of that vile country maiden in Paradise. The name of the village alone should have been a warning to me. But, oh, the neck that maiden had! Gently toasted a golden cream it was, from a sunny spring spent planting her backyard garden, her juicy veins throbbing with hot invigorating blood, and displayed by a silken nightgown open to her collarbone.

There she lay, asleep, alone in her soft bed, *The Blood of Art* open on her lap, her head turned slightly to the side, her long dark hair fanned on the pillow, out of the way, her veins irresistible, virtually pulsing with youth.

How was I to know she was a vegetarian, and consumed garlic until her blood was a veritable toxic river of that vile herb?

I had been watching her for some weeks as I hung from the eaves of the small barn behind the three-story, century-old farmhouse, swirling each night outside her lighted window while she prepared for bed. Now I know why her husband stays up late, watching ice-hockey or baseball matches.

Garlic. There are no children.

Then came the night when the late spring air was sufficiently warm for her bedroom window to remain open. I entered, and without caution, guzzled that deadly brew from the luscious veins of her golden neck.

It was a miracle I survived. I managed to crawl to the window, then fell two stories, landing on my shoulder, dislocating it—in a garlic bed. From there I dragged myself out of sight behind a row of spruce trees, while her husband investigated the noise beneath her window.

"Hmph. Probably a raccoon," he muttered, then returned to the ice-hockey match.

I remained hidden until the horizon in the east began to soften, then desperately, using the spruce boughs for assistance, I hauled myself to my feet and staggered along the empty sidewalk of Paradise to where I had left my car among a sprawling collection of derelict vehicles in front of a long-deserted garage. My ancient black Mercedes Benz did not look out of place.

I drove slowly to my mansion on the outskirts of Bridgetown, weaving over both lanes of the empty grey highway, my strength ebbing. I managed to reach my residence just as the sun peeked above the tattered maples and oaks at the edge of my unmanicured grounds, lush with last year's dead weeds. Then I slept until well after midnight.

I arose weakly at three the following morning and struggled to the bathroom, leaning against the walls, hauling myself along by grabbing the edges of doorways screened with cobwebs. I returned to bed and slept the day away. I did not awaken again until after dusk, feeling as weak as the previous night, dizzy and short of breath.

A week later my health was only slightly improved. It was a totally dark night, the stars and moon smothered by a blessing of thick clouds that hurled rain triumphantly against my black windows. The exuberant wind had ripped trees from the ground and snapped electrical lines. The entire town was completely, wonderfully dark.

Although I was near as frail as on that first night, the weather cheered me somewhat. It was a good night to partake of some fresh air, and to feed my pet turkey vultures.

So I staggered across my overgrown front yard, trampling my beautiful dead grass, until I reached the edge of the property where the long brown grass was dappled with vulture droppings. I left the rotten meat beneath the skeletal poplar tree where they preferred to roost, then, my task completed, I staggered back across my dead lawn, breathing with difficulty and muttering to myself.

A young Mounted Police officer in a cruising patrol car, surveying the damage from the storm, must have spied me stumbling through the knee-high brown grass in front of my mansion. When he stopped his cruiser and approached to assure himself of my well-being, I was bitterly cursing garlic, and comely vegetarian maidens who used that cursed herb for birth control.

Against my feeble resistance he forced me into the back seat of his cruiser, and drove me to outpatients' at Soldiers' Memorial Hospital, where they gave me a transfusion of blood—as satisfying for me as it would be for a drunkard to consume whisky through a tube in his arm, and low-quality whisky at that. Three days later they transferred me to the secure wing of the End of the Line Nursing Home.

My health improved only marginally and, much to the consternation of the nursing staff, I slept during the daylight hours and haunted the corridors at night with the help of a clumsy contraption called a walker. In the beginning they scolded me severely, but eventually they acquiesced and allowed me to prowl the empty corridors.

However a considerable amount of time elapsed before I could convince them to address me as "Count." Even so, they continued to disparage the black suit that hung loosely from my now gaunt frame. I had worn those same black vestments for over a century, even when I slept away the daylight hours with my hands folded on my chest. I had no need of blankets. My black suit provided sufficient warmth.

One evening, in a vain attempt to entertain two of the younger nurses with a dollop of Transylvanian humour, I requested tea and strumpets with clotted blood. They looked at each other aghast and scurried from my room. Apparently Transylvanian humour is not to their taste.

I require no mirrors, for I throw no reflection, which presented a problem shaving whilst I lived alone in my pleasantly dilapidated

Bridgetown mansion. I overheard the nurses one evening remarking on the patchwork quilt of beard, moustache, and sideburns I had sported on my arrival at The End of the Line Nursing Home. I had always used a barber until I moved to North America, something that idiot Stoker neglected to mention. But at the nursing home, a nurse shaved me every evening, bending over me as I reclined in an uncomfortable armchair. The nurses' bare throats, mere inches away, teased and tormented me until I hyperventilated, and they had to withdraw a step until my breathing returned to normal.

Stoker. There were numerous errors and omissions in the hateful book that ignoramus had penned purely out of spite, solely because I had captivated Madame Stoker. What a fine, delicate neck that lady had! Her blood tasted of strawberries. The ending of the book was particularly galling. My death was not only inaccurate, but childish, merely wishful thinking on the part of a third-rate hack.

But now it is different—death is approaching. My hair has thinned. I can feel deep lines on my face, and creases corrugating my forehead. My formerly majestic moustache is now white and dishevelled, stained with yellow. My eyes are dim and lifeless, sunken into my bloodless face.

Yes, I am dying. I need blood. Young blood. But young blood is a rare commodity at the End of the Line Nursing Home.

Oh, I tried older blood, from ninety-four-year-old Gertrude down the hall, one midnight when the night staff was less than vigilant. But the side effects of her medication almost caused me to expire. It took weeks to crawl away from death's door, and I still have not recovered from the ordeal. I suspect some of her medication contained garlic.

Some evenings I ask the night nurse for tomato juice, not to drink—I despise the ghastly stuff—but to stare at, and remember, and dream of yesterdays. Blood is so good!

I remember a particular comely wench in London and chuckle inwardly, a rare occurrence since that fateful night in Paradise. 1954 it was. It transpired she was an inveterate coffee drinker; and having feasted on her blood I was unable to sleep the entire day. Oh what delightful memories!

11:55. Impending midnight. The most agonizing time of night. The time of night I should be feasting on some youthful maiden's blood. I rise unsteadily from my bed, smooth down what is left of my hair and grasp the handles of my walker. Slowly I emerge from my room, wondering which nurse is on duty. Perhaps she can provide me with a glass of tomato juice. But tomato juice is not what I crave—not even close.

I proceed down the corridor behind my walker. The glassed-in nurses' office is empty. I peer into the darkened common-room, and there she is: the young one, the one called Blanche, the one with hair the colour of cinnamon falling below her tender shoulders, the one with full red lips, the pretty one with the faint faraway smile in her quiet brown eyes, eyes that are now closed in blessed sleep.

I approach silently. Her young neck, free of her cheery pastel top, is snow white, with veins of robin's-egg blue warbling beneath the tender skin, tantalizing me. Fortunately there is no sign of a crucifix. A Baptist no doubt. I stand above her, staring, her delicious neck beckoning, her young bosom gently rising and falling.

Oh, to sink my teeth into that juicy vein, to drink that sweet blood, to be young again and—best of all—to make that delicious young maiden my slave. My heart races with the thought and my hands sweat. I can feel a trickle of saliva escape from the corner of my mouth and slowly slide down my chin, but I am too enthralled by her naked throat to wipe it away.

From behind her I manoeuvre my walker alongside; cautiously, silently. I must not wake her. Not now I am so close. I grip the handle of my walker nearest the maiden and lean toward her delectable neck, ignoring the pain in my back. I open my mouth. My teeth touch her pure skin.

Without waking, she swats at her neck, thinking a fly has landed there perhaps, and I lurch backwards, grabbing the handle of my walker to remain upright as my false teeth clatter on the hardwood floor.

Yard sale

K.R. Byggdin

Connie.

There it was, out of place but unmistakable. Her youngest daughter's name written in black ink on a square of masking tape. The tape was affixed to the base of the brass floor lamp Dot had almost knocked to the ground when she stumbled just now. All those twelve-hour nursing shifts at the Yarmouth hospital had taken their toll on her body. Although Dot had retired years ago, her aches and pains had not.

Recently, her doctor had prescribed orthopaedics to help her sore knees and shins. They had begun to throb something awful whenever she tried to take in an exercise class in the rec room of her building, or walked down to the little shop on Main Street that sold English Rose tea in little paper bags. Her favourite.

While the new shoes did ease the pain somewhat, they were bulky and made Dot a bit uneven on her feet, like she was walking on a floating dock. She did not tell her pedorthist this when he brought her in for the fitting. She didn't want to seem ungrateful.

Dot set the lamp upright again and went into the kitchenette of her little suite to fix herself a cup of tea. Then a thought struck her. She moved back into the living room and looked behind the large flat screen TV her husband had bought just before he died three years ago.

Cathy.

Another square of masking tape. This one belonged to her middle child, who lived up in Cole Harbour where her job as a social worker kept her too busy to visit very often, or so she said.

Whenever she did come down, Cathy always went on what Dot secretly called The Enhancement Rampage. Throwing away perfectly good slacks that just needed some new elastic sewn into the waistband. Glueing glow in the dark protective bumpers on the corner of every side table, counter top, and nightstand. Filling the suite with time saving gadgets and gizmos Dot could never figure out how to use, no matter how many hours she spent reading the manuals and pushing buttons.

The old grandfather clock to Dot's left chimed the hour.

Suspicious now, she opened the little glass door that housed the weights but didn't find any markings. Still, best to be sure.

She went to the suite's front entrance and opened the door. Peered down the hallway in both directions. Empty.

She returned to the clock and clasped her arms around it in a feeble imitation of a bear hug. Dot knew she shouldn't do this on her own, could fall and break a hip or put her back out if she wasn't careful, but curiosity got the better of her. Besides, it had been a long time since she had done anything this adventurous with her day.

Throwing her weight into it, Dot was able to rotate the clock ever so slightly to the left. The chimes bonged in protest and the pendulum swung widely from side to side. She held her breath and waited. After a moment or two, everything settled down.

She went into the bedroom and opened her nightstand drawer. Found the flashlight her granddaughter, Connie's girl, had given Dot on her last birthday. It had a big, easy-to-click switch on the top for her arthritic fingers. A very thoughtful gift.

Dot turned the flashlight on and shuffled back into the living room, directing the beam of light between the wall and the clock. There, at its base, Connie's name appeared again.

Connie, her youngest daughter, lived in town and checked in weekly on Dot, but only because she worked here in the retirement home, washing sheets and scrubbing toilets for the residents. In effect, she was paid to spend time with her mother. Connie's visits were always quick and businesslike. She bustled about in a tidying frenzy, never really sitting down to chat about her life or reminisce about the good old days over a cup of tea.

Dot looked around the room. Her eyes were drawn to the Maud Lewis painting. She had purchased the piece directly from the artist on a whim for five dollars, during a drive down the Old Post Road back in the 60s. An autumnal landscape, with a harbour full of sailing ships, surrounded by trees with brightly coloured leaves. Her husband didn't think much of it at the time, but she liked the way the artist had captured the scene. It reminded her of her childhood, vibrant and idyllic.

She walked over to the painting and took it down from the wall. Turning it over in her hands, Dot discovered a bidding war. Several pieces of dry, yellowed tape were attached to the back of the frame. Connie's name had been written down first, then crossed out. Underneath this was a second note.

Connie, don't be greedy. You're already getting the lamp and the clock and a lot more besides. I'm sorry, but we need to be fair about this. XOXO Cathy

A third piece of tape from Dot's eldest daughter, Carol, had settled the argument. She was a divorce lawyer who had done quite well for herself during the acrimonious negotiations with her own three ex-husbands. She lived alone in an upscale Toronto neighbourhood ironically known as the Bridle Path. This was an endless source of mirth for Dot.

Carol hadn't been down to visit her mother since the Christmas before last, the year Dot had moved into town from the family home on Shipwreck Road in Robertsport. She couldn't keep up with all the housework anymore, and besides, what was the point of staying in that big empty place all by herself with only the memory of her husband to keep her company?

Sorry my darling sisters, but you're both wrong. This would look absolutely stunning over my fireplace in the front sitting room. I've already redecorated with a colour palette that matches the piece perfectly. You can have the rest, sell it or

> *pass it down the line to your great-great grandchildren for all I care, but I'll have the Lewis. Don't worry, I'll pay the shipping costs when the time comes. –Carol*

"When the time comes." So, this was it. Her daughters had parcelled off her life before she was even gone. Without realizing it, Dot had somehow ceased to be a mother. She had become instead the caretaker of a miniature museum, curating exhibits of her children's favoured knickknacks and antiquities until her life lease ran out and the items on loan were distributed to their designated owners.

The home phone rang. The call display system Cathy had set up for Dot announced that her granddaughter was calling. She hurried to pick up the receiver, did her best not to sound out of breath when she answered.

"Oh, Kaitlyn. Hello, dear, how are you?"

"Good, Nan! Just wanted to check in and see how you were doing. I hope you don't think I've been ignoring you. It's just been crazy around here with finals coming up and everything."

Bless her heart. Kaitlyn had phoned her nanny almost every day since she left home last fall for her first year of university up in Cape Breton. Dot felt very lucky to have such a kind-hearted and attentive girl for a granddaughter.

"Oh no, dear, no, you need to focus on your studies and keep your grades up. Don't worry about me, I'm getting along just fine. Have any summer plans yet, do you?"

"Well, I'm not sure," Kaitlyn answered. "I've really been enjoying my volunteer gig at the thrift store this semester. They want me to stay on but it doesn't pay so I'll have to get a real job somewhere too, maybe a restaurant or something. I want to try and do that study abroad thing my friends keep talking about next year. I'd love to see Europe or Asia, anywhere new, really. A girl can dream, right? But yeah, for now it's just helping out at the thrift store and then we'll see what happens."

The thrift store. This gave Dot a sudden idea.

"That's good, dear. Now Kaitlyn, I keep meaning to ask you

something. Where did you say you got that nice writing desk of yours for your dorm room last year? Like the buy and sell column in the paper, but on the computer? Sounded like Kejimkujik."

Her granddaughter laughed. "You mean Kijiji?"

"Yes that's it. Do you think you could put together an advertisement for me?"

"You mean a posting? Sure Nan, what'd you have in mind?"

"Oh, just some things here and there. A little yard sale to clean out the clutter. Except I haven't got a yard anymore," Dot said with a chuckle. "Anyways, that doesn't matter. I'll tell you what, why don't I text you the full list?"

Cathy had thought a cellphone would be useful for Dot to have in the event of some sudden emergency, but had neglected to show her mother how to actually use the darn thing when she dropped it off during her last trip down to Yarmouth. The machine had stayed in its box until Kaitlyn came home from school for her spring reading week. She had sat down and patiently walked Dot through how to make calls and even write little messages to people.

"Sounds good, Nanny!" Kaitlyn said with a laugh. "Oh, and if you remember how to take photos on your phone it'd be good to send me some of those, too. People are more likely to get in touch if they can see what things look like ahead of time."

By the time Dot had finished photographing everything and writing up the details of her online yard sale, it was almost midnight. When she woke up the next day she found a response from Kaitlyn to all her texts.

> *Wow Nanny, looks like u were busy last nite. U sure you want to get rid of all this??*

Dot typed out a response as best she could. It was hard to see the little keyboard properly, even with her trifocals balanced at their usual sweet spot on the tip of her nose.

> *Yyes I am SRUE.*

She watched the status of the text change from *Sending* to *Sent*. Then she thought of an important addendum.

>*PS- Plees don't tell yur mother or aunts abuot all this. I dnot wantt any fuss. Loveyou, Nan.*

It only took a few hours for the news to spread. Dot marvelled at how much more efficient the world wide web was compared to the *Tri-County Vanguard*.

People came from all over to take home a piece of the plunder: Digby, Shelburne, even one man from Truro. He actually paid over the asking price for the grandfather clock. Said he wouldn't feel right paying her any less, that he was still getting a steal of a deal.

When it was all over, Dot sat down in her one remaining arm-chair and smiled. She felt light and free. She rummaged through her pile of manuals, even more useless to her now that she had sold off most of Cathy's unfathomable gadgets.

She found a blank page between the English and French sections of one pamphlet and tore it out, then grabbed a pen to write a note. Tomorrow, she would put on her new shoes and wobble down to Main Street so a lawyer could do things up properly.

>*This is the last will and testament of Dorothy Elvira Spinney née Nickerson (revised).*
>
>*First, the money. Split it up equally amongst yourselves and enjoy it. You know what they say. 'You can't take it with you.'*
>
>*To my youngest daughter Connie, I leave a box of letters that your father and I exchanged when we were young. Here's one family heirloom you won't have to dust or polish.*
>
>*To my middle daughter Cathy, I leave my faithful wrist-watch. It can't tell you the weather or the news or glow in the dark, but it's kept me on time for forty years and if you wind it once a day it should do the same for you.*
>
>*To my eldest daughter Carol, I leave my assortment of tea cups and saucers. Some of the patterns are quite nice, though*

there aren't many matching sets anymore and I doubt they'd fetch much at an auction. I do imagine, however, that they'd look absolutely stunning over your fancy fireplace in Toronto if you wish to display them somewhere.

Finally, to my granddaughter Kaitlyn, I leave my Maud Lewis painting. May this cheery scene remind you to never stop dreaming in technicolor.

All my love,
Nanny Dot

At the wake house

Trena Christie-MacEachern

David brushed his bangs out of his eyes and stared at the boys cycling behind the community hall. They whizzed by at lightning speed, the wind in their faces, and he envied them. He didn't want to be here of all places, and told his mother he wasn't feeling well. Matter of fact, David hadn't felt well since the phone call four days ago.

"Sandy's gone," his mother had told him.

"Gone where?" he had asked.

He wished he was playing catch or watching TV or, better yet, hanging out with Mattie, eating hot biscuits right out of the oven with butter dripping down his fingers. But he wasn't. He was here, waiting in the line-up with his mother to bid his farewell.

Heat came to his cheeks when he looked down at the clothes his mother had borrowed for him. "You have to look respectable," she had said.

His pants legs dragged underfoot despite Janet's efforts (she used tape to try and remedy the hem). The shirt cuffs had to be rolled up too, and the tie, well, David tucked it into his belt which he had tightened to the second last notch to keep his pants from falling.

Once he was inside the hall, the peppery smell of incense wafting through the air made David's nostrils flare. Then he saw the casket and his eyes watered.

Had it only been four days since he last heard Sandy's voice? Was any of this real? Who's going to grill the hamburgers, or take them to practice, or know where all the camping gear is? Like, all of it.

David stepped out of line and sat on one of the chairs. Its seat was made of pressed wood and it had metal legs. It wobbled when he sat down, but he didn't want to move to another. He didn't want people gawking at him, staring at the dress clothes that didn't fit, and asking him questions they already knew the answers to.

After a few minutes, his mother came up to him. "Aren't you going to pay your respects to Mattie and his family?"

David shrugged.

"Well, I have to get to work now, David. I'm already late. Faye said Glenda will be here later. You can hop a ride with her. Okay?"

And then she was gone. He wanted to run after her, call out her name, but he remained frozen and silent in his chair. He squeezed the seat so tight his fingers started to cramp.

He watched Mattie shaking hands with people he didn't recognize. His friend stood poised but rigid, and didn't look his way. David wondered if he had done something wrong. Did he embarrass his friend by the way he was dressed? He knew his hair was a bit straggly (his mother's words). She said he'd get it cut the next pay cycle, or if she did well on tips.

An older woman, who had sat near him with two others, interrupted his thoughts. "You're Earl's boy."

David nodded.

She stared at him with droopy blue eyes; her grey hair was wild about her head, like she had let it dry in a windstorm. David expected to see a leaf fall out on the floor.

"Same stamp," she said to the others.

The three bobbed and blinked, passing information with their eyes, like Morse Code.

"Where's your father at now? Does he help your mother at all?"

Just in the nick of time, before David had to respond, his classmate, Sprout, wandered over. "Whad'ya-doin'-sittin'-there?"

David didn't answer Sprout, either.

"Come on, then. Follow-me."

He led David to the back of the hall, into a small room with a tiny window. In it was a smorgasbord of platters and dishes, of sandwiches, and biscuits, some buttered, some with jam, slices of orange cheese, a hunk of homemade, squares, cookies, and a cake with raisins in it. Tea was steeping in glass pots; coffee perked in silver urns.

Sprout pulled back the plastic wrap on a plate and inspected the contents of a sandwich before taking a bite. "It's always tuna or egg."

"What are you doing?" David gasped. "It's funeral food."

"Relax. It's for everyone. Help yourself."

Although David was hungry, he resisted the urge to dive in like his classmate. He settled on a large molasses cookie.

He was readying to bite when Sprout asked, "Did you touch him?"

"What?"

"Sandy. Did you touch him? I did. My mum did, too."

"No," David said. Then he asked, "What'd it feel like?"

Sprout thought for a moment, chewing and swallowing before answering. "Remember when we made ashtrays in Art class?"

David furrowed his eyes then recalled the texture. It was smooth and cool to the touch. He nodded.

"He felt like that."

David looked at his cookie. He suddenly lost his appetite and threw it into the garbage bin. "I don't believe you."

"See for yourself."

"No." David shook his head.

"Oh, for Pete's sake! You chicken? He's not going to open his eyes and get mad at you." Sprout laughed. David didn't. "Oh, come on!"

Before David could argue, Sprout began pushing him toward the front of the hall, where Sandy's casket was. They were making a ruckus and heads were turning when an older man in a suit coat came up to them.

"Boys! That's enough. Where's your parents?"

Sprout pointed to his, standing and talking to another man and a woman. David looked down. He tried tucking his dress shirt back in, in an attempt to look respectable. His hands shook and his armpits sweated and he didn't want to get in trouble, here, of all places.

"Where's yours?" the man asked.

"She had to um, leave, for work."

When David looked up, the man nodded slowly, acknowledging his identification. His stamp. "Well, this isn't a playground, boys. I think you know that."

He stuck his hand in his pocket, pulled out two bills. "They need milk for the tea. Run over and get a carton, and keep the rest. Get yourself a little something."

He was handing the money to David but Sprout pulled it from the man's fingertips and turned toward the door. "Come on, scaredy cat. We don't have all day. My parents will be leaving soon."

They bought two small cokes, a bag of chips, a couple of gumballs, and three packages of M&M's, one for Mattie, with the left-over change.

Sprout had to leave. David passed his time waiting at the back of the hall for Glenda. He sucked on the chocolate orbs slowly, savouring them, as they melted inside his mouth.

When the package was empty, he looked up and saw that he had a clear view of the casket. He thought it time to say his good-byes but he should get closer.

David took a deep breath and a step forward. No one paid him any attention so he moved another step. Brilliant red blooms draped over the casket like they too were in mourning.

It was then he noticed how different Sandy looked. The man there seemed larger, swollen. He didn't wear his hair the same, and his face looked tight and pained. Like he had swallowed something distasteful.

That's when David thought of an idea what to do with the last package of candy.

He raised his hand as he moved a little closer, shuffling his feet like they do in step-dancing lessons. His arm trembled when his fingers grazed the stiff cuff on Sandy's uniform.

Just when his hand hovered over Sandy's, Mattie leaned in beside him. "What are you doing?"

"I'm uh, just, giving this to your dad." He showed him the brown package. "I got it for you, Mattie, but thought. I don't know. Maybe your dad would like it."

"That's stupid. Dad can't take it with him." Mattie's lips were pressed in a hard line.

"I know. I'm sorry. I just remembered the last time we had them and he said, 'next time, we'll practice catching them in our mouths.' Remember?"

David laughed oddly, but then the air in the room shifted. Mattie closed his eyes and his face contorted. His body shook and he grunted and squeaked, sounding more like a wounded animal.

His mother and sisters descended like crows around him and David backed away, further and further until he was out of sight, alone, in the hallway by the bathroom.

On the drive home, David was quiet. With fall, the dark nights came early. He squirmed, knowing he'd have a long wait alone. He wished he had somewhere else to be.

On these nights when his mother worked late, he'd often stay at Mattie's. Mattie's house was always warm and bright and full of people. The TV was on or the radio, and Faye always had something cooking. The dog barked to go out or be let in, or to be petted, and David liked that.

Glenda turned on the wipers, "Hope it doesn't rain for the funeral tomorrow," she said.

David rested his head on the window, listening to the rain and the radio. Then he shouted, "Glenda! Stop the car!"

He thrust open the door and vomited. He spat on the side of road, and on the tire, and on the borrowed shoes. He remained bent over till he could catch his breath and stop retching.

When he finished, he wiped his mouth with the sleeve of his shirt and Glenda passed him a package of tissue.

"Did you have anything to eat at the wake house?"

"Just some chocolate."

"Oh, must have been the chocolate."

"Yeah, must have been."

Helen's roses

Marilyn A. Jones

"The tide starts in soon! Remember to be careful!"

Making her way to the beach, Jenny smiled as the memory of her grandmother's warning echoed in her mind. Having lived a lifetime on the shore of the Bay of Fundy, Grandma instinctively knew the comings and goings of the tides, their pleasures as well as their dangers.

Folks had to be hardy to survive living along this shore, with winter winds that lifted the snow and drove it with such force that a person would try to make themselves smaller, hunched into jackets to lessen the blow of stinging, smothering blasts of white. Blown-over trees, missing roof shingles, broken fence posts and telephone poles were all evidence of this harsh and destructive season. Early spring days were fraught with worry as Grandma, like many wives along the shore, struggled to peer through thick fog, trying to glimpse the fishing boats that carried husbands and sons home.

But a little later, when the spring brought songbirds, when summer's balm and autumn's bounty followed, it brought healing and strength back to all living things. So many memories.

Jenny, the granddaughter closest to Helen's heart, remembered the time she came to spend yet another day with Gram, wandering the beach to collect pieces of driftwood, filling pockets and a basket they carried between them. While they stood at the edge of the low tide mark, Helen fell when she lost her footing on the slippery seaweed.

Jenny was near tears as she helped her grandmother hobble over rocks on their way home. At the hospital they learned Helen's hip wasn't broken but badly bruised.

The doctor warned against beach combing. All her life she'd been able to walk, and even run across the beach, not stopping for slippery seaweed because slipping along was more fun. A person could go faster! Her Grandma was going to miss her beach walks.

Now one of Helen's favourite pastimes was gone the way of other activities, but she felt consoled thinking she could enjoy many others. She enjoyed all seasons, even winter, now that she could sit in the comfortable chair by the window with the wood-stove crackling and her favourite books close at hand. Plenty of time for walks when warm summer days coaxed, or when fresh autumn air smelled of apples and fallen leaves.

One clear summer day, Helen set out once again to admire the beauty of her world. Some years ago, she had been surprised to find a beautiful rosebush growing at the lower end of a long-forgotten farmer's hay field. She wondered why anyone would plant a rosebush there, so close to the bay, then decided it could have been the work of a bird dropping seed.

She preferred taking walks accompanied by her walking stick only, so this discovery was to be her secret, just as during her childhood when she discovered one of those especially beautiful tree stumps, evidence of trees blown over years ago. A stump wore a blanket of soft green moss, tempting Helen to stop and admire the unusual shape that reminded her of an old castle. She loved decorating those stumps with pretty leaves and stones, perhaps a marble or shiny penny from her pocket, then calling it her 'secret'.

So on this fine day Helen tottered off toward the old field, taking time to note each flower along the way, admiring every bird in sight, stopping only when she reached *her* rosebush. She talked to it now, as friends do, complimenting the handsome shinygreen leaves, the lovely large and aromatic red blossoms Rugosas are known for. At the end of summer, when fat red hips shone like rubies in the sun, she'd put a few in her pocket to be nibbled on later.

Saying goodbye to her rose bush, waving a greeting to the gulls that glided over the water, she smiled, then turned and headed for home.

On that warm and breezy day, Jenny arrived just in time to see her grandmother disappear behind some bushes where the bottom of her field met the bottom of the long-deserted farm property. Curious, she decided to follow her, even after guessing correctly that her grandmother would probably not be pleased about being followed.

The path was rough but pleasant and she followed at a discreet distance, giving her grandmother space. Before long, she saw Helen standing near the edge of the old field, seeming to converse with someone; however, there was no one in sight.

Watching quietly, Jenny inched a little closer. It became apparent by her actions that her grandmother was talking to a rosebush!

Jenny hurried away before Helen could notice her, smiling to herself and thinking, *It's okay, Grandma. I won't tell anyone. It will be my little secret.*

The winter of Helen's seventy-fifth year was especially cold, with strong winds piling snow into heavy banks surrounding the houses, with some reaching the windowsills. The bay's high tides seemed vicious, with breakers exploding against rocks, throwing spray high and producing foam that flew gracefully through the air. Electricity was off for days at a time, phones worked sporadically, roads were blocked.

Everything became a challenge; patience grew thin. Folks became listless and discouraged.

Then, just as it happened for eons, winter weakened, seas calmed, winds lessened, spring rains comforted, summer sun promised to make the world warmer. And it did.

It was time to shake out the kinks and start walking again, and Helen was on her way to visit her rosebush.

But it wasn't there! The rosebush she loved was gone from sight! Breathless when reaching the edge of the field that had nourished her rosebush, she was astounded to see an emptiness, a depression in the earth.

But what's this? A rosebush growing on beach rocks? Yes, the violent motion of high tides and strong waves had broken away part of the bank, taking everything with it, including the rosebush.

And there it was, its roots still clinging to the rocks that embedded the sandy banks, then travelling into the rough gravel that part of the Fundy beach was known for. It seemed to be thriving, extending new shoots that had already taken hold, supporting small new bushes, one of them already flowering.

Helen felt like cheering.

Each time she visited her rose bush, Helen thought about how brave and determined this plant must have been to struggle through the process of re-establishing. She stood still, reflecting how precious life is for all species.

"So carry on, little rose bush!" she would call down to her friend. "Defy relentless winds, salty waves that soaked your leaves and flood your roots, summer sun that makes the rocks so hot! Withstand long days of cold fog, sleet, and snow. I have survived a lifetime on the Fundy shore, more than fourscore and ten, and you could be close to matching that number. It will be interesting to see which one of us will have to admit first that we just can't do this any more!"

~

In the funeral parlour, a modest group of family and friends waited to say a final goodbye to Helen. In the first row, sitting close to her mother and siblings and taking comfort from their presence was Jenny, holding a wad of damp Kleenex.

Up front, Helen lay in a pink casket with her hands folded gracefully. While waiting for the service to begin, those present admired the strategically placed sprays of flowers that the town's florist had delivered. White baskets held perfectly arranged hothouse flowers that had been pampered and protected, the bright colours and added greenery combined to make arrangements as beautiful for this funeral as they had for many others.

One arrangement, however, didn't measure up to the rest, or so some critical people whispered to one another, wondering who would bring *that* to the funeral. And look at that old vase! But they had to admit the roses looked so alive they seemed to glow with life, radiating a feeling of warmth.

As Jenny sat in the family pew and listened to the service, her eyes rarely moved from the blossoms from her grandmother's secret rose bush, the tough little Rugosa that had given Helen years of pleasure. Her heart told her they belonged where, if possible, Helen could look down and see them, smile, and send greetings to her friend on the rocky Fundy beach.

In the company of old men

Pam Calabrese MacLean

My words are too quick for Frank. It is always later, while he ice-fishes with his grandfather, or helps the old sawyer next door put in his winter's wood, or sits through the long yellow evenings of summer in the company of old men, that he hears in one of their voices the words I've spoken.

Like the time all five cows took sick just a week after I'd told him I thought the feed had gone off. I started making hot bran mash and Frank took the tractor over to get old Jonah. Frank and I both trusted him.

Jonah said, *Feed's gone off.*

My God, Annie, Frank said to me after he'd driven Jonah home, *how could we be so stupid? Lucky guess to start with that bran.*

There were other times, other cautions. Spaces too wide between the boards in a stall, horses fed too hot, animals left unattended, predators not reckoned on. Most things got put back together, one way or another.

Not the mare, though.

We'd only had her long enough to know she was afraid of everything. Sometimes, when Frank was driving the team, she wouldn't understand what he wanted. She'd get so panicked she'd just lie down and shiver. Stayed down twenty-two hours once. Nothing he'd say could get her up.

Another time, he was so mad I knew he was going to beat her. It wasn't his way but she'd pushed him. I could hear his voice rising up out of the trees.

I had to get to him quick. I could smell the sweat of them both as I ran along the woods road leaving a trail of skirt and shirt and white cotton.

I made love to Frank that day, not ten feet from where the mare lay, wild-eyed and snorting.

Things smoothed for a while and I let myself believe there were changes. One evening at supper, Frank asked my opinion. And he waited, his eyes never leaving my face.

Mare's got quite a cough, he said. *Any ideas?*

Well, the hay seems real dry and she's not used to standing in. She needs green grass.

He knew that already so I wondered if he just wanted to argue. Wanted an excuse to spend the evening away.

I knew my tone had been wrong the minute he spoke. *I'll tether her out,* he said with his voice gone flat.

I could watch her for an hour or so.

Christ, Annie, she'll be alright. You can't be making a baby out of everything.

The mare did fine. Just two nights on the grass and her cough seemed better.

Third morning, Frank's shadow moves along the kitchen counter. He beckons from the veranda. I can't read his face but I think he's excited, has something he wants to show me.

As I go to him, I remember another summer morning, when we were first married, how he'd burst into the house and taken me by the arm. He'd come across a doe and her twin fawns sleeping in a small clearing just beyond our pond.

We ran, holding on to one another and trying to be quiet, but when we reached the spot, the long grass had already begun to stand again, and the earth was cool.

I'd never seen Frank that happy. We made love where the deer had lain.

This time his face was different, and as I wiped my hands and moved out onto the deck, I thought maybe we'd left things too long

I couldn't make sense of what I saw. I kept looking at Frank. Then at the mare. Frank's eyes were glassy and wide, mocking hers. And even though his mouth was clamped shut, hers open, the tongue, green and swollen, their faces were the same dead faces.

We caught hold of each other but, anxious for comfort, we turned away.

I couldn't bring myself to leave Frank in the days that followed the mare's dying. He was almost broken by the dragging of her body up the woods road and into the small clearing. Nor the days that followed while he watched pieces of her disappear.

I thought I'd call one of the old men. Jonah maybe. He could talk to Frank. Help him understand what needed to be done.

I'd just picked up the phone when the dog dragged one of the mare's legs into the yard and I was surprised to learn that I didn't want Frank to understand. Understanding meant I'd have to stay, work things out.

I just stood there, the phone beep-beep-beeping, too tired to put it back. I was tired of everything, all the time. Tired of the living, tired of burying the dead, tired of trying to raise things up again, tired of other peoples' dreams, and tired of thinking it was always up to me.

I began to talk to him about my leaving.

~

No one knows for sure I've gone. Nothing about Frank or his life changes.

I realize I've been wrong all along. Never have my words been too quick. Rather they've been too slow.

And it is not now, but a moment years later, that he will look up from his book, or drop the hoe between neatly laid out rows of corn, and reach with his whole body to catch the sound of my leaving.

Wormhole

Marie Mossman

I stood with my friend on rough field-grass close to my family's home. His face belonged on *Mad* magazine's cover.

He pointed to the ground and said, "If you dig down far enough, you'll come to China."

We had heard Chinese people could keep eggs edible for a hundred years, but my concept of China lacked further details, and I imagine his did, also.

Seven decades later, when we were less confident about facts, my friend nodded his head toward the door which opened onto the powder room in his newly-purchased farmhouse. "It's chilly in there, 'cause there's no insulation where it backs onto the porch. But go ahead. Use the toilet. The dark box is my worm condominium."

"I want to try worms, too."

After I closed the door, I heard constant chatter from somewhere. My gut knotted as if I were walking alone on a street after dark.

"Did you turn the radio on?" I asked, when I came out of the tiny room. "Did someone drop in?"

"Why?"

"I heard voices," I said.

"I didn't mention them, 'cause I wanted to see if you heard them, too. They're louder when no one else is in the house. It must be something an electrical wire's picking up."

He shook his head in puzzlement, then said, "What do you think of my composting worms?"

"Amazing. There's no smell."

The next time I visited, my friend said, "It's creepy. I'm still hearing voices when I go in the powder room. It's not the wiring. I had it checked."

I would hear the voices every time I used his powder room toilet. They seemed to come from the worm condominium.

"The leggy ones confine us," a voice said. "They never give us enough protein. They feed us on mushy lettuce junk, 'cause we eat it like greedy childlings. We need protein!"

"My wormhole is the way," a louder voice said. "The answer to our need for protein. I have quantum knowledge, and I have the key. Listen to me."

All the other voices were silent. The loud one continued, "The leggy ones'll come to this room. It's their habit. The toilet has a compelling call for them. I'll open my wormhole to Mars. You'll chant, 'free trip to Mars' over and over, so the leggy ones hear, but do not hear. They absorb such messages all the time from their brain-draining toys.

"I'll switch my wormhole key to travel mode. In seconds, they who now confine us will arrive in our underground pen on Mars. We'll turn our tormentors into protein. It'll be mega times more efficient than munching our way to China for an old egg. Follow me! Follow now!"

My friend and I no longer hear voices in his farmhouse.

234

About the authors

Jeremy Akerman is an adoptive Nova Scotian who has lived in the province since 1964. In that time he has been an archaeologist, a radio announcer, a politician, a senior civil servant, a newspaper editor and a film actor.

Moose House published three Jeremy Akerman books in 2022: his memoir *Outsider* and the revised editions of *What Have You Done for Me Lately?* and *Black Around the Eyes*.

Melissa Armstrong enjoys writing with a touch of humour about everyday ordinary events. She has been published in Canadian Stories (canadianstories.net) for her memoir 'Selling a home, not a house', and 'Her'. 'Her' is also featured on story-quilt.com, a sister site to Canadian Stories.

She likes to collect craft and art supplies and on occasion use them, mostly yarn, clay and paint. She also likes gardening while she and the chickens listen to audiobooks.

Melissa lives on the French Shore with her family, too many chickens, ducks and two sassy cats.

Bob Bent was born in Amherst, lived most of his life in and around Lawrencetown, and now lives in Middleton and Cottage Cove, Nova Scotia. He has had stories published in *The Nashwaak Review*, *All Rights Reserved*, and *Feathertale Review*; a piece of non-fiction in *The Barnstormer*, and a series of travel/running articles in *Run Nova Scotia Raconteur*. *Moose House Stories Vol. 1* features two of his stories.

A collection of whimsical stories for children and grandmothers, *Have Yourself a Silly Little Christmas*, illustrated by Andrea Wood, was published in 2013. He published a collection of serious short stories, *The Last Time I Saw Alice*, in 2018. His first novel, a humorous espionage/hockey thriller entitled *Spy on Ice*, came out in 2020.

Chris Bristol worked at many professions ranging from gas jockey to deckhand to computer programmer. Now retired, he has decided to pursue his lifelong love of writing and is fulfilling his dreams of exercising and publishing his imagination.

K.R. Byggdin grew up on the Prairies and now lives in Kjipuktuk (Halifax), where they recently completed studies in English and Creative Writing at Dalhousie University. Their writing has appeared in *Moose House Stories Vol. 1* and in other anthologies and journals across Canada, the UK, and New Zealand. Their debut novel *Wonder World* is available from Enfield & Wizenty.

The daughter of a documentary director and niece of a Time Lord, **Clo Carey** has moved across the Atlantic three times. Her love of books led her to a career in the book trade. She currently works at South Shore Public Libraries, and is a member and mentor of The South Shore Scribes and Writers Ink.ie.

Clo has been writing for years and has a number of novels, short stories and creative non-fiction pieces to her name.

Trena Christie-MacEachern loves Halloween, wine, and writing fictional stories with a twist. She's a member of the Writers' Federation of Nova Scotia and two writing groups. A substitute teacher and rural mail driver, Trena lives on Cape Breton Island with her song-writing husband and her blue-eyed Border Collie, Lucy.

Her work has appeared in *Galleon*, *The Inverness Oran*, *Cape Breton's Christmas*, and *Community Voices*. Let the trumpets sound: this is her first paid writing gig!

William Dockrill began his writing life as a radio copywriter. The CBC produced and aired two of his short stories for *Book Time* and *Atlantic Airwaves*, and a radio play for its Halifax station. He won the Writers' Federation of Nova Scotia's short story competition in 1995, following a second place finish the year before.

His work includes a social history of Bear River, *Water Under the Bridge* (2001), an on-going blog for Mapannapolis.ca, and two drawer novels which may yet see the light of day. He lives in Granville Ferry.

Leah Benvie Hamilton has always lived in rural Nova Scotia. Now retired, Leah worked in the field of home care. Besides writing stories, she is an avid gardener, quilter and rug hooker. Leah has a memoir piece published in the anthology *Country Roads*, and a story in the online journal, *The Bangalore Review*.

Tara G. Harris lives and writes in Bridgewater, Nova Scotia. She studied English Literature at Acadia University and Memorial University of Newfoundland where she focused her studies on the works of Newfoundland women writers. She is a member of Newfoundland's Qalipu First Nation, established in 2011. As she grew up in small town Newfoundland, the challenges of living in rural communities have always been a subject of personal interest. Relationship to place and the role of place in shaping personal identity in Atlantic Canada are among the themes she hopes to explore.

Her creative nonfiction piece "Lucky Strike" was published in the Fall 2021 issue of *Understorey Magazine*.

Linda H.Y. Hegland is an award-winning poetry, lyric essay, and non-fiction writer who lives and writes in Nova Scotia. She writes the occasional short story. Her writing most often reflects the influence of place, and sense of place, and one's complex and many-layered relationship with it.

She has published in numerous literary and art journals and has had work nominated for the Pushcart Prize. She has previously published two books of poetry, *Bird Slips, Moon Glows* and *White Horses*; and a book of lyric essays, *Place of the Heart*.

Jan Fancy Hull Jan Fancy Hull lives in a log chalet beside a quiet lake in Lunenburg County, Nova Scotia, where she has written non-fiction, award-winning poetry, short stories, and novels.

In former lives, she worked as a radio broadcaster, arts administrator, sailing tours skipper, and employee benefits broker.

During the winter, Jan watches snowflakes fall as she writes. In warm months, she carves Nova Scotia sandstone into sculptures. She enjoys the occasional round of golf, and drifting on the lake in her little boat, which she claims is a great place to edit.

In 2022, Jan received the Rita Joe Poetry Prize for her poem,

"Moss Meditations."

Moose House publishes many, many of Jan's books.

Marilyn A. Jones was born and raised in Cape Breton, a coal-miner's daughter. Her education completed, she moved to Halifax, where she was employed as a stenographer for several years, and from there to Cottage Cove, Annapolis County.

A long-standing member of Authors' Ink, a writers' group, she has published four books: *Stories to Tell*, volumes 1 and 2; *Aunt Toni's Diary*; and *Growing up in Cape Breton*. She has also contributed to newspapers, including the Middleton *Spectator*, *The Grapevine*, and a monthly newspaper, *Shoreline News*.

An avid reader, she enjoys playing the guitar, gardening, and watching the fishing boats on the Bay of Fundy.

Grace Keating grew up in Antigonish, at the tail end of a large family and a long line of story tellers. Add to that, a forty-plus year career in costuming for film and television in Vancouver, where real life is fabricated and fantasy becomes real. From this wealth of raw material she creates stories both rich and diverse, giving unique perspectives on human nature and the intricate weaving of relationships.

Grace has had several stories published in various collections, including *Moose House Stories Volume 1*, and has also produced a series of chapbooks. She is a co-author of the Moose House novel *Less Than Innocent*.

Grace is recently retired, which, she is finding out, is the last stop on the great procrastinator's journey.

Grace Keddy is a retired LPN who saw an ad for a writers' course at the local museum. She signed up and the rest is history, as they say.

John MacEachern was raised in the small farming village of Kleinburg Ontario, twenty-five miles north of Toronto. After graduating from Cornell University he spent his entire life in the hospitality industry, eventually owning and operating two of Canada's finest country restaurants: The Doctor's House in Kleinburg and the Captain's House in Chester, Nova Scotia.

Upon retiring he pursued his two passions: art and writing. He paints primarily watercolours but has also done many pastels and egg tempera works. He has written two novels: *The Hat Trick Murders* and *The Blood of Art*, as well as many short stories.

He lives with his wife, Barbara, in Nictaux Nova Scotia. They have four children and five grandchildren.

Carolyn MacIsaac lives in rural Nova Scotia with her husband of over 50 years. They have three children and six grandchildren. Carolyn enjoys writing something she can jot down in an afternoon and has published short stories in *Our Canada*, *The Lost Children*, and *Where Pines and Maples Grow* (a book the Pictou County writers' group produced for Canada's 150th birthday). She has written two novellas. She also writes the weekly mission statement for Bethel Baptist Church, where she is a member.

Carolyn loves the outdoors and enjoys snowshoeing, hiking, biking and kayaking.

Virginia MacIsaac enjoys visiting attics, reading mysteries, and listening to stories about the past. She worked as a rural mail driver, as an archivist in a community archive, and now does bookkeeping, grant writing, and heritage projects. She contributes to the *Inverness Oran* column "And Then Again" and started freelancing non-fiction in 1984. This is her first fiction publication. She and her husband live in rural Cape Breton and have two grown sons.

Pam Calabrese MacLean is the author of two poetry books and two children's books. Moose House published *Sofa*, a collection of her short plays, in 2021. She is a co-author of the Moose House novel *Less Than Innocent*.

She lives in Nova Scotia.

Tracy Matheson appreciates living and connecting to the land with her family in the territory of Mi'kma'ki known as Nova Scotia. She says writing chose her. She has a self-taught practice with short stories and poetry at its core. With 30 years of business management and entrepreneurship, Tracy's passion for social enterprise and advocacy projects is rooted in creative arts and building healthy communities. She is Reiki Master and Yoga / Meditation guide. Her goal is to inspire others to harness their inner artist.

Tracy writes with a local group called the South Shore Scribes.

Roberta McGinn lives in Dartmouth, NS with her husband Bill, Maggie Mae the dog, and two cats. She is currently working on her first novel.

Marie Mossman lives with her feet planted in Nova Scotia's soil. Her experiences with worms, who live in a soil-filled container, sparked the question: 'What if these bottom dwellers demanded more than blended organic vegetables?'

You may never trust another worm after you read the answer.

Moose House published Mossman's first novel, *A Rebel for Her Time*, in 2020. She is working on the sequel.

Mossman is a co-author of *Less than Innocent*, a COVID-lockdown romp available from Moose House.

Annette Muise was born and raised in Yarmouth, Nova Scotia. She lives there with her husband and two daughters. She has always loved exploring nature and these adventures often inspire her writing and the nightly bedtime stories she creates for her daughters.

Each year Annette and her family enjoy the sapping experience at her sister and brother-in-law's maple ridge. This annual tradition was the inspiration for her story.

When **eloise murray** retired from a profession with a publish or perish expectation, creative writing was the third dimension of her plan for the future. It was preceded by digging in the earth and creating folk art for family and friends. The novel she wrote during COVID, *Another Beginning*, kept her grounded.

Two of her stories appear in *Moose House Stories Volume 1*.

Carolyn Jean Nicholson worked in the health care field, teaching in post-secondary education, and ministry in The United Church of Canada. She followed in her mother's footsteps in researching her Nova Scotia ancestors, resulting in her first book, *William Forsyth: Land of Hopes and Dreams*. Moose House will publish her second book, *Traitors, Cannibals, Highlanders, and Vikings*, in 2023. She is a co-author of the COVID lockdown novel, *Less Than Innocent*.

After graduating high school, **Thibault Jacquot-Paratte** left his native Annapolis Valley, first to do a work term in translations in Cameroon, then to live in a van all around North America, then to do a Bachelor's and Master's of Nordic Studies at the Sorbonne before returning to Nova Scotia and the valley in 2018.

His first three plays came out in 2016-2017, followed by his collected verse, *Cries of somewhere's soil* (2020); a miscellany, *Souvenirs et fragments;* and the novel *A dream is a notion of* (2022).

Dozens of his short stories and poems have appeared in journals and anthologies, including *Moose House Stories*, Volumes 1 and 2. He is a co-author of the Moose House novel *Less Than Innocent*.

He recently co-edited a charity anthology for Ukraine, *Il y a des bombes qui tombent sur Kyiv* (2022). He writes in both English and French, plays music, tells jokes both good and bad, and likes to spend time with his wife and their daughter.

Danielle Pierce was born and raised on the South Shore of Nova Scotia, and now calls the Annapolis Valley home. When she's not writing, you might find her walking her dogs or reading novels; if you can't find her, she's probably run away to a cabin in the woods or convinced someone to go to the beach.

Rose Poirier spent her youth in Cape Breton, swatting flies. She's now in Halifax with her son, hubby, and GPS-tracked cats. After decades in Public Relations and teaching communications, she recently wrote for Cape Breton anthologies. Rose has a penchant for researching family ghosts. And a yen to return to the UK, where her life changed.

Linda Turner and her Acadian partner raised their family in Rogersville, New Brunswick. A letter found in Australia and written from Pictou on New Year's Eve, 1840 enabled her to discover the town's captivating history, which prompted a move there in 2017.

Michelle Wamboldt was born and raised in Truro, Nova Scotia. She is a graduate of Dalhousie University and the Humber School of Journalism in Toronto. Her debut novel, *Birth Road* (Vagrant Press/ Nimbus Publishing), was released in April 2022. Her fiction has also appeared in *The Dalhousie Review*.

Michelle has lived in a small rural community on the beautiful South Shore of Nova Scotia for the past 25 years. She is currently working on her second novel.

Anne MacLeod Weeks taught advanced writing for forty years and thought it was time to do some writing of her own. Living on the South Shore, she spends her time writing, photographing, and hiking with her Jack Russells. She has published in a variety of educational and professional journals and had a short story appear in *Down in the Dirt* magazine.

James O. Weeks taught English in secondary schools and community college for forty years. He published articles in professional journals and short genre fiction (*Wilderness Tales*) while teaching young adults about writing.

Beyond the classroom, Jim worked as a swimming pool manager, camp counselor, and liquor store clerk, and for twelve years was a driver and pump operator for a volunteer fire department.

Jim and his wife (a fifth-generation Nova Scotian) live in Lunenburg.

Moose House will soon be publishing his first novel, *Nodding's People*.